LIGHTING THE WAY

GLENDA C. MANUS

First Original Edition

Copyright© Glenda C. Manus 2014

All rights reserved.

South Ridge Press Publications
2014

This book is dedicated to my daughters, Laura Whittaker and Krista Cook, my encouragers.

A SPECIAL THANK YOU

To the women in our Tuesday Morning Bible Study Group for your prayers and support. Our spiritual journey of reading and studying God's word together has inspired me to follow God's direction.

To Laura, Krista, Pat and Linda, for reading the manuscript and making honest and helpful suggestions

To Cherie Steele Photography for providing the front cover photo taken of the stained glass windows inside Van Wyck Presbyterian Church during the 2013 Christmas season.

To my lifelong friend, Marlene, for always being there with a caring heart and words of encouragement.

To my husband, Henry, for believing in me.

And especially to God, whose gentle prodding takes me to places I would never dare to go alone.

CHAPTER 1

He let himself in at the kitchen entrance of the parsonage and stood there listening for a while. No one heard him come in, which didn't surprise him with all the noise they were making. Just a few minutes earlier, he had met his father in the courtyard of the church with his parka pulled closely around his ears and walking briskly in the other direction.

"They're like a gaggle of geese in there, son. If you value your sanity, you'll go for a walk with me instead of opening that kitchen door." His father was right, of course, but it amused him to see that his wife, Liz, had jumped right in the middle of the fray and was holding her own in the bombardment of conversation between his mother and two sisters. Liz was sitting on a bar stool at the counter peeling and slicing apples while Irene Clark was giving instructions to her daughters on the fine art of making pie crusts so flaky they would melt in your mouth.

"There you are," his mother said when she noticed him at the door. "Your father walked out of here just when I needed him most. We've put the turkey in the brine, but we need your help lifting the bucket and putting it in the refrigerator. I've cleared some space and moved a shelf around to make room. It must weigh a ton."

"Not quite a ton," he said, with a quick wink at Liz, "but too much for any of you to be lifting." He lifted the five gallon bucket with ease out of the sink and with a little wiggling around, he finally made it fit in the space his mom had cleared out.

He walked over to Liz, standing behind her and massaging the back of her neck as his mom and sisters exchanged smiles and glances. "Our first Thanksgiving with Liz in our family," he said, unaware that they were looking at him in amazement. He, who had been so nonchalant about dating and more so about marrying, had turned into a hopeless romantic.

Irene Clark felt a warm place in her heart as she watched her only son with his new bride. She knew love when she saw it. She'd experienced close to fifty years of that same kind of love with her husband, Will. But enough of the mushy stuff - it was time to get moving.

"Rock," she said, "Would you get the potatoes out of the pantry and start peeling them? And be sure to put them in ice cold water so they won't turn brown before we cook them in the morning."

"I knew I should have gone for a walk with Dad," he said. "Why am I always the potato peeler?"

CHAPTER 2

"*A merry heart maketh a cheery countenance: but by sorrow of the heart, the spirit is broken.*"

- Proverbs 15:13 KJV

Two hundred miles northeast of Park Place, South Carolina, Maria Ramirez cowered in the corner of the kitchen waiting for the next blow - it had been several minutes since he last hit her. With her hands clasped together at the back of her neck and her elbows covering her face, she was lying in a fetal position on the floor of the apartment she shared with her husband, Ernesto. She was afraid to lift her head, fearing any movement on her part would set him off again. She had listened as he walked away, but waited until she heard his loud snoring before she dared to get up.

He was lying flat on his back on the sofa just a few feet away. His drunkenness was obvious - his breath and clothing reeked of the cheap whiskey he had consumed before coming home from work.

There had been no provocation for his actions. She had prepared his dinner and was wiping the splatters from the stove when he walked in. The radio was tuned to one of the local Hispanic stations and she was singing along with the music. He had grabbed her suddenly by the hair and pulled her around to face him, cursing all the while. "Where have you been? I've been trying to call you?" Before she could answer, a blow to her face knocked her off balance and she could taste blood on her lips. His fists were large and the second punch had knocked her to her knees and he had seemed surprised when he looked down to find a chunk of hair that he had ripped from her scalp in his left hand. The look in his eyes showed a fleeting glimpse of remorse, but then he left her crumpled at his feet. He hadn't given her a chance to tell him the phone was out of order.

She got up and walked gingerly past him and made her way to the bathroom where she cleaned away the blood from her mouth with a damp cloth. She wet the cloth again and pressed it against her bleeding scalp, then parted her hair from the other side to cover the spot where he'd yanked it out. She steadied herself against the sink and in a moment the feeling of nausea and lightheadedness was gone. Listening to the gasping snores coming from the other room, she knew from experience he would be out for a while, so she gathered some clothing from the closet, some personal things from her dresser, and some toiletry items from the bathroom. After stuffing them all in a backpack, she took a quick survey of the room to see what else she might need. The music box was on the nightstand - she couldn't leave it knowing Ernesto would probably smash it to pieces when he found her gone. It was a delicate china figurine of the Virgin Mary holding her infant child. When it was wound up, it would turn on its base, playing a sweet melody as it turned. It was special because it had been a gift from her father one Christmas when she was a child - a year when money was tight and she wasn't expecting a gift. She held it in her hands for a moment, then reluctantly put it back in its place. Sighing, she knew she would probably never see it again, but she had no space to pack such a fragile item. She picked up her backpack and walked out of the room. Ernesto's heavy winter jacket was on the coat rack in the hallway and she pulled it on.

The smell of burning food was strong. She ran to the kitchen where a pan on the stove was beginning to scorch. She turned off the burner and set the pan aside. When Ernesto had come home, the fried plantains had already been topped with ground beef and cabbage and were warming in the skillet ready to eat. Now they were ruined, but it no longer mattered. Her appetite was gone and she wouldn't be around when he woke up.

A case of bottled water was on the metal cabinet beside the stove and she put two bottles in her backpack along with some candy bars from a bowl on the table. Ernesto's wallet was on the counter where he took it out of his pocket when he came home each night. His pocket knife and some change were beside it.

She grabbed the wallet and the coins and slipped them into one of the jacket pockets. On second thought, she pulled the wallet back out. She opened it up, searching frantically for her immigration card that Ernesto carried with him at all times. It was his way of controlling her. She found what she needed folded in one of the seams and took it, along with some of his money, then put the wallet back on the table. Putting it all in her pocket, she quietly opened the apartment door. As she backed out the door, she heard more cursing and a retching sound as if he was going to be sick. She froze in place, but when he started snoring again, she closed the door to the tiny studio apartment and moved quickly toward the outer stairway. The elderly neighbor across the hallway opened her door and looked out. Their eyes met, and she looked at Maria with compassion. "Go fast, little one," she said, "and may God travel with you." Maria nodded and waved a tentative goodbye. She never wanted to see this place that held so many unhappy memories again.

CHAPTER 3

"Whether you turn to the right or to the left, your ears will hear a voice behind you, saying, "This is the way; walk in it."

- Isaiah 30:21 NIV

In nearly every household in town, a Thanksgiving noonday feast with tables laden with the customary turkey surrounded by cornbread dressing, cranberry sauce, mashed potatoes, giblet gravy, candied yams, green beans and a few other favorite family recipes had been served and eaten. The dining room sideboards were filled with pies and cakes waiting for sated appetites to be revived a little later. In most of these households, several generations had come together to thank God for His many blessings and were now breaking up into clean-up crews. The lucky and the lazy were gathering in living rooms talking to grandparents or playing with babies. There would be laughs and giggles when grandpa started snoring in the recliner as the turkey's natural sedative, tryptophan kicked in.

It was almost the same scenario that was taking place in the Presbyterian Church parsonage in Park Place, South Carolina as the Clark clan gathered after their huge Thanksgiving feast. Will Clark watched his family as they sat around the large mahogany table in the dining room. They would have two more days together before they had to leave to go back to Marietta, Georgia. He watched his new daughter-in-law, Liz, who seemed to be at ease with everyone - not an easy task with the Clark clan. He and his son, Rock, were quiet and mild-mannered. His daughters, now they were a different story. They had taken after his wife, Irene, in both looks and personality. A social butterfly was the perfect cliché to describe his beautiful and charming wife. Lisa and Allison were just eighteen months apart in age and had always been best friends as well as sisters. The two of them had married well. Lisa's husband, Robert was a pediatrician, and Allison's husband, Mark was an attorney for an Atlanta law firm with a satellite office in Marietta. He and Allison had a daughter, Gillian, and a son, Chase. Robert and Lisa had just one, Rachel, and their topic of conversation at the moment was that it was about time for them to give her a little sister or brother.

Will noticed Rock and Liz exchanging smiles and wondered what it meant. Could they be trying for a child also? Now that would put Irene in a tailspin. He decided to keep this tidbit of information to himself. Irene would blow it all out of proportion.

He and Irene had discussed Rock and Liz just this morning as they had their coffee before the others had awakened. "She is a treasure," Irene had gushed. "I've never seen our boy so happy." Will had agreed and now as he watched their easy bantering back and forth, he knew Irene was right. Liz was definitely a treasure in the life of his son. A minister needed a wife, and Rock had taken his own sweet time finding one. Just when he and Irene had given up hope, it happened that God had it under control.

The children were getting restless. Gillian came up and whispered in his ear, "May we be excused, Papaw?"

He looked at each one of his grandchildren. They all had the same pleading look.

"Well, of course you can," he whispered back. "Y'all run along outside and play. Papaw's going to sneak into your Uncle Rock's office and take a nap in the recliner."

"I won't tell anyone," Gillian whispered back. Giggling with excitement, three sets of feet scampered to the kitchen door and slammed it on the way out.

Thanksgiving was not a custom the people of Honduras celebrated, so as Maria Diaz-Ramirez stood all alone on the corner of Church and East Main Street, she was puzzled as to why no one was out and about. The stores and restaurants were all closed and she was hungry, a feeling that rarely subsided now that the baby growing inside her was so near at hand. She had two candy bars and a bottle of water in the backpack holding her belongings. She was holding out on those until her hunger pangs hit the emergency level, and they weren't quite there yet.

She was standing in front of a building with a name she had seen before. The US Postal Service emblem looked the same as the bright blue and white logo on the building in Raleigh where Ernesto sometimes went to send money back to Honduras for his sister. *Park Place Post Office* was in big letters on the sign out front. She glanced inside and was surprised to find this place seemed to be as empty as all the other buildings she had passed on Main Street. She often lost count of the day of the week. One day seemed to just slip into another. Wednesday, she thought, or maybe Thursday. Whatever day it was, she knew it was not Sunday because the churches all stood empty. She had walked through the town looking for a Catholic church, thinking it may be possible to get help from a priest if she could find one. She had found four churches, but they were all Protestant. She couldn't keep walking much farther - she was tired and hungry and running out of money.

She had used ninety-seven of the one-hundred and twenty dollars she had taken out of Ernesto's wallet yesterday when he fell into a drunken slumber. Eighty-two dollars had been the cost of the bus ticket from Raleigh to Charlotte and she had eaten out of vending machines at the bus station at midnight and then had breakfast at a Waffle House on Independence Boulevard earlier in the morning as she was making her way out of Charlotte on foot. As she sat in the booth eating alone, she had overheard at the table beside her a young Hispanic couple speaking of a new job they were taking on a horse farm in Sparta, South Carolina. She asked them if they were heading there now and when they said yes, she made a quick decision and told them she had family in Sparta. "I'm looking for a ride," she said. "I don't have much money left, but I'll give you what I have."

The young woman looked closely at Maria's bruised face. "Si," she said. "You are welcome to come along with us." After paying their checks, they walked out to a black Toyota. The young man opened the back seat door on the passenger side. "I'll make room back here," he said. He moved a few bags around and took her backpack from her. He put it on top of some blankets stacked on the other seat and she got in. She was surprised when only forty-five minutes later, they arrived in Sparta. She had hoped it would be much further to the south. She wanted to be as far away from Raleigh as possible. Ernesto had been drunker than she had ever seen him, but she knew when he woke up, he would start looking for her. The couple offered to drop her off at her relative's home, so after driving around for a while, she pointed out a house in a run-down neighborhood and they stopped to let her out. They would not accept her offer to pay them for the ride. She watched them drive away and started walking back to the highway. If she stayed in Sparta, she may run into them again and they would ask questions. They had asked too many already about the scrapes and bruises on her face. The sky was overcast and the air was brisk, but Ernesto's jacket was thick and provided all the warmth she needed.

Just a few miles east of Sparta, she saw a sign pointing to Park Place. Thinking it was a park where she could rest for a while before trying to find shelter for the night, she followed the direction of the sign and was surprised to come up on a little town. To Maria, it seemed like a mirage in the middle of a desert and something about it called out from behind her in a whisper like the wind saying, "Maria, this is where you stop running." But now that she was here, she had no place to go.

Hearing the sounds of children playing outside a house near the pretty church with the bell tower made her homesick for her family in Honduras. Her family was poor, but they were happy together. Her father had arranged for her marriage to Ernesto Ramirez, a man more than twice her age, because he had promised he would take her back with him to the United States and see that she got an education so she could live a better life.

Ernesto was a US citizen, having been born in Texas to an American missionary who had married his father, a local Honduran construction worker. Senora Ann, Ernesto's mother, was a good woman and had taught the children in the village to speak English. She was of the Protestant faith and even though most of the villagers attended the Catholic church, they learned some valuable lessons on faith and salvation from the teachings of Senora Ann. Maria knew she would be disappointed if she could see what had become of her son.

After Maria married Ernesto, she received a visa from the American Embassy and when they reached North Carolina, Ernesto petitioned the immigration office for her to have resident alien status as his wife. After three years, she would be eligible to apply for US citizenship.

But things had changed soon after they settled into their apartment. He had started drinking heavily and with the drinking came the dark moods and then the beatings. He became jealous and wouldn't allow her out of the house unless he was with her. Her dreams of going to school were dashed and she felt like a prisoner. He told her if she tried to run away, he would divorce her and she would be put in jail and then deported. Being deported sounded heavenly to her after the abuse, but she could not bear to think of being in jail. Ernesto made it sound as if she would be starved and tortured. She had to think of the baby.

The shriek of a little boy's laughter brought her out of her deep thoughts and brought back memories of another little boy's laughter. "Ah," she said aloud in her native language, "mi hermano pequeño," and then in the English she had learned from the kind missionary - "my little brother".

She wiped the tears from her eyes and walked up the steps of the post office. The door's mirrored image showed a young girl looking back at her. Because she was barely five feet tall and somewhat undernourished, her mid-section made her look slightly overweight rather than pregnant. The couple who had given her a ride hadn't seemed to notice her condition. The reflection showed a pretty face, even with the bruises - the face of a child who would turn seventeen on Christmas Day.

She tried the handle of the door, and to her surprise it opened. The lobby was large with bright shiny boxes with keyholes lining the wall to the right. There was a table with a trashcan underneath, and on the table was a sales catalog and a large box. She looked inside the box and realized she had come to a place where miracles happen when she saw four large loaves of bread and a package of sweet rolls with a sign saying '*Free - day old bread. Please take it or I'm going to give it all to Louise Ledford's chickens - pronto*' and it was signed, '*Betty*'.

Maria knew how to speak English, but she had difficulty learning to read the English words on paper. She recognized the words free, bread and chickens. She didn't see any chickens, but the bread would be her dinner. The dark corner in the back couldn't be seen from the windows so she took her bread and sat cross legged on the floor, leaning against the wall. She opened her backpack, dug out a bottle of water, made the sign of the cross, and thanked God for his blessings in providing food and shelter for the night. After eating, she thumbed through some of the catalogs until the sunset lost its glow beyond the building across the street. She made a pillow of her backpack and wrapped warmly in the jacket with the hood over her head. The sun shining in the window all day had warmed the tile and although it was hard, she settled in and fell into a dreamless sleep - the best sleep she'd had in a very long time.

She awoke to the sounds of a clicking noise coming from the wall behind the shiny boxes. She pushed herself up to a sitting position. The tile floor had cooled considerably during the night and she was chilled. The noise on the other side of the wall sounded as if someone was stuffing the boxes with papers from the other side. She tried not to make any noise and picked up her backpack, stuffed the pack of sweet rolls and a loaf of bread inside, and zipped it up. She walked very quietly to the front trying not to make a sound, but she tripped over the leg of the table. She heard a voice from the back, "Who's out there so early this morning? Don't you know I haven't even got the mail put up and I'm not opening this door until 8:30!" Maria ran for the door and made it out before anyone could see her. She rounded the corner, slipped down the back alley and hid behind the dumpster at May's Flower Shop until she was sure she hadn't been seen.

Maybe it was against the law to sleep in the building, she thought. This strange country had so many laws. She watched, but no one came out behind her, so after a few minutes, she slipped from behind the dumpster, crossed through the intersection and walked down Church Street in the direction of the church with the big bell tower. Maybe it would be open and she could go in and light a candle. Si, God had brought her to this little village and He would see her through her trials.

CHAPTER 4

"*I will both lie down in peace, and sleep; for you alone, O Lord make me dwell in safety.*"
- Psalm 4:8 NKJV

After her scare of being discovered, Maria hurriedly walked along Church Street. Something about the church building ahead was comforting - maybe it was the familiarity of the bell tower - a structure much like the church in her village in Honduras. She looked at the large house where the children had been playing the day before. It was quiet this morning, and with the sun not quite over the horizon, there was no one up and stirring and there was no traffic on the street. The temperature was below freezing, but the heavy hooded jacket was warm.

The entrance to the church was right beyond the house. There were iron handrails on each side of the steps leading up to the double front doors and when she reached the top landing, she tried each of the door handles. The church was locked. She had looked forward to the quiet sanctuary of the church and was disappointed. Maybe there was another entrance. The doors were never locked at her church back home. As she walked around the building, she found two other entrances, but they were locked also. Going around the corner, she saw a set of steps leading down to a heavy metal door on the far side of the church near the house. She walked down the steps and tried the door. It opened and she walked inside. It was a large basement - about eight feet high on one end but gradually lowered to only about three feet high on the opposite end. There were heat duct pipes running the length of the area and large rolls of insulation stood in a corner on the concrete floor. A worn rug and some carpet scraps were in another, and a tall ladder was stored near the door. It was slightly musty, but with the small amount of heat escaping from the ducting system, it was not unbearably cold. It was not a perfect place to stay, but it would do until she could....well, what could she do? She had nowhere to go.

She walked back outside, hoping to look around before anyone started stirring. The bread and sweet rolls she had grabbed from the post office would do her a day or two, but she knew bread alone was not nutritious enough for the baby she was carrying. The garbage cans behind the house were so full the lids would not close. She watched carefully for any sign of people stirring about, and when she did not see anyone, she furtively walked across the back yard and opened one of the cans. In the top bag, there were a few clear plastic plates of food that had barely been touched. Wouldn't it be nice, she thought, to have such an abundance of food that you would think nothing of throwing it away? In her home village, food was never wasted. Any leftover scraps always made their way into an omelette or a tortilla. She lifted the trash bag out of the container and hurriedly made her way back to the basement with it. When she got back inside, she searched through the bag for food that looked edible. She picked out several slices of turkey, a discarded bag of slightly wilted lettuce, two over-ripe bananas, and a plastic container almost full of pimento cheese. A peanut butter jar still contained a spoonful or two. She couldn't afford to be picky - she had never had a need to eat discarded food before, but knew she must eat for the baby to be healthy. She continued to go through the bag. There was a bag of apples beginning to soften with a few bad places needing to be cut out. Apples had been scarce where she lived in Honduras. They only grew in the mountainous regions, but occasionally her father would bring some home and she loved them.

The weather overnight had been cold enough to keep the food in the garbage can from spoiling and if she rationed the things she had salvaged, she would have enough to last for a few days. She stayed inside for the remainder of the day and tried to fix a comfortable place to sleep. The insulation had a backing on it, so she unrolled a long section and threw the carpet scraps on top of it for a bed or for sitting.

As the morning progressed, the big house and the one behind the church had people back and forth visiting all day. It made her homesick for her own family. Her body ached from sleeping on the cold hard floor of the post office, so she curled up on the insulation, finally feeling some warmth and went sound asleep.

Main Street was alive with shopkeepers decorating their storefronts. Crowder's Feed and Seed's windows were already decorated. A Red Flyer wagon with a big bow on the handle was filled with Breyer Horses of all sizes and shapes. A large Santa figure stood beside it holding a sign reading 'Hold Your Horses - Santa's Comin'. The other window had two bright and shiny bicycles, one pink and one blue, with silver bows tied around the handlebars. Two large stuffed horses were propped up on the seats. A brand new wheel barrow held bags of deer corn and horse feed, and boxes of amaryllis bulb kits were stacked on a small table.

Junie Crowder was hanging a wreath above the front door while his wife, Kathleen was supervising the hanging. Reverend Rock Clark, the Presbyterian minister in town, was watching the scene unfold.

"Dad-blame it, make up your mind, woman! I'm 'bout near freezing to death perched up here on the top rung of this ladder." The ladder looked to be about as old as the store, so Rock hurried over to steady it.

"Get down from there, Junie - I'll hang it for you."

"Rev Rock, there's just no pleasin' this woman. I might as well stay up here or she'll be making you say bad words too. Kathleen, this is exactly where we had it last year. The nail's still here."

Kathleen looked skeptical. "Then the wire must have stretched 'cause it's hanging too low. See if you can twist a knot in the wire, Junie. That's all it needs."

Junie handed the wreath carefully down to Rock. "I can't twist knots and stand up here at the same time. See if you can do it."

Finally, the wreath was in place, and with Junie down off the ladder, the three of them stood back and admired it. Junie walked up a little closer to the door. "Those little hammer and wrench ornaments you ordered look real nice, Kathleen."

Kathleen cocked her head and looked at her husband of forty-six years. "Well, at least you're sayin' something complimentary now, instead of calling me a dad-blamed woman."

Junie walked back to her and put his arm around her. "Aww, Kathleen honey, I was just bein' impatient like always. I didn't mean nothin' by it. I'll get up on a ladder for you any day of the week."

Rock said his goodbyes and walked on down the street before things got too mushy. He would come back later.

May Ferguson was in the window of her flower shop when Rock stopped to admire it. Her window had won the Blue Ribbon awarded by the Park Place Woman's Club for three years running for Best Display, and from the looks of this one, she was a top contender this year as well. The Main Street storefront display windows were tall and wide. These old buildings were much the same as they had been a hundred years before when each business owner was competing for customers, and a surefire way to draw them in was to have what they wanted and needed in plain view as the shoppers walked by. Not much had changed, except now the owners had to compete with the shopping mall in the neighboring town of Sparta. The people of Park Place were fiercely loyal to their Main Street business owners though, and didn't mind paying a little extra for their wares in order to keep their town alive and their businesses healthy.

Last year May had decorated using a Victorian Christmas scene but this year, it was more of a country Christmas theme. A vintage door with green chipping paint and a brass doorknob was propped in the center of the display area with heavy wire strung from the ceiling holding it up. A simple evergreen wreath with pine cones, red berries and a large red and white checkered bow hung from the door. Two vintage step ladders were standing like teepees on each side of the door and each rung held evergreen plants and a few poinsettias trimmed with the same ribbon pattern as the wreath. An old Hoosier cabinet was in one corner holding simple country themed gift items such as candles, soaps, and lotions. A huge taxidermy moose head was nailed on the wall of the other corner and strings of popcorn ran through its antlers. Santa figures and angels were on the shelves of a bookcase made of old orange crates. A large tree trimmed in multi-colored lights, strings of popcorn, pine cones, and red berries glowed softly behind the display.

When May saw him standing there, she motioned for him to come inside. As he stepped inside the door, the smell of gingerbread cookies assaulted him and all of a sudden he was starved.

"Are you making gingerbread?" he asked hopefully.

May laughed. "No, that's a candle I'm burning. Smells good, doesn't it?" Rock tried to hide his disappointment, but May noticed. "I do have some chocolate chip cookies and some hot chocolate, but I don't suppose you would be interested," she teased.

"You supposed wrong, my friend. I'm always interested in cookies." She stepped out of the window and walked with him to the back of the shop. During the Christmas season, homemade cookies were made fresh daily for her customers and Rock had become a good one over the last few months. She had made several flower deliveries to the little cottage behind the church when it had become known that the Presbyterian preacher was courting the young lady who lived there, and the deliveries continued after they were married celebrating each month's anniversary. She knew it would slow down after a while, but for now it was exciting to witness the romantic notions of the middle-aged preacher. Everyone in town had once thought he was destined to be a lifelong bachelor.

"How's Liz?" she asked as they sat at the small table drinking their hot chocolate. Rock picked up a cookie and started munching. He was finding it increasingly hard not to blurt out the little details about how Liz was doing in her pregnancy. He was so excited - he wanted everyone in town to know, but they had agreed to keep it under wraps for now. It had caught most of the townspeople by surprise when after years of being a bachelor, their favorite preacher in town had married the young widow next door. And they were going to be even more surprised when they found out a baby was on the way.

"She's fine," he said. "She's excited about getting a Christmas tree up. I can't believe how much Christmas stuff she's accumulated over the years. All I brought to the marriage was a shedding three foot artificial tree and about ten ornaments. I plan to take it out of the attic and set it out by the curb with the garbage. I hope someone takes it off my hands."

"I'm so glad you two got together. The whole town had you as an item way before either one of you realized you were destined for each other, but we were beginning to wonder if it would ever come to pass."

"So am I, May. I was just too busy to see what God had in store for me, but never again will I get so occupied with things that are not my business. I'm changing my meddling ways and refuse to get involved where I'm not needed." He stood up and put his napkin in the trash can.

"That'll be the day," May said and walked him to the front door.

"It's true - I've changed. I promise - scout's honor," and he held up his hand.

"It'll take more than a Boy Scout pledge to convince me," she said raising her eyebrows. "You just always seem to find places where your help is needed whether the person knows it or not." She reached up and flipped the Open side of the sign on the door to face the outside. "We wouldn't want it any other way."

"Nope, those days are over," he said. "By the way, I'd say your display has a good shot at the blue ribbon again this year." She walked with him out the door and looked at her window from the outside.

"Just a few more ribbons and greenery and I'll be through. I wish I could have found a deer head instead of a moose though. Our grandson in Montana brought Jeff the moose head the last time he came home for a visit," she said. "I'm glad you stopped by, Rock. Tell Liz I said hello."

Rock continued his stroll down Main Street, stopping and talking to the business owners he saw outside. Sam Owens was standing outside Banty Hen Antiques, a store he and his wife Valerie had recently opened. The building had formerly been a big chain jewelry store, but when a spot became available in the Sparta Shopping Mall, the business had closed shop and moved.

Sam had propped a large vintage Flexible Flyer sled against the building and was busy tying a ribbon around the runner. Part of the window looked fresh out of an early 1960's magazine. A large aluminum tree with foil needles stood on the left side of the window and was illuminated from below by a revolving color wheel. Vintage blue and silver Shiny Brite ornaments hung from its branches with their colorful, graphic boxes sitting underneath.

A gate and a small section of a white picket fence separated the display and took the viewer back into the 18th century to the Victorian Era where a cardboard fireplace created a peaceful scene with needlepoint stockings hanging from an old mantle with chipping paint. An antique feather tree stood beside an elegant sideboard which held all shapes and sizes of Dickens style Christmas carolers and Department 56 snow villages. A Lionel train set was spewing steam from the engine car and making its way around the track circling the tree.

Hmm, he thought, May's Flower Shop is in for some stiff competition. Sam and Valerie Owens were members of the Methodist church. Junie said they both had recently retired, and when Valerie spotted the empty building, she had pestered Sam to lease it and open it up as an antique shop.

Sam stood up from tying the bow and bumped into Rock. "Excuse me, Rev Rock. I didn't see you standing there."

"My fault entirely," said Rock, jumping back. "I was so busy window gazing, I didn't realize I was about to step on you."

"And I was in my own little world. Valerie's working me to death getting the store ready for the big event. We opened a couple of weeks ago, but she thinks having a Grand Opening with coffee and cookies will get more people in. She's already put it on Facebook and has it in the Park Place Gazette. It's scheduled for next Saturday - hope you and Liz can drop by. We miss her at church - you stole her away from us. I know she loves antique furniture and we've got some nice pieces."

"I'll tell her, Sam. She would love this store. We'll be moving back into the parsonage after the remodel and I'm sure she'll want to change things up some."

"Anytime Rock, we would love to have both of you drop in."

"I have a feeling our church calendar is going to be hectic, but maybe we can squeeze in a little time before Christmas." He looked down at his watch. "Oops, I've got to get home. My parents are here visiting and I've been gone so long, they'll think I'm ignoring them. I'll see you next week." He waved to Valerie who was standing in the window and hurried toward home.

CHAPTER 5

"*B*lessed are the meek, for they will inherit the earth.*"*
- Matthew 5:5 NIV

Maria watched from the open vent cover in the basement as a man and woman left the big house and walked hand in hand down the path toward the smaller house. They had been back and forth all afternoon. It must be a large family, she thought. An older man had come outside for a while - then several other adults had gone back and forth from the big house to the cottage. The children had slammed the kitchen door each time they went out and back in.

She waited a while after the lights went off and seeing no activity in the big house, she took her two water bottles to the spigots right outside the basement door and filled them. Then she put the trash bag outside on the steps to keep the food items cold where they wouldn't spoil. The weather was already below freezing. Wrapping the coat tightly around her and pulling the hood up over her ears, she finally got warm and drifted off to sleep. She dreamed she was back home in her parents' house in the bedroom she shared with her little brother. She felt safer than she had felt in a long while.

The next morning was bedlam in the parsonage. Irene was giving orders and had assigned each person, right down to the grandchildren, a role in getting the house back in shape from their visit. "What should we do with all this food?" Lisa asked as she and Allison worked on their assigned duty of cleaning up the kitchen.

"Mom's already taken care of it," Allison answered. "She asked Liz about it last night. She took some things back to the cottage, but she asked if we would freeze the leftover turkey and ham for sandwiches and soup later. There was a whole pan of cornbread dressing left - we may as well freeze it too. This freezer is bigger than the one they have over there. If there's anything perishable, put it in sealed plastic bags and it goes in the big trash can out back. The garbage pick-up only comes once a week. Apparently raccoons are a problem here so the sealed bags deter them from getting into the garbage. She said sometimes the raccoons will carry the whole trash bag away if they smell food in it and they'll find stuff strewn all over the lawn."

Will had walked in to get a bottled water from the refrigerator. "So that's it," he said. "Raccoons! I saw a bag of trash out back of the church when I first walked outside this morning, but now it's gone."

"Maybe Rock saw it and picked it up," Allison said.

"Probably," said Will as he walked outside to empty another bag of trash. As he put the bag in the container, he could hear a beeping sound at the front of the house. He walked around the corner and looked out to the street where a blue truck was backing up. A porta-jon was on the back. The driver motioned him to come to the window.

"Where do you want this thing?" he asked.

"I have no idea," Will said as he dialed Rock's number on his cell phone, "but I'll find out."

"I'll be right over," Rock said from the other end of

the phone line.

Rock was pulling on his jacket as he walked out the door of the cottage. Will met him halfway. "What are you doing with a porta-jon?" he asked.

"The re-model of the kitchen and bathrooms," he answered. "They'll have the water turned off for a good bit of the time, and the workers will need a bathroom." He directed the driver to unload it at the very back of the house near the trash cans. "At least it won't be seen from the road," he reasoned. "They're not very eye-pleasing, are they?"

"That's an understatement," his father said.

"We'll be over to see you off - what time do you think you'll be leaving?"

"Forty-five minutes, tops," he said. "Irene's got to have everything spotless before we leave."

"I told her not to worry so much with it. The remodelers will be making a mess in a few days anyway."

"You know your mother, Rock. She's a clean freak. I've got to get the rest of the stuff in the car - see you in a bit."

Rock walked back to the cottage and Will went back in the house to get another load of suitcases to pack in the car. It seemed like a bottomless pit of suitcases had appeared again after he had already made two trips to the car earlier. "Irene," he yelled back towards the bedroom. "I didn't know we owned this many suitcases!"

She came out of the bedroom. "We don't, you silly man. Those came from upstairs. Robert is running the vacuum and Mark is cleaning the bathrooms. It won't hurt you to carry their suitcases out since they're busy cleaning, will it?"

"I don't suppose so, as long as I don't have to put anything else in my car."

"Don't be grumpy, my dear! Run along now."

"Yes, Ma'am," he said under his breath.

Maria had slept later than she planned and the people inside the big house were already stirring as she hurriedly pulled the trash bag back inside the basement. She would not be so careless again. With a plastic fork, she scraped the remainder of the peanut butter from the jar and spread it on one of the apples to eat for breakfast. She heard a noise outside and looked through the vent and watched as a large truck dropped off a small blue building like the ones she had seen when she had gone with Ernesto to one of his worksites, but she wondered why. Did they not have toilets in such a large, fine house? But it would make her life simpler - she had worried over what she would do without a toilet.

The family seemed to be leaving. She watched as they brought suitcases outside and put them in the trunk of their cars. There were three children and six adults. The man and woman living in the small house had come to see them off. They said their goodbyes and the two cars drove away.

CHAPTER 6

"*He who finds a wife finds a good thing and obtains favor from the Lord.*"
- Proverbs 18:22

"Deck the halls with boughs of holly, Fa-la-la-la-la La-la-la-la." The tune was slightly off key, but Rock kept singing. "Tis the season to be jolly, Fa-la-la-la-la La-la-la-la." His look was smug as he stood back from the tree with obvious satisfaction. "The lights are all strung, Liz. Now it's your turn to hang the ornaments." His left arm was crossed over his chest, and his chin rested on his right hand as he gazed at his handiwork. Then he turned around and looked at her, waiting for her to respond. She was getting the gold beaded garland out of the box. "Well, what do you think?"

"You're not getting off that easy, Buddy-roe. This is a joint effort - we both hang the ornaments."

"Both of us? You've seen how long it's taken me with the lights. The one string alone was a nightmare. I changed out the fuses and replaced half the bulbs and it still wouldn't light up."

"And then I came along and wiggled it and voila! It lit right up. I must have the magic touch."

"You do!" he said, and pulled her into his arms. "The magic touch indeed."

Liz felt the magic all the way down to her toes as his kiss intensified. He held her for a while longer, then slowly relaxed his hold and looked into her eyes. "This isn't going to get the tree decorated, is it?" For a moment she was lost in his eyes, but reluctantly pulled away.

"No," she sighed. "I suppose not. I really want to get this finished since I have to go back to work Monday."

"I'm sure your students don't like going back after the break any more than you." He looked down at her and felt a wave of tenderness wash over him. Every day with Liz was more special than the day before. At forty-five, he had lost all hope of finding a wife, but God had other plans. He felt a sense of peace and contentment he never dreamed possible. And she literally took his breath away every time they kissed.

"Oh, they'll be zombies on Monday. It's going to be hectic - the semester is almost over, exam time is upon us and there are only three weeks until Christmas vacation. I think I see some backrubs in your future."

"I think I missed my calling," he said, "if my backrubs are anywhere near as good as you say they are, maybe I could moonlight as a massage therapist."

"Oh no," she said, "you know what they say about doctors and dentists - they're so busy fixing other peoples' problems, they don't have time to treat their own. I don't want to share my masseur."

"Don't worry," he said, snickering at the thought of patients lining up outside his office for a back rub and his secretary's reaction. "Reva would run them all away."

"I would hope so," she said with a grin. She closed the lid on the tote the lights had been in and put it aside.

"You know, just a few days ago, a four day school break seemed long and luxurious, but this one's gone by in a blur. Just think, tomorrow's Sunday, and you know how fast Sundays come and go."

"The days have gone by in a hurry, haven't they? That tends to happen when my whirlwind family comes for a visit."

"I'm glad your mom and sisters were such troopers to come up on Wednesday and get all the preparations done for Thanksgiving dinner. I'm not sure I could have done it with this morning sickness. Just the thought of cooking was about to do me in."

"You got over it a hurry when all the food was spread out on the table. You ate almost as much as I did," he teased.

"That'll be the day when I can eat more than Rock Clark," she said. "Reva had you spoiled when I married you - feeding you chicken and dumplings and peach cobbler all the time. Besides, I never said I had trouble eating it - just cooking it. Seriously, Rock - I've never had such a feast. Growing up, we just didn't do traditional Thanksgiving meals. Living on the coast, our holiday meals usually involved seafood of some sort cooked by my dad. Then after Ron and I married, we just continued the Low Country cooking tradition."

"Seafood sounds good. Right now I'm sick of turkey leftovers. My family is just the opposite - they're steeped in tradition. The Thanksgiving menu never varies - year after year it's the same things. Turkey, dressing, giblet gravy, mashed potatoes, green beans made by Mom. Then a broccoli casserole, candied yams, deviled eggs and yeast rolls made by my sisters."

"You forgot about the pies - I've never seen so many pies in my life. I'm glad we used the parsonage for our gathering - we never could have squeezed your family in this tiny place. And I loved the luxury of having two houses so we could sleep everyone - much nicer than having them stay in a hotel room. It was a good way to get to know your family. I really like your mom and sisters." She paused for a minute. "You're right though, I did feel like I'd been in a whirlwind when they left this morning."

"Well, you were a big hit with the family. Mom gushed every chance she got about how wonderful you are and what a lucky man I am. I couldn't believe it - Irene Clark has never called anyone wonderful - except maybe her grandchildren. This was your first holiday with them - just you wait until we all go on vacation together next summer. The Clark clan comes from far and wide for this trip - you won't know what hit you."

"They won't know what hit them, you mean. We'll be adding two to the family vacation and one of us may be noisy."

"Two?" He looked puzzled and then it dawned on him. "There will be two - you and the baby!" He looked at her tenderly. "Does it not seem surreal to you that we're having a baby? All these years of being a bachelor, I never thought I would have kids of my own."

She smiled at him. "It seems that way to me too. The years I spent with Ron - always hoping for a baby, but it never happened. We went to doctor after doctor and they couldn't find anything wrong. We prayed for a baby and I would get angry with God for not answering my prayers."

Hearing Liz talk about her years with Ron was natural to Rock. Ron had been his best friend until he died suddenly of a heart attack and left Liz a widow at thirty-six. In the two year period since Ron's death, through their common grief, their friendship had grown stronger. Before either of them realized it, they had fallen in love.

"God didn't ignore your prayers, Liz - He just knew the big picture and you didn't."

"I'm not doubting God's plans, Rock. Here we are now - you and me. And within the first month of our marriage I became pregnant. Yes, it does seem surreal." She gave him a quick hug. "Now on with the tree. Did you get all the boxes out of the attic?"

"Yes Ma'am - I even took the lids off so you could get started."

"Where's the angel?"

"What angel?"

"The one that's supposed to be sitting on top of the tree."

"You didn't tell me about an angel."

"I shouldn't have to. Everyone knows you can't have a Christmas tree without an angel on top."

"Well, yes - now that you mention it - everyone does - except maybe me." He snapped his fingers and looked at the top of the tree as if waiting for something to happen. "Oops - the magic's not working this time. You find the angel and I'll get the step ladder back out." He opened the front door and walked out on the porch to retrieve the ladder.

"I love you, Rock Clark. You're the angel," she yelled after him, and then quietly whispered a prayer of praise to God for bringing such a good man into her life. Ron had been the love of her life and when he died, she never dreamed there would be another. She knew in her heart Ron would approve.

The angel was wrapped in tissue paper and was in the box with her Christmas village accessories. This was the same angel that had adorned her grandmother's tree and her great-grandmother's before. It was one of the few things she had asked for when Nana Ruth had passed away. It was at least ninety years old according to her mom. Rock walked back in with the ladder and watched as she turned the angel over gingerly in her hands. Just the day before he had heard her tell his mother the story. When she was a child, helping her grandparents decorate for Christmas, she had accidentaly broken one of the wings. Her grandfather had repaired it with glue and neither of them had told Nana Ruth. She suspected she knew though, because since that day, the right wing had been a little crooked, but through the years, it had become part of its charm. "It just shows no one is perfect," Grandpa had said as he placed it on the tree. "Not even the angels." He had climbed back down the ladder then and scooped Liz up in his arms. "Isn't that right, Lizzy-Bell? Now let's go get some hot chocolate!"

"Isn't it funny how the little mistakes and accidents we made as children seem to stick with us," Irene had told her. "But it sounds like your grandpa was a kind and sensitive man, and his actions are what make this a special memory for you and not an unpleasant one."

As Rock had watched the two most important women in his life interact with each other, he knew they would become fast friends.

Rock took the angel to the top and leaned into the tree. He stretched as far as he could without tipping over to put it on the top. "Perfect," he said. As he started back down, he bumped the light strand he had worked on and the lights went back out. "Now this is enough to make a preacher cuss," he said.

"Don't you even think about it. Anyway, I think you only have one bad word in your vocabulary," Liz replied back. The lights flickered again. "Oh, they're back on. What did you do?"

"Just used some of my magic," he teased. He had just wiggled them again.

"Something must be loose in there. Do you think we should throw away that strand?"

"What? After all my hard work? No way!"

"Seriously, Rock, there may be a bad connection - you know, like an electrical problem. I've heard a lot of fires have started with Christmas tree lights."

"Just with the old lights from years ago - they really were a fire hazard," he said. "They're much safer now." He lifted the garland back out of the box where she had dropped it. "Let's get started so we can finish up tonight." They worked together for over an hour, stopping only to drink a cup of hot chocolate and reminisce about Christmases past. Theo gave them a little help by swatting at the bottom ornaments. When they finished, they sat on the sofa and admired the transformation of the living room. Two stockings were hanging from the mantel. A wreath with a natural winter theme, pine cones and a large red bow hung over the fireplace and Rock's tiny nativity set was on the small parlor table. The mirror on the hall tree reflected the poinsettia on its bench giving the illusion of two of them instead of one. The gas logs, along with the lights from the tree gave the room a soft and cozy glow. Liz had not put up a tree since Ron died and Rock only had what he called a Charlie Brown tree that he sparsely decorated each year.

Rock turned to Liz as he remembered what she had

said earlier. "What kind of bad word do I have in my vocabulary"? He looked worried.

For a moment she looked puzzled, but then she remembered and smiled. "Oh yes, *Rats!* You're always saying *rats.* I don't like rats, and it creeps me out every time I hear the word." She laughed as he looked relieved. "Please refrain from using it anymore, would you?"

He shook his head and rolled his eyes. "I refuse to let you deprive me of my bad word. Rats, rats, and more rats. Did you know the Romans considered rats to be good luck, and there's a National Rat Day, and that rats are extremely intelligent animals, and they have poor eyesight and are colorblind.... "

She put her hands over her ears. "Enough already! I promise I won't complain about your occasional use of the word, if you promise not to share anymore rat facts."

"It's a deal."

Liz stretched her feet out towards the gas logs for warmth. "By the way, the poinsettia May brought by today is beautiful - I don't suppose you had anything to do with that?"

"Who, me?" He was rather proud of himself for thinking of calling May. He looked over at the poinsettia on the bench. It was nice - he could always depend on his favorite florist to send the best. He had been rusty in the romancing department before Liz came along, and he knew he still had a long way to go.

Liz yawned. "The tree looks nice. I'm glad we tackled it tonight."

"So am I," he said. "I could sit here all night looking at it, but tomorrow's a busy day." He stood up and offered his hand to pull her up from the sofa. He turned off the Christmas tree lights and put his arm around her. As they walked down the hallway, he whispered in her ear, "Now, about that kiss we started."

"Ah, yes," she said, and pulled him toward the bedroom door. He looked back - Theo was fast asleep under the tree.

CHAPTER 7

"**A**nd *also that every man should eat and drink, and enjoy the good of all his labour, it is the gift of God.*"

- Ecclesiastes 3:13 KJV

Rock opened the outer door to the post office, trying to sneak in unobserved to check his box, but Betty had seen him on the sidewalk from the window and was at the door waiting for him.

"Come on inside, Rev Rock - we've got something exciting to show you."

"It must be important to make you come outside to get me. What's up, Betty?"

"It's Wanda's books! She just got two big boxes and she opened one up. Get in here and see it. It's a right spectacular show - she's whoopin' and hollerin' something fierce."

Betty was right - Wanda was fluttering around and holding her heart. "I just can't believe it, Rev Rock. I've been waiting on these books for over two months. First, it wasn't formatted right and I had to change it. Then they sent me the proof and I found some mistakes. I thought I was never going to get them published. Look! It's got my name on it. My name, *Wanda Burns*. It's just giving me such a thrill to see my name on this book." She was holding the book out for him to see. The front cover was a photo of a fishing boat overlooking a serene coastal village, and it was titled, *The Ghost of Craggy Point*.

Rock reached over and gave her a hug. "Well, the title sure makes me want to read it. Congratulations, Wanda. I'm excited for you - when are you going to have them for sale? I want an autographed copy."

"Oh my, I hadn't even thought about it. I'm going to start practicing on my signature - I've got such sloppy handwriting. I'll let you know when I get them inventoried and up for sale. Thanks for wanting to buy one!"

Rock turned back to the counter. "Have you forgiven her for not having you as a character in her book, Betty?"

"Aw, shush! I was just teasing about being mad. Anyways, she's going to put me in the next one, aren't you Wanda."

Wanda laughed. "Yep, I think we've had plenty of things happen in Park Place recently to write about." She looked up at Rock. "Don't worry - it'll be fiction and I won't make it so as anyone would know who you are, Rev Rock."

Rock rolled his eyes. Lord help us, he thought. What are we in for? "Wanda, Park Place is so small, how can anybody here not know who we are?"

Betty piped in, "Well, I'm going to be in it for sure. And I don't care if you do use my name. When they make it into a Hallmark movie, I want Gladys Knight to play my role in the movie."

"Gladys Knight?" Rock asked. "I thought she was a singer."

"Well, I was thinking about Kerry Washington, but she's just a little bit too naughty to play me." She lightly touched her curls and held her face up in profile. "Don't you think I look a little like Gladys Knight?"

Rock didn't want to put his foot in his mouth, so he was glad when Jerry Mabry, who had walked in during their conversation, started slapping his knees and laughing. "I think you should just go for the big guns, and get Oprah." It was all over then. Rock joined in and laughed so hard, he snorted.

"Hmph," Betty said. "Y'all won't be laughing when I'm a celebrity."

Wanda chimed in, "Betty, don't get ahead of yourself. I haven't even written the book yet."

"Well, all I can say is, you better be gettin' busy."

Rock walked out the main door and into the lobby to check his box. "Yep, best entertainment in town," he muttered to himself. He walked down the steps and headed down the street. He hadn't meant to be in the post office so long. He was late for his Monday morning gathering at Crowder's Feed and Seed. He walked in at 10:05 and a chorus from the back greeted him in unison, "Where you been?"

At 10 o'clock sharp on Monday mornings, a few of the locals gathered inside Junie and Kathleen's place of business. The gatherings had started out with just three men and had now grown to five. Jenny Braswell called it their Social Hour and was happy to get Larry out of the house for a while, but was happy to see him when he returned an hour or so later with little tidbits of town gossip. Fred Laney's barbershop, a few miles out of town, was closed on Mondays, so Fred always came in to buy laying mash for his hens and hung around for the conversation. Rock had dropped in one day to buy a water hose when he still lived in the old parsonage, and Junie, the owner of the store, had invited him to join their group.

Last year, they had taken in a new member, Cap Price, who needed their help during a bout of depression after his wife had passed away the previous year. Cap now had a new lease on life. With Rock's help, he had reconnected with an old friend, Madge Johnson, and after a brief whirlwind of a romance, had married her, and as he liked to say, was 'happy as a pig in slop'.

His new wife was the topic of their conversation today. "Madge got some high-falutin' remodeling company from up in Charlotte to come by and give us an estimate for gutting the whole house and starting over. I told her I couldn't afford to pay for it, but she's got more money than Carter's got liver pills, so she's bound and determined to do it. I'm not complaining, mind you. She can do whatever she wants to do if it makes her happy. Of course, Madge is happy all the time anyway. " When he grinned, Rock could tell he had paid a recent visit to a dentist. Where the gaping hole had once been, there was now a bright and shiny tooth.

"We're going to live in her house while they do the remodel."

"So, she's not going to sell her house?" Rock asked.

"Nope! She's keepin' it so as when her son and his family visit for the holidays, they can stay in it. She's got two grandchildren in college and they're gonna come stay for a week during their Christmas break. Bill and Selma will be up to spend the night on Christmas Eve and stay through the twenty-seventh." He sat there for a moment in reflection, then looked up at Rock. "Me and Josie didn't have any children - never did figure out if it was me or her, but it don't matter. We were content as long as we had each other. But Rev Rock, it's sorta' nice being a part of a big family. I'm lookin' forward to this Christmas like never before. Is it wrong of me to be thinkin' like that? Am I being disrespectful to m' Josie who I was happy with all those years?"

"No, Cap. I think Josie would be glad that you've moved on with your life and have a new family. It's not taking anything away from what you had with her. She'd want you to live your life to the fullest."

"You know, I think you're right. I was beginning to dry up like an ol' prune. I can't for the life of me understand what Madge sees in the likes of me."

"She sees your good heart," Rock said, and meant it.

Fred Laney piped in. "Quit your blabbering, boys. Y'all are gonna' make me cry."

"Now that I've got to see!" Larry Braswell said and took out a freshly pressed handkerchief from his pocket and handed it to him. Fred swatted it away.

"Get that thing away from me," he said. "You've probably been blowing your nose on it."

Junie shouted from the cash register where he was ringing up the sale of a roll of twine and a horse pick. "Am I gonna' have to come over there and break it up between you two? I'll swanee, you're as bad as two kids."

Larry stuck his tongue out at Fred and put his handkerchief back in his pocket. "I hear there's some more remodeling around town fixin' to start," he said, looking at Rock. "Bring a woman into the mix and before you know it, you'll be appearing on that TV show Jenny likes to watch - Design on a Dime. She's bound and determined to turn our house into some modernistic Scandinavian retreat complete with George Jetson furniture and one of those little wood stoves that goes from the floor to the ceiling. I don't know what she's going to do with all that antique furniture she was so wild about buying just two years ago."

"You can sell it on Ebay," Fred said. "I've heard of people making a killing selling stuff they find around the house."

"I do well just turning a computer on, and I don't even want to learn how to sell stuff on Ebay. Nope, that's going to be Jenny's problem. That is, if she ever gets around to starting this project. Right now it's just in the dreaming stage." Larry turned back to Rock. "What kind of remodeling are you doing to the parsonage, Rev Rock? I heard someone say that Jay Harvey is the contractor the Session decided on. He's a good one, all right."

"He's starting today, as a matter of fact." He looked at his watch. "I'm sure he's there by now - he said 9 o'clock, but I've been gone all morning. We're doing just a few minor things - mostly in the kitchen."

"Well, that shouldn't take long. Maybe you'll be in there by Christmas," Larry said.

"Jay said it would be mid-January. He's also going to remodel the master bath. There's just a shower in there right now, and Liz wants a tub. The rest is just cosmetic. It's time for a new paint job inside the whole house. I'm not in any hurry to move back in, but Liz will love the extra space. I love it right where we are." Again, he almost slipped up and said something about Liz wanting to get started on the nursery. I'm not good at keeping secrets, he thought.

Fred and Junie joined in the conversation about how a woman is never satisfied with the way her house looks. "You get one project completed," Fred said, "and then it's time for another."

Rock was at ease with the easy bantering. Just a few months ago, he would have felt, as Reva put it, like a third wheel if he had joined in with the others talking about their wives. It was a good feeling.

CHAPTER 8

"And let us not grow weary while doing good, for in due season we shall reap if we do not lose heart.

- Galatians 6:9 NKJV

Maria awoke to the sound of a man's voice. She jerked her make-shift bed of batted insulation and carpet scraps back into the corner they came from and hid behind one of the large concrete supports in the church basement. After a few minutes, she realized the men were not as near as she had thought, so she came out from her hiding place and walked over to the air vent so she could see outside. The vent was partially closed from the outside, but she pried it open a bit and saw a white van parked in front of the big house. There was an American and two Hispanic men getting tools and ladders from the van. The Americano was unlocking the back door of the house and the others began taking the tools inside.

This had been the third night Maria had spent in the basement. She knew today was Monday, because yesterday there had been much activity in the church building. The parking lot had been full and she had observed people going in and out of the church during the morning hours. But best of all was the music. The bells in the bell tower had sounded eleven times and then the glorious music had begun. She could not hear the voices singing, only the music - but it was enough. The first hymn was familiar and she sang it quietly in her native tongue as the music played. Her voice was sweet and clear.

Oh Ven, Oh Ven, Emmanuel.

Rescata del mal a Israel.

El vive en un exilio triste.

Desde el dia que tu te fuiste.

Oyen su voz, Emmanuel.

Aqui te espera Israel.

She pulled the bed back out and sat down. Her stomach was growling and she remembered she was almost out of food. There were three sweet rolls left ‐ a little stale, but still good. She carefully wrapped two of them back up in the cellophane package and ate the other. The sweet rolls, along with one lone apple was all she had left to eat.

It was not in her character to be bold or deceptive, but Maria had decided she would do anything within her means to care for her baby.

Pulling her backpack out from under the insulation, she opened it up and emptied the contents. When she started gaining weight, Ernesto had only allowed her to buy two pairs of maternity pants and two oversized shirts, but when she had grabbed things out of the closet, she had taken one of his flannel shirts along with her own. She took a quick inventory of the items spread out before her. The flannel shirt along with one pair of pants, one shirt and underwear were there ‐ the other clothing she was wearing. She wished she had a way of taking a bath ‐ she felt dirty after three days of wearing the same clothes.

She had bathed as much as possible at the water spigot each night using a washcloth she had brought from the apartment, but what she really needed was a shower, and she would have to find a way to launder her clothes.

She counted out the little bit of money she had left. She had two tens, three ones, and $4.25 in change - so little, she thought, but with a determination much bigger than her stature, she planned what she would do. One day at a time, Maria, she thought. God will get you through one day at a time.

She was desperate to get out of the dark, dreary basement. Remembering a dollar store she had passed on the outskirts of town, she decided that a brisk walk would do her good. She needed milk, and she found herself craving a good hot meal. She had slept as close as possible to the heat ducts but she never seemed to get warm. She was beginning to feel the constant cold in her bones. She put the money in the pocket of her coat and looked out to see if anyone was watching. The men in the van were no longer outside. She hurriedly scrambled up the steps into the sunshine. Instead of walking to the street in front of the church, she decided to go through the small alley she had spotted behind the parking lot at the back of the church. The church chimes had just struck eleven times. She hoped she would blend in with the lunch time travelers on the street.

Rock and Cap were the last to leave the feed and seed store and they walked out together. Cap's old truck was parallel parked out front. "Do you want me to give you a ride?" he asked Rock.

"Thank you, but no, the walk will do me good. It's just a little over a block."

"I'll see ya' next week, if not before," he said. "Madge has been on me about going to your church with her and I might take her up on it next Sunday. I'm not going to change my membership at the Methodist church just yet, though. They've been awfully good to me."

"That's something for you and Madge to work out, Cap. Maybe for the time being, you can just go with her one week, and she go with you the next. You know you're welcome to join ours any time, but I'm not going to try to persuade you one way or the other. You already have a good church home and Bob Hartley is a wonderful minister."

It was because of Bob that Rock and Cap were now good friends. Suffering from a deep depression after his wife had passed away, Cap had caught the attention of the Monday morning men's gathering at Junie's store. He had not been eating properly and had lost weight and let his appearance go downhill. Bob Hartley's broken leg had prevented him from checking on Cap, so Rock had offered his services and with Bob's approval, he had gone to visit Cap. That one visit had started an avalanche of events both negative and positive. Rock had opened up a can of worms in a land scheme involving a former lady friend, which in turn led to an attempted poisoning meant for him, but almost doing in his cat, Theo instead. The positive outcome was that Cap and Madge Johnson had reconnected and in a whirlwind of a senior romance, had gotten married just a few months back.

"I 'preciate you not pressurin' me, Rev Rock. I reckon we'll figure it out sooner or later."

Rock walked past the post office and turned onto Church Street. He started to go in the office to see if Reva had any messages for him, but his growling stomach guided him past the office and up the little path toward the cottage. He heard the chimes as they rang. Eleven o'clock, he thought. I'll eat lunch and then go to the office. As he started up the steps, he glanced toward the church. He stopped and watched as a young Hispanic girl walked across the parking lot and into the alley beyond. His first thought was that she may be skipping school, but then again, she may be older than she looked. She probably just took a shortcut through the parking lot, he thought, and the growling of his stomach shook the thoughts of the girl out of his mind.

Rock sat at his desk listening to Reva fuss and fidget, all the while holding a calendar almost up to his nose. "Thanksgiving's barely over and there are only twenty-five days until Christmas," she said, pointing to the appointment book and pushing it closer to his face. "Do you have any idea how many things you have on your calendar?"

"I'm sure you'll tell me. Hold it back a little, Reva - I can't see...or breathe." He studied the calendar. "Looks just about like every December since I've been here," he said.

"But there's so little time."

"Hmm. Thirty-one days in December. As I recall, every December has thirty-one days, Reva. So what's so different about this one?"

"I give up! You're just being smart-alecky today, yes you are!"

Rock laughed. "Calm down - I'm just teasing. I know exactly what you mean. It does seem like we have less time. Thanksgiving fell late this year - the 27th. The first Sunday of Advent was yesterday and tomorrow's December 1st." He shook his head and sighed. "The season is coming at us like a freight train."

"Now, you're getting it," she said. "I've made a copy of December's calendar and I'm going to scotch tape it right on your desk just so you don't forget something. By the way, have you had lunch?"

"Thanks for staying on top of things, Reva. I know I don't tell you enough, but I appreciate everything thing you do," he said, as he watched her tape the calendar to the glass top covering the antique oak desk where he sat. "And yes, I just finished eating another turkey sandwich."

"Well, at least I don't have to cook for you anymore," she said. "I told you Miss Liz would fatten you up, didn't I? Pretty soon, you're gonna' have to move this desk out from the wall or you're not going to be able to sit behind it anymore." She snickered and walked back toward her office.

Surprised, he looked down at his waistline. "Well, I don't think I've gained any weight," he said, but she had already gone out of hearing distance. He tucked his thumb under his belt. Hmm, he thought, it is a little snug, and the Christmas goodies would be rolling in soon. He decided to not worry about it until after New Year's.

Reva walked back in with a cup of coffee and put it on his desk. "I just made a fresh pot, and I brought us a pan of cinnamon rolls from home this morning. I made 'em from scratch, just like you like them." Her face beamed. Her homemade cinnamon rolls were famous in

Park Place. "They'll be ready in about seven minutes - they're in the toaster oven now."

"What are you doing to me? First, telling me I'm gaining weight, and now tempting me with cinnamon rolls. You know good and well I can't resist those things."

"Just trying to keep you happy," she said.

"Keep it up - I'm not complaining. Liz is..." For heaven's sake, he did it again - he almost said that Liz was gaining weight, so why shouldn't he.

"Liz is what?" Reva asked.

"Liz is not going to have much time to bake things. It's the end of the semester and she's swamped with testing stuff." Whew, that was close, but he thought he did a good job of covering it up. He put his reading glasses back on and looked down at the paper on his desk. "Let's look at this calendar together. What are all these parties you've put on here?"

She smiled and picked up her copy of the calendar. "Now that you've got yourself a wife, this is what happens. You get invited to all the Sunday School parties. Before, you were a third wheel so you didn't get any invitations."

"A third wheel? I think I liked it better that way," he said. "Do we have to go to all of them?"

"You askin' the wrong person," she answered. "You need to talk to Miss Liz about that."

"Reva, I wish you would just call her Liz, instead of Miss Liz. That sounds sort of stuffy."

"Stuffy, schmuffy," she said with her hands on her hips. "I don't call you Rock, now do I? I've always called you Rev Rock, and I'm gonna' keep 'a doin' it, just like I'm going to keep calling her Miss Liz."

"Yes ma'am," he said. "You just call her whatever you

want." He had never won an argument with Reva yet, and it was too late to start trying now. He looked back at the calendar. "What's this on Friday? It just says 'Poles'."

"That's when we start putting up the poles for the Lighting the Way ceremony, which by the way, is not this Sunday, but the next. We always do it on the third Sunday of Advent, you remember."

"Why are we putting up the poles a week early this year?"

"You askin' too many questions, but I'll answer you anyway. Grady Parker's going to be out of town the following weekend and he's the one that owns the big auger for digging the holes. You don't want to be diggin' those holes by hand do you?"

"No ma'am. That contraption of Grady's makes it too easy." The Lighting the Way services were Rock's favorite part of the Christmas activities. The four churches in town were all located within a four block radius of the center of town and they all participated in the services. Poles with lanterns were set up a few days before, lining the walkways of each church and on the lawns of the homes in between. They started in the courtyard of Park Place Presbyterian at 4:30 p.m. with a blessing for the services and then started lighting the candles in the lanterns before walking into the church for a fellowship of song and worship. From there, they continued lighting candles until they reached the next church, with services in each of the four churches until they reached the final church, White Pines A.M.E. Zion. There, it ended with a spirited rendition of "Go Tell it on the Mountain" sung by one of the older members of the church with everyone joining in on the chorus. All denominations worshiping and singing together - it was a wonder to behold - and the spirit of Christmas was ignited in the hearts of each and every person who attended.

"And this Saturday, the men and women meet at the church at 10 a.m. to put the tree up in the sanctuary for the women to decorate," Reva said. "Saturday night is when the Sunday School parties begin." She winked at him.

"Don't even go there," he said. "We'll see about that."

"Then the next week is Lighting the Way. We have the Children's Home Christmas party on Saturday, the 20th at 2 p.m.; the Christmas pageant and the soup and chili supper on the evening of the 21st; and finally Christmas Eve services at 6 p.m. on the 24th. You're going to run yourself ragged, yes you are - and you're gonna' take me right along with you. Why, I'm plum tuckered out just looking at this calendar!"

"And all the in-betweens," Rock said. It seemed like every year during the Christmas season when everyone was busy and rushed, a few tempers flared and there were fires to put out.

"Come on over here, Reva. We're going to need all the help we can get to wrangle through this calendar. Reva knew what he was up to and walked over and reached both arms over the desk. Rock stood up and caught her hands in his and they both closed their eyes. "Lord, this is the season where You sent Your Son to save all mankind. Help each and every one of us to be reminded of this as we keep our hectic schedules. Keep us focused so that our mind is on You and give us the peace and grace to get through these busy days. Lord, I thank you for Reva and I ask you to bless her as she gives so tirelessly of herself. Work in the hearts of our congregation as they go about doing Your work in the wondrous days ahead. In Your Son's name we pray. Amen."

Reva squeezed his hands and then turned them loose. "Thank you, Rev Rock. Let's get started - it's full speed ahead." He heard the timer for the cinnamon rolls and made his way into the kitchen. He may have to let his belt out another notch, but that's what the notches were for, he thought. The fullness of his December calendar called for a cinnamon roll... or two.

CHAPTER 9

T he Lord God said, "It is not good for the man to be alone. I will make a helper suitable for him."

- **Genesis 2:18 NIV**

"It would be rude to miss the Christmas parties," Liz said as she set the table for dinner. "Especially since we've received invitations. And you know what that means, don't you?" Rock shook his head. He knew he was about to find out, and he didn't think he would like the answer. "If we go to one, we have to go to them all." Rock dropped his head and slumped.

"Seriously? How are we going to have time? You should see what Reva has on that calendar."

"Oh, it won't be that bad - I think it'll be fun. I'll call Reva tomorrow and write all the dates on my calendar. Besides, it's just the newness of it all, and I doubt they'll even think of inviting us next year."

"If you say so," he said, looking hopeful. "I'll pour the tea. You go ahead and sit down. I can tell you've had a long day." He pulled her chair out from the table and she sat down. He put ice in the glasses and sliced a lemon, then poured the tea. A pot of vegetable soup was on the stove and he ladled up a bowl for Liz and then one for himself.

"Ah, just the way I like it," he said after taking a big swig of the iced tea. "Sweet... you haven't lost your touch."

"You should know," she said. "You drank gallons of it

on my front porch last summer."

"I liked your tea just fine, but I think it was the company I liked better," he said. "And look where it got me."

"And look where it got me," she teased, patting her stomach. "It was the tea, I tell you. You told me yourself it was addictive. You hardly noticed me at all."

He thought back to the subtle signs last summer when he realized he may be falling in love with her - the inner joy he felt when he was with her, the electrifying sensation when their hands accidentally touched, the quickening of his heart when he took in the scent of her perfume. "Oh, I noticed all right. I just didn't think I stood a chance."

He blew on his spoon and tasted the soup. "Delicious! You made a huge pot of it - either you're extremely hungry or you think I am."

"Well, you always are." She put her soup spoon to her lips. "Ooh - too hot!" She put the spoon back on the saucer holding the bowl. "It needs to cool off. I made enough so you could have some for lunch tomorrow and there'll still be enough to freeze for another meal. I made banana bread too."

"Reva thinks you're fattening me up," he said. "Do I look like I've gained weight? My belt does feel a little snug."

"You can afford to gain a few pounds, Rock. It's because you've been eating regular meals lately instead of eating on the run. When your body adjusts to your new eating habits, the weight gain will slow down."

"Good! I don't want to have to buy new clothes."

"I think I'm going to be the one buying new clothes,"

she said as she put both hands on her waistline. "I've already had to start using rubber bands to expand the buttons on my pants." Rock had an overwhelming desire to get up and pat her stomach too, but thought she may be getting tired of him randomly putting his hands over her baby bump every time he was in the same room with her. He couldn't help that he wanted to be a part of every single day of their baby's development. She kept her hand on her stomach and noticed he was watching her. She smiled. "Well, what do you think?"

"I think you're quite possibly the most beautiful pregnant woman in the world and that I'm definitely the luckiest pregnant woman's husband in the world."

She laughed. "Eat your soup - it's cooled off enough now."

He considered eating their meals together to be one of the better perks of marriage. He had eaten alone for so many years - most of the time taking his plate to his study to eat as he worked on his sermon. The kitchen in the new parsonage that he had lived in the past five years was just too cold and impersonal. He had asked the Session about making a few cosmetic changes to it before they moved back into it, and they had agreed to hire someone to do it. Liz had planned out the project and had decided that simple things would make a big difference. The cabinets would be painted a robin's egg blue; new, softer light fixtures would replace the big industrial ones; and new curtains would be hung along with white plantation shutters to give it all a French Country look rather than the current industrial restaurant look. The stove would be changed out for one more suitable for cooking for a small family. The large gas range had been an extravagance when they built the parsonage. He could never understand who they thought was going to cook on it. He could have made do with a one-burner hot plate. But now it would be put to good use. The stove in the church kitchen was too small and in need of new burners, so the plan was to move the one from the parsonage over to the church.

Liz had picked out custom made plantation shutters for the kitchen and the contractor had already ordered them. She was looking forward to the move so she could start working on the nursery, but Rock was enjoying living once again in the little cottage that had been the church parsonage when he first moved to Park Place. It felt like home.

"How was school today," he asked.

"Tiring! All I wanted to do was sleep. I had lunch with Jody in the teacher's lounge and I kept nodding off. I just couldn't keep my eyes open."

"Is that normal?" He looked at her with concern.

"Jody says that's how she first knew she was pregnant the second time around - she would fall asleep at the drop of a hat. She says it will last through my first trimester and maybe into my second. The good news is that today was the first day I haven't felt queasy - I'm hoping my morning sickness is over." She stopped eating and reached for the saltines. He watched as she crumbled the crackers into her soup bowl and ladled another large spoonful of soup on top of them.

"Rock, it feels so strange - here I am almost old enough to be Jody's mother - well, not quite, but she's a lot younger than me, and I'm the one asking her the questions about the side effects of pregnancy. She's twenty-four and already has two little boys, and I'm almost thirty-eight and having my first. And get this - Tina Watson, is only a year older than me and she just had her first grandchild. This is making me feel ancient."

Rock knew that Liz was just nervous. On their first ob/gyn visit, Dr. Alexander had told them that at age thirty-eight, her pregnancy was considered high risk. The risk of having a miscarriage was higher at that age, and chromosome abnormalities occurred more often in babies born to older mothers. Rock had spoken to him later and told him that he could have been a little more diplomatic. He was worried that it had taken away some of the joy she'd felt about becoming a mother.

"I know it's frightening to her," he had told Rock. "But she needs to know all this upfront so she can take the right steps to staying healthy. Gestational diabetes occurs more often at that age, so it's important that she eats the right foods and doesn't gain a lot of weight. I'm sorry, sometimes I don't have the best bedside manner, but I'll try to be more encouraging on her next visit. More women are waiting until they're in their thirties and early forties to have children now, and they're having perfectly healthy babies."

Jody was the only person Liz had told about her pregnancy. She was Liz's guidance secretary and they were good friends. She trusted Jody to keep it quiet. Since there was a greater risk of miscarriage, she and Rock had decided not to announce it just yet. They would wait until mid-January, when Liz was in her second trimester. It had been hard keeping it a secret from his parents when they visited last week - he wanted to shout it from the rooftops.

"You're not ancient! Look at me if you want to see ancient. People will think I'm her grandfather."

"Her? Do you think our baby is a girl?" she teased.

"Well, it's a fifty-fifty chance, isn't it? No, I haven't really thought about it - but we could do the old trick with the needle and thread, holding it over your wrist and if it swings one way, it's a girl. If it swings the other, it's a boy. My mother swears by it. She predicted all her other grandchildren's sexes before my sisters had their first ultrasound."

"Well, she'll be disappointed if she doesn't get to predict ours. We'll break the news to them when we go visit the week after Christmas. My doctor's appointment is on December 27th, but I'm not scheduled for an ultrasound until the next month. We'll go to visit my parents first, if you don't mind. Mom's not going to believe it - she's given up hope of ever being a grandmother."

"And then on to give the good news to my family," Rock said. "I can't wait to see Irene Clark's reaction." Rock was glad he had scheduled almost two weeks of vacation after Christmas. It would give them ample time to spend with both families.

He got up from the table and emptied what was left in his bowl into the sink disposal, then picked up her bowl and did the same. "Go sit down and put your feet up. I'll clean up the dishes and then bring a glass of milk and a plate of banana bread into the living room. Oh, and turn on the Christmas tree lights on your way in."

"I could get used to this," she said. "But I'm not promising you I'll stay awake for the milk and bread."

When he walked in with the tray fifteen minutes later,

she was lying on the sofa with an afghan pulled up to her chin and snoring softly. Theo was curled up beside her doing the same.

He put her plate and glass on the end table and took his to the recliner. "Well I can tell I'm in for an exciting evening," he said, and turned on the evening news. Theo heard him and got up and stretched. He jumped from the sofa on to the arm of his chair and before Rock knew it, he had almost tipped the glass over trying to drink the milk. "You crazy cat," he said and swatted Theo off the chair. He took his glass of milk into the kitchen and poured it in Theo's dish with Theo right on his heels. He washed out his glass, poured himself another and walked back into the living room. Liz was still asleep. He sat there watching her and tried to remember a time in his life when he had been so happy. None came to mind.

He had turned all the lamps off and relaxed in the glow of the fire logs and the lights from the Christmas tree. As he looked at all the little touches of Christmas displayed around the room, he suddenly thought about his musical nativity pyramid still sitting in his attic. During one of his childhood Christmases spent at his house in Montgomery, Alabama, he had spent the whole afternoon winding it up and replaying it. His grandfather had told him it was made of sixteen different types of wood from the Bavarian forests of Germany. The base layer held the basic nativity scene figures in the stable, the second tier held the shepherds and sheep figures, and the third tier held the wise men. When the mechanism was wound up, the bottom and top tiers revolved in one direction and the middle tier went in the opposite direction. The music was to the tune of Silent Night, his favorite Christmas hymn. When his family was packing their suitcases to go home, his grandmother had brought it in his room wrapped carefully in tissue paper. "Take good care of it," she had said - and he had. He would get it out of the attic tomorrow when he went over to check on the remodeling progress.

What a difference a year makes, he thought. This Christmas was going to be so special with someone to share it with. He was still amazed at how everything had transpired. At the age of forty-four, he had still been a bachelor, and mostly content with his life. Then the auto accident involving Holly Spencer, a stranger in town, and her daughter, Abby, had shaken things up a bit. Rock was ultimately appointed as their guardian ad litem helping to make medical decisions for Holly and being a source of comfort for little Abby.

But to Rock, the biggest series of events had started as innocent conversations between two lonely people on the front porch of this very house he was now living in. He and Liz were friends. "Strictly platonic," he had told anyone who asked. The front porch was the allure he had told himself, and the iced tea and good company kept him coming back. Thank God, he had come to his senses and realized he was in love with her. He remembered the very day he had realized it. She had gone up to her mountain cabin and had stayed much longer than planned. A three day visit had turned into weeks and through a series of mishaps, mixed-up feelings and no communication, he almost let her slip right through his fingers. He had been so busy trying to solve everyone else's problems that he couldn't identify his own. When he was finally still long enough to hear God's voice, he found his direction and came to realize that love was right there in front of him all along.

He would never forget her reaction when he finally showed up at the cabin. Earl, her friend and neighbor who had suffered a brain injury when he was a child, was sitting in a tall rocker on the porch carving one of his nature creations out of wood. Earl stood up when Rock walked up the steps. Rock motioned with a finger to his lips. "Where's Liz?" he whispered. Earl understood and whispered back, "Miss Lisbeth is getting coffee for her and chocolate for me. She's been looking for you many, many days. I'll go now." Rock nodded, shook his hand, and whispered a silent thank you.

Earl turned around and started walking away. On second thought, Rock called back to him. "Wait a minute, Earl. Can I borrow your baseball cap?" Earl smiled and handed it over. He donned the cap and moved Earl's rocker so that it was facing the trout stream and only the back of the rocker was visible from the door. He started whistling just as Earl had been doing. He heard the screen door bang behind him and glancing sideways in her direction, watched as Liz walked across the porch. There had been a recent rain shower, and cooler temperatures had greeted him as he drove up the long, winding road that led to the cabin. Liz was wearing a flannel shirt over a school spirit t-shirt and a pair of faded jeans. His heart did flip-flops as he sensed her coming closer. She walked over and put the hot chocolate on the porch rail, and said, "Here's your cup, Earl - it's pretty hot so be very, very careful." It couldn't have worked better. She had not even looked at him.

As she turned to walk back to the swing, he spoke in

a normal voice and said, "Thank you Miss Lisbeth, but I'm tired of being very, very careful." He watched what seemed to be in slow motion as her coffee cup slipped out of her hand and fell toward the floor. In one fluid movement, he got up from the chair, moving swiftly to swoop her out of the way so she wouldn't get burned.

"You know how to make a grand entrance, Reverend Clark," she said, not bothering to move away from his embrace.

He reached down and brushed away the strands of hair that had fallen across her face and brushed his lips against her ear and whispered, "I've missed you Liz Logan, and...," he paused for a moment but decided to just do it and not drag it out, "and I love you." Caught off guard, she pulled back and looked at him, total surprise in her eyes.

"I must be losing my hearing, Rock Clark. Please repeat that." He smiled at her and started to say it over again, but she put her finger up to his lips. "Never mind, it could never come out that perfect again." They stood there just holding each other as if turning each other loose would break the spell.

He had no idea how long they embraced, but they both heard it at the same time - Earl was ringing the bell on his bike and shouting for all the valley to hear, "Miss Lisbeth and Rev Rock are in love. Hip, hip, hurray!"

Rock laughed. "I think Earl is a prophet," he said, and got down on one knee. "I'm going about this all wrong - I don't even have a ring yet - but Liz, I've already waited too long and I can't wait any longer. Will you marry me?" For a moment she stood still, not saying a word and he was afraid he was going to be humiliated and have to run home like a love sick puppy. But then she spoke.

"Aren't you even going to ask my father for his approval? That's what all good Southern men do." She stood there looking serious and he wondered if he had breached some sort of etiquette - he thought the approval thing was meant for young women who still lived with their parents. He was relieved when she laughed and said, "Of course I'll marry you Rock Clark - I thought you would never ask."

Theo woke up and stretched, but Liz was sacked out. Rock watched as the cat walked across her chest. He made his way to her face and stopped, standing there as if trying to will her to wake up. He reached down and purred in her ear, but she just covered herself up even tighter in the blanket and swatted him away, never waking up. He finally gave up and walked across the back of the sofa, then leapt in the air to the back of Rock's armchair. From there he made his way into his lap.

"You should have stayed where you were, Theo," he said as he pushed him aside. "Since all is quiet, I'm going to work on my sermon." As he reached his hand out to the side table to pick up his Bible, Theo attacked it. "Ouch," he said, pulling it back. "You shouldn't have done that, Old Boy. Now you're confined to the laundry room for the rest of the night." He picked up the fidgety cat making sure he wasn't within range of his teeth and claws and walked through the kitchen to the laundry room. Checking to see that he had plenty of food and water, he put him down and shut the door. He looked down at his hands and didn't find any shed blood. Since Theo's stay in the animal hospital during the summer, he had settled down. He still swatted at Rock when he walked by, but now he was more playful than vicious, and when he bit, his bites were just nibbles. Rock remembered the days it had not always been that way, especially the few months after he had rescued him. At least now when he bit, he knew when to stop.

When he got back to his armchair, he said a prayer thanking God for the blessing of Liz in his life and finished by asking for guidance while he prepared for his Sunday message. The tranquility that filled the room was complete and as usual, the words spilled forth onto his notebook.

CHAPTER 10

"**A**nd my God shall supply every need of yours according to his riches in glory in Christ Jesus."

- Philippians 4:19

Maria's day had been productive. The Dollar Store shared space in a small strip mall with Kit's Thrift Shop and BJ's Diner. A bridge rebuilding project was underway nearby and there was a steady stream of Hispanic workers in and out of the restaurant. She was afraid that because she was alone, she would be noticed, but there was so much activity that no one paid her any attention at all, especially in the back booth that had been conveniently empty. She was relieved when she saw the prices on the menu. The few times she and Ernesto had eaten out in Raleigh, the prices were outrageous. He would complain loudly that he had to work all day just to pay for one meal.

She scrolled down the menu. Her spoken English was excellent, but reading in English was more difficult for her. She had learned English by hearing it spoken - not from seeing the words on paper. Studying the menu, she saw that she could get a plate of three vegetables and one meat for $4.50. She wasn't sure how much sales tax would be, but if she had water with her meal, it shouldn't be much more than $5. She thought of the things $5 would buy in the Dollar Store and hesitated, but only for a moment. She had no way of heating food and what she needed more than anything was a good hot meal.

The waitress was a woman in her late forties with a

bright red apron and hair almost as bright. When she came to get her order, Maria looked at the menu and tried to read the words aloud. Two middle-aged men dressed in camouflage had just come in and settled at a nearby table. Maria had seen them drive up in a pick-up truck with a gun rack on the back window when she was walking in. One was wearing an orange toboggan and made a point to speak loudly.

"If they're gonna' come over here and live, they need to learn to speak English. I'll betcha anything she's illegal." Maria blushed and moved further back in the corner.

The other one piped in, "They need to send 'em all back home. We don't need the likes of 'em over here." The waitress walked over to their table and put her hands on her hips.

"Listen boys, if you can't think of anything nice to say, we don't need the likes of *you* in here. You can just take your business on down the road."

"But Kit, there ain't nowhere to eat for twenty miles."

"Y'all shoulda' thought about that before you opened your big fat mouths. Burt Mason, I'm ashamed of you, but I don't expect much more out of your sidekick Carl, here." She turned around and gave the one she called Carl a pitiable look. "Any man that would run off and leave a pregnant wife for another woman is a low-bellied skunk in my book." Carl looked like he wanted to crawl under the table.

"That was eight years ago, Kit. Ain't you ever gonna' forget that?"

"Not when it was my baby sister, I won't. Why I oughta' run you out of here anyway, I'm getting mad just thinking about it. Just keep your mouths shut, you hear?" Both men nodded meekly.

Maria couldn't believe what she had just witnessed. A tiny woman, not much bigger than herself, had just dressed down two grown men and got away with it. If she had talked to Ernesto like that, she was sure she would be dead by now.

"Honey, don't pay any attention to those two. Do you understand English?" When Maria nodded, she continued, "My name's Kit Jones. Me and my husband, BJ, we own the thrift shop next door and this restaurant. I don't usually do any waitressin', but we're shorthanded today. Our kitchen helper quit this morning and BJ dragged me in here to help. I can't work with that hard-headed man in the kitchen, so I sent Becky, our waitress, back there, and here I am taking orders." To Maria, it looked like Kit was giving the orders. She would give anything to have that kind of confidence. Kit sat down on the bench beside her. "What's your name, honey?"

"Maria," she answered, and held her head up proudly, hoping to win the respect of this marvelous woman.

"Glad to meet you Maria. Now, let me help you with your order."

Maria finished her meal, cleaning her plate - even sopping up the last bit of gravy with the last of the biscuits Kit had brought out. The restaurant was warm and most of the lunch crowd had cleared out including the rude men at the other table. She waited for a while for Kit to bring her check, but when she didn't, Maria walked up to the cash register to pay.

"Your check's all paid up, honey. You don't owe a thing," Kit told her after she finished ringing up the customer in line ahead of her. At Maria's surprised look, she told her, "Burt Mason's normally a decent sort of man - it's just that the company he keeps is a bad influence, that's all. He felt bad about showing out like that and asked me if he could pay your bill after Carl had paid and walked out. I'm just sorry it happened and hope you'll come back." She tidied up the area around the cash register and looked back up at Maria. "Are you married to one of the workers from Performance Bridge Company?"

Not knowing what to say, Maria hesitated but then half nodded.

"Then you must be staying over at the State Park in one of those construction trailers with your husband. I heard the construction company rented out all the campsites for their workers for the winter months. That's a pretty place over there. Now, if you need a job and all your papers are in order, we could use a kitchen worker in the back. That hard-headed old man I was talking about is my husband, and he's not so bad to work with. Sometimes the two of us clash when we're together twenty-four / seven, if you know what I mean." Maria nodded. "Just think about it, honey, and the next time you're in here, let me know. We pay cash, but we just want to see your visa papers or we could get in trouble with the immigration people. I understand all the bridge workers have been checked out, so I'm sure you're ok, but we still want to glance at 'em if you're interested in working."

Maria had never heard anyone talk so much and so fast in all her life. All she had to do was nod, and this lady kept talking.

"Look's like you're the last customer for a while. I'll

get Becky back out here and I'm off to open the shop back up. You ought to come with me and look around. You might find something you need. Just go on out front and wait for me to come unlock the doors."

Maria was embarrassed that the man had paid for her lunch. She didn't like accepting charity - her father had always managed to provide for his family. He was poor, but a proud man and he instilled this in his children. But it was helpful and she was appreciative - it would mean she could buy more food at the Dollar Store and maybe get something from the thrift shop. She walked outside and waited for Kit.

BJ came out to the front and Kit handed him the cash register box. He stood a head taller than his petite wife. He reached down and kissed her on the top of the head. "Pretty big crowd we had in here today. This is the first time I've had a break. It's a heck of a time to lose Lois! She said there was too much work to do and she couldn't handle it."

"Don't be so hard on her - she's gettin' a little age on her and doesn't handle stress very well." She took off her apron, folded it up and put it under the counter. "I don't figure we'll have too many more customers since it's almost two o'clock - maybe just a late straggler or two. Becky can handle it from here. I'm going to go open up the shop."

"Who's that you were talking to?" he asked.

"Her name is Maria. She says she's with the bridge builders, but there's something different about her. She has bruises on her face that look suspicious, and I don't think she's eaten a bite all day, the way she tore into that plate of food. Burt Mason and that trashy ex-brother-in-law of ours were giving her some grief over the way she speaks English. I wanted to pick them up by the seat of their pants and throw them out on their heads."

Her husband laughed. "Knowing you, they would have probably rather had a head bashing than one of your tongue lashings."

"I'll admit, I did lay it on pretty heavy." She sighed. "You know, a sermon that Rev Rock preached about a month ago stuck with me. You remember the one about Christians and racism? No, I don't expect you do - you were probably dozing." She gave him a look of consternation, but then laughed. "Anyway, it was about how God made all people of all colors and races and no-one should be discriminated against. It was from Leviticus. I went home and read the whole chapter. One verse I remember was '*do not mistreat foreigners living in your land*'. That sermon has made me look at people in a new light, BJ, and it just makes me mad when I see it all around us."

BJ rubbed the top of her head. "My little spunky redheaded fireball has a warm and fuzzy heart."

"Shh...don't tell anyone," she said and put her finger over her mouth. "I've got to get out of here. I told Maria I would open up the shop so she could look around. Maybe I'll find out more about her."

"Just remember, Kit. Whatever it is, it's not your concern. Don't be sticking your nose in somebody else's affairs."

Kit feigned a look of surprise. "Who - me? You can't be talking about me," and she flipped her hair up with her right hand and sashayed right out the front door. She wondered what he would think if he knew she had practically offered the girl a job.

Maria was waiting at the entrance of the shop when Kit arrived to open up. She turned the key in the lock and held the door wide open for Maria to walk in first. "Honey, you just look around all you want. I've got a little bit of everything in here. If it's got an orange tag, it's half price."

Under different circumstances, she would have loved to shop in Kit's little store. Her prices were reasonable, but she had nowhere to put anything and no money to spend. As she walked back to the front of the store, she spotted a shelf that had camping equipment. A green sleeping bag was on the bottom shelf and she reached down to check the price tag. "Nobody camps in the winter, so all that stuff is 75% off. It's all used, but I laundered the sleeping bag, so it's fresh and clean," Kit called out from the back where she was hanging some shirts on a rack. "What does the tag say?" she asked.

"Ten dollars," Maria answered.

"Woo hoo! It's your lucky day," Kit said, walking over to where she was holding the sleeping bag. "That's only $2.50 - less than $3 with sales tax."

Maria picked up a flashlight marked $2 from the same shelf, and a summer scented candle in a jar from another sale shelf. When Kit rang it all up, it was only $3.98. Maria gave her all the change she had in her pocket. Kit counted it out, rang it up and gave her a quarter and two pennies back. Maria was happy with her purchase and gave Kit a dazzling smile. "Can I leave this here while I go to the store next door?" she asked.

"Hey, you've been holding out on me," she exclaimed. "You speak excellent English! Are you sure you don't want a job?"

Maria looked at her, hesitating before she spoke. "Do you think I could?" she asked. "I haven't worked before."

"I know you could do it," Kit said. "But do you have your papers in order? We don't want to get in trouble with Immigration."

Maria pulled out the card that she had taken from Ernesto's wallet. Kit looked it over and compared the photo on the card with the girl in front of her. "It all looks in order. I'll need to talk to BJ about it. Come back Thursday and I'll introduce you to him. If all goes well, we'll put you to work on Friday."

"I think you must be an angel," Maria exclaimed, and she walked out the door.

Thirty minutes later, Maria came back in the shop with a small bag of groceries. She spread out the sleeping bag and placed everything in it and rolled it back up. Kit helped her to position it over her shoulders like a backpack, and as she pulled her arms through the straps, Kit noticed for the first time her bulging stomach. Uh oh, she thought. That's not chubby, that's pregnant. And here she'd gone and got herself right in the midst of it, despite BJ's warning, by offering her a job, but there was just something about her that tugged at her heart. She had learned that her heart tugs were usually God moments as if He was trying to get her attention. When the door shut behind Maria, Kit picked up the little bell sitting on the counter. "Kit, old girl," she said aloud as she rang the bell. "She thinks you're an angel so I guess you're gonna have to earn your wings."

Maria carefully watched the parking lot and surrounding area from her vantage point amongst the magnolias. When she was sure no-one was looking, she walked casually to the side of the church and then ducked down the steps to the basement. The white van was back at the big house, and it conveniently cut off the view of her hiding place from the church office. She was proud of her purchases, especially the sleeping bag. It was nice and thick and would keep her warm. With a little luck she would have enough food to last now until Thursday, when she would go back to the restaurant to see if she had a job. Her biggest fear was that Ernesto may have reported her missing and handing over her papers to Kit would cause the authorities to be able to find her. She would just have to take her chances. God had brought her this far, so she would not give up now.

CHAPTER 11

Jill Cooper sat across from Rock's desk and waited patiently for him to finish his phone call with the person on the other end. "Thank you for agreeing to help, Holly. I know you and Jill will work well together..... Yes, I'm sure you'll do just fine. Give my love to little Abby. Goodbye now."

"Good news," he said as he put the phone back in the cradle and turned to Jill. "She said she would help you with the children's Christmas pageant. She'll meet with you Sunday after church."

"That's a relief," Jill said as she scribbled on her notepad. "I panicked when Julia told me that she and Jim would be spending Christmas in Australia with their son this year. They're leaving on the fifteenth and won't be back until January 1st. She's always helped me and I knew I couldn't do it by myself."

"I think it'll be good for her," he said. "She seems to have fully recovered, and according to Maura, she needs something to do that will make her feel as if she's contributing to the community after everything that was done for her while she was in the hospital."

"I'll enjoy working with her, Rev Rock. It seems like just yesterday that we were praying so hard for that girl to live. I remember sitting in her hospital room while she was in a coma - a stranger to her, but feeling such a strong connection through our outpouring of prayers."

Rock started thinking back. It did seem like yesterday, not almost seven months ago, that the mysterious young woman, Holly Spencer, had been involved in an accident on the highway and suffered brain trauma that left her in a coma for almost two months. Her five year old daughter Abby was not injured, and had won over the entire town with her brave persona and charming ways. Holly had come with purpose to the town to try to find Abby's father's family when she herself had been diagnosed with cancer. With Holly in a coma, no-one knew how to find a next of kin to make decisions. Rock never suspected that her family connection was right in front of all their noses all along. That's one time, he thought, that my meddlesome ways paid off.

Jill said something and he realized his mind had been wandering. He turned his attention back to her. "I'm glad she agreed to help," he said. It wouldn't seem right without a children's Christmas pageant."

When Jill left, he started to rise from his chair. He felt a sandwich in the refrigerator was calling his name, but the minute he stood up, Reva called out, "Next..." and Tom Sinclair walked in and plopped down in the comfortable arm chair. Reva walked in right behind him, carrying Rock's ham sandwich and a diet coke. "We're playing musical chairs today, aren't we?" she said and handed his food across the desk.

He turned to Tom. "This woman can read my mind," he said. "All I have to do is think about a sandwich and she makes it magically appear."

Tom laughed. "We'll have to start calling you Jeannie," he said. "Do you wiggle your nose when you do your magic?" he asked, looking at Reva.

"I'm going to wiggle both your heads if you start talking about magic," she said. "Next thing you know, you'll be talking about voodoo and hocus pocus. That stuff scares me." She pretended to shiver and then laughed. "Nah, I know you're just kidding. I don't need any magic working with Rev Rock. I can read him like a book." She walked out but left the door open between their offices.

Rock pushed his sandwich to the side, but popped open the drink can. "Go ahead and eat your sandwich," Tom said. "You can eat while we talk." Tom was the chairperson of the maintenance and grounds committee, but Rock had told him one time that the committee should be called the Catch-All committee, because everything that didn't fall under a specific category seemed to get shifted to maintenance and grounds.

"It can wait," he said. "I'm not that hungry," but his growling stomach told a different tale.

"Do you have another one of these?" Tom asked, holding up a green piece of paper titled *Calendar of Events*.

"Yep, right here on my desk where Reva taped it so I wouldn't lose it," he grinned. He started trying to peel the tape off the desk.

"I might steal her away from you and pay her a lot more to work for my construction company," Tom teased.

"Don't even think about it," he said with alarm.

Reva came back in. "I know y'all are talking about me, she said. I can feel it in my bones." She handed Rock another copy of the calendar of events. "I knew you would try to take that tape off, so I brought you one you could hold in your hands." She glanced down at the peeling tape, then popped him on the hand. "See, I knew it!" She smoothed the tape down and walked back out the door.

"How does she do that?" They both laughed because

they had said it in unison.

Calendar of Events for Park Place Presbyterian

- Friday, December 5 - 10 a.m. Put up poles for Lighting the Way

- Saturday, December 6 - 10 a.m. Decorate Church, 6 p.m. Young adult Sunday School party

- Saturday, December 13 - 10 a.m. Christmas Parade; 5 p.m. Senior Adult Christmas party

- Sunday, December 14 - 4:30 p.m. Lighting the Way ceremony begins

- Saturday, December 20 - 2 p.m. Children's Christmas Party

- Sunday, December 21 - 5 p.m. Christmas Pageant, 6:00 p.m. Soup & Chili Supper

- Wednesday, December 24 - 6 p.m. Christmas Eve Service

- Saturday, December 26 through Sunday, January 4 - Rev Rock on Vacation

Tom looked at the list of events and took a deep breath. "Wow," he said. "That's quite a list."

Rock assured him that the only thing he was in charge of was to coordinate with the other churches in the pole digging on Friday, and scheduling with the churches and community organizations who would light the candles on the weekends leading up to Christmas. After he left, Rock ate his sandwich and opened the door to the outer office. Reva's hands were flying over the keyboard when he came in. Without skipping a beat, she called out, "There's some sweet potato pie in the refrigerator."

He stopped mid-stride on his way to the refrigerator. "How do you do that?" he asked incredulously.

"What?" she asked. "Oh, it's easy. One measly sandwich is just not going to cut it with you. I could hear your stomach growling from the other room." He shook his head and opened the refrigerator door and stood staring at a pie whose presence lit up the room.

"Never mind," he said. "Just keep doing it," and he used the knife on the counter to cut himself a slice about the size of South America shown on the map above the microwave.

"Hmm... just a few days under seventeen." Kit was looking at the date of birth on Maria's immigration card. "Wow, your birthday is on Christmas day. It must be nice to share a birthday with Jesus." She looked down at the child standing before her and smiled. "We can only employ you five hours a day until you turn seventeen, but we can work with that."

Maria was relieved - she was desperate. Her money was gone except for three dollars and some change, and her food supply was down to a can of beans and some dried fruit she had bought from the Dollar Store. She had taken great care to clean up and look presentable. After her successful outing on Monday, she had started getting out of the dark basement during the day. Each day, she went a little farther on her daily walk, just getting a feel for the layout of the town. The Laundromat she had discovered was located beside the dry cleaners on Elm Street and just yesterday, she had taken her clothes there to launder. She had brought along a washcloth, a hand towel and shampoo, so while the clothes were in the machine, she went to the cramped little bathroom and took a sponge bath and washed her hair in the sink. The room was warm and cozy from the heat of the dryers. Maria towel dried her hair the best she could and sat in one of the chairs until it had dried completely. The pleasant humming of the washer was soothing and the stress from the last few days seemed to melt away. She stayed seated long after her clothes were laundered and she fell asleep in her chair right after she put them in the dryer. A young Hispanic woman had finally touched her gently on the shoulder and awakened her, asking if she would take her clothes out of the dryer so she could use it. It was a restful place - somewhere she could spend time during the day and not bring attention to herself.

Kit handed the card and the copy of the application for US residency back to Maria. "We're busiest in the kitchen between 7 a.m. and noon, so that should fit the five hour time frame just fine. Now it's time to go over and meet BJ. Just smile and act happy - his last kitchen worker was a grouch." Kit laughed and Maria couldn't help but laugh with her. "That's right, honey! Flash that gorgeous smile with those beautiful white teeth and he'll be spellbound." She walked out the door with Maria following right behind.

Kit was right, BJ thought. The little dark-haired girl with the snowy white teeth had won him over right away. He could see she was eager to please and he felt she needed the job in the worst kind of way. He had reservations but he kept them to himself.

The crowd had thinned out and Maria and BJ sat down at a table. Kit walked in the kitchen and served all of them up a plate of fried chicken, mashed potatoes and green beans. They discussed her responsibilities as they ate. "I can't do it all," said BJ. "This week, I've been doing food prep, cooking and washing dishes. It's about to wear me out. Becky helps when she can, but she's got her hands full waiting tables and working the cash register. Can you manage preparing the food and washing dishes?"

"Oh, yes," Maria said. "I've worked in the kitchen with mi madre all of my life." BJ smiled, thinking that was not a very long time at all considering her age.

Kit watched the two of them as they interacted. They'll get along famously, she decided. Maria was cleaning her plate, and Kit had a gut feeling she was eating for two. She didn't know how far along she was - because of her undernourishment, it could be farther than she appeared to be. Should she ask her about it, she wondered. No, she thought - if she wants me to know, she'll tell me. She got up and started gathering up the plates, balanced them all on her arm and took them back into the kitchen. She brought back a piece of apple pie on a paper plate wrapped in plastic wrap and handed it to Maria. "You can take this with you for dessert." At least with her working in the restaurant, she could make sure she got enough to eat.

"She'll be starting tomorrow morning at 7 sharp and work until noon," BJ told her. "She knows it's temporary, but if we still need her after Christmas, she can work longer hours." He got up from the table and walked over to the cash register. He wasn't sure this was going to work

- she was just a child, but he knew there was no point in protesting. When Kit made up her mind, it was a done deal.

"I'm probably going to live to regret this," he muttered as soon as Maria and Kit walked out the door.

"What's that you say?" It was Walt Carrington who had come up to the counter to pay his check. He held his hand to his left ear and adjusted the hearing aid as it squealed and squawked.

"I was just asking if you enjoyed your lunch." BJ said a little louder.

"I did, but next time don't cook the chicken livers quite so long. They were a little on the rubbery side."

CHAPTER 12

T herefore, *as we have opportunity, let us do good to all people, especially to those who belong to the family of believers.*

- Galatians 6:10 NIV

It had been another long day for Liz, but as she walked in the front door of the cottage, her frustrations melted. The smell of oregano and tomato sauce greeted her and she instantly felt better. She put her purse and folders on the bench of the hall tree and hung her jacket on the coat rack Rock had brought from the parsonage. The jacket wouldn't be needed tomorrow except for the early morning hours. A weak weather system had brought in some mild temperatures and the next few days were going to be in the mid 60's.

"I'm home and I smell Italian," she said as she made her way back to the kitchen.

Rock was standing over the stove wearing the chef's apron his father had given him for a wedding present. He wiped his hands on a kitchen towel and met her halfway for a hug. He sniffed her hair, and then her neck. "Hmm," he said. "I don't think you smell Italian at all. You smell like my wife Liz, right down to the sweet scent of camellia blossoms." He held her close and she sighed, long and deep, and then breathed in his scent as he lightly brushed her cheek with the short end-of-day stubble that had grown out since his morning shave.

"This may be better than what you've got cooking in

the pot on the stove," she said as she snuggled closer in his arms.

"Hold that thought," he said as he broke away for a moment. She watched as he drained the spaghetti noodles into a colander and then poured them back into the pot. The sauce was bubbling in the saucepan when he poured it over the hot noodles, stirred it a time or two and then covering it with a lid, he turned off the burner.

"It'll stay warm for a while," he said as he gathered her in his arms. "Did you hold that thought?"

"Yes, and I let my imagination run wild," she said as she took his hand in hers and pulled him down the hallway. "There's just something about a man who cooks!"

Tom Sinclair's farm tractor looked a little out of place on Church Street, but it was a welcome sight to the men who had taken it upon themselves to dig holes by hand in years past for the poles that held the lanterns for the Lighting the Way ceremony. Tom's son, Pete, had rigged up a contraption on the back of the tractor that held steady the drill and auger as they spaced the holes every twelve feet, lining almost two city blocks. They started at Park Place Presbyterian and continued down Church Street, turning right on Hampton Avenue to the Methodist church on the corner of Hampton and Congress. They continued digging holes up Congress to Cornerstone Baptist Church and there they stopped. The AME Zion and the Reformed Presbyterian churches were a few blocks to the south - too far and not enough poles to continue digging holes. But each of those churches participated by putting their own poles and lanterns out front.

Tom and Pete were wiping sweat from their brows. The temperatures were exceeding expectations and Liberty Bank's flashing sign was announcing 12:47 p.m. and 68 degrees. They had finished digging the holes and had grappled with the poles that were stored in the basement of the Methodist church. Each church had asked for volunteers in dragging the poles out and putting them up, but this year with the work being done on a weekday while the kids were in school and the workforce at work, the pickings were slim. Rock scanned the crowd and he and Pete were the youngest ones there. As a matter of fact, he and Pete were the only ones under sixty-five there, he thought, with most of them being in their seventies. He could feel a back-ache coming on.

Walt Helms, the pastor at Cornerstone drove up in Rock's pickup truck with one load of the poles. Macy Turner, the moderator for the Presbyterian Women drove up right behind him.

"Be careful - you'll damage the cat food cans and the globes won't fit into the openings," she said. "They're a little snug already." She went to the back of the truck and started inspecting them.

Walt whispered to Rock. "If cat food cans could talk," he said. "We've been bouncing those poles around all year long - hope she doesn't notice." He took his baseball cap off and brushed it against his pants. "It's dusty down there." He rubbed his hand through his hair and put the cap back on. "Every time we need something out of the basement, we roll 'em to the other side. They've got rolled around a lot this year. I think it's time to store them somewhere else. We're adding some more insulation under the floor joists next month, so they'll have to be taken out anyway."

"We can store them," said Rock. "There's nothing but a few paint cans and a ladder in our basement. We rarely go down there unless we need the ladder - which we'll probably need tomorrow since we'll be putting up the Christmas tree in the sanctuary. It's a ten-footer."

Rock looked up and saw that Betty from the post office was standing with Macy. "I closed the doors for lunch," she said. "I'm here to help."

"You can start standing the poles up in the holes we dug," said Walt.

"Hmph," she said. "And get my nails messed up? I think not!" She held out her hands for Rock and Walt to see. "I just paid $35 for these beauties, and I'm not going to break 'em on those old brittle poles." She sneezed. "And this dust! It's done made my allergies act up!"

"Well, what did you have in mind?" Rock said.

"I'll just stand here and look pretty," she said, and patted her new bob hairstyle with both hands. She turned around to see who was among the working crowd. "Hmph," she said again. "I've changed my mind - I'm going to lunch. There ain't nothin' but a bunch of old white men out here," and she walked off in a huff.

Walt hooted and hollered and slapped his hands on his knees. "What are we gonna do when she retires?" he asked. "She lives out of town and we won't see her much anymore."

"Don't worry," said Rock. "She won't stay away. She'll be buying her a house in Park Place just so she can aggravate us."

"I hope so," said Walt as he got back in the driver's seat of the pick-up. The men followed him on foot up the streets putting out about ten poles at a time, while some of them started placing them in the holes to come back later and pack the dirt in around them.

The poles were simple - they were four foot lengths of black PVC pipe with a small block of wood wedged down into the pipe. A cat food tin was nailed to the block of wood, and when put in place, a candle would be set inside the tin and a glass globe on top. The Woman's Club would decorate each pole with ribbons and bows and when the candles were lit each night, it was a sight to behold. People came from all over town through the streets to see the candles beckoning them from one church to the next.

Walt pulled Rock's pickup into the church parking lot. "Let's break for lunch," he said. "I'm about pooped."

"So am I - Spread the word. Let's meet back here at 2." He rounded the corner of the church and cut through the parking lot to hit the path to the cottage. He decided to make a sandwich and a glass of iced tea and eat his lunch on the porch. The rocking chairs looked inviting with the sun filtering in through the trees. With his mind on the chicken salad waiting on the top shelf of the refrigerator, he opened the front door and walked in, not even looking in the direction where the young girl was waiting in the copse of woods for everyone to clear out so she could make her way to the church basement. She had worked for five hours, and then walked home. Her legs ached and her feet were swollen. All she wanted was a nap.

Maria's day had gone by in a blur. BJ had insisted she take a break at 10 a.m. between the lunch and breakfast crowd. He had fixed her a huge breakfast, going heavy on the grits since he had half a pot left. "Bacon or sausage?" he had asked. She shrugged, so he gave her two pieces of each. She had already sliced tomatoes and shredded cheese for the lunch salads, so she sprinkled cheese on her grits and put two slices of tomato on her plate. "I'll be making fresh biscuits for the lunch menu, so if you want some of these, help yourself," he told her, as he opened up the warmer to reveal ten or twelve biscuits left from breakfast. "Otherwise, I'll be throwing them out."

"Can I take some home with me?" she asked.

"Sure, I'll put 'em in a plastic bag and you can pick 'em up when you leave," he said as he started bagging them up. "How 'bout if I put this leftover sausage in there too?" he asked, holding up the tin pie plate from the griddle. She nodded, and he wrapped the sausage in foil and put it in the bag with her biscuits.

At noon, Kit walked in ready to take over. She had locked the thrift shop so she could help Becky wait tables during the busy lunch hour. It was time for Maria to go home. Everything had been prepared in the kitchen and all BJ had to do was cook. He came out from the kitchen, opened the cash register and paid her for her day's work. Her hand trembled as she held it out for him to count out the money - $40, a little more than he had told her.

"You did a real good job today, Maria, and we had a big crowd. My brother's boy helps me on Saturdays, but I'll need you back on Tuesday - we're closed on Sundays and Mondays."

She smiled and nodded, "I'll be here."

"How did she work out?" Kit asked as the door closed behind Maria.

"She's a hard worker, that's for sure. I explained each thing to her one time, and she took off like a little Ninja. It made me tired just watching her. The way her eyes lit up when I paid her makes me think her husband must be on short hours. I think she really needs it."

"Me too. I hope I'm wrong, but I have a feeling all's not quite right at home."

"Hey, I need to place my order over here," a voice cried out from the far right table. It was Jim Cunningham, one of the foremen from the bridge construction project.

"Hold your horses, Jimbo. I'll be right over!" Kit put her apron on and picked up her pad and pencil. "I'll swanee, I've never seen such impatient people in all my life."

"And I've never seen such a fireball of a redhead," he said as she arrived at his table."

"You just wish your hair was half as pur-r-ty," she said with her slow Southern drawl. "Now, just what did you want to order, gentlemen?"

The foreman looked at the menu, sighed and closed it. "What I'd really like is Chicken Liver Tortellini with balsamic vinegar, brown butter and sage," he said and looked up at Kit expectantly. Kit looked down at him as if he had sprouted a new head. Jim could no longer keep a straight face, and started laughing. She put her pad in her apron pocket and said, "You been workin' on that bridge in New York too long. Just for that, I'm bringing you some cold grits and meatloaf."

BJ yelled from the kitchen, "We're out of grits."

"Thank God!" was all that Jim Cunningham could think to say. He smiled up at Kit. "Surprise me."

Kit looked at the man sitting at the table with Jim. "How about you, honey? Do you want something fancy-schmancy too?"

"No, I'll have what he's having."

She turned around. "This is y'all's lucky day," she said and marched back to the kitchen whistling 'Onward Christian Soldiers'. "Pig's feet and sauerkraut," she yelled to BJ.

"Coming up," he yelled back.

Jim cringed and looked at his lunch companion. "You never know what you're gonna get in here," he said and shook his head. Ten minutes later, Kit walked back to the table with two plates piled high with pork chops, mashed potatoes, green beans and corn bread.

"Order's up, boys, I'll refill your iced tea" she said as she put the plates in front of them.

"I'm beginning to like pig's feet and sauerkraut," Jim said to the other foreman. They laughed and dug in like they hadn't seen food in a month.

"Just a little to the left - ahh, that's the place." Rock was sitting sideways on a kitchen chair and Liz was massaging his back. "This is the last year we're going to set up those poles on a Friday if I have anything to say about it. With today being a school day and working day, all the fit and able crowd was nowhere to be found. They're the ones who run around trying to compete with each other over who's going to get the most done. We old men usually just sit back and watch, which is exactly what some of them did today. Ouch, now a little to the right - oh yeah, that's better."

Over his shoulder, Liz was rolling her eyes and trying not to laugh. "Poor baby," she said. "I suppose you're hurting too much to go to the Sunday School Christmas party tomorrow night."

Rock looked back at her hopefully. The thought of his aching muscles making him miss the party made the hurt almost worthwhile. Just when he thought he had an easy way out, her mischievous eyes gave her away.

"I don't think so," she said, giving him a few karate chops on his shoulders. "My backrubs are awesome. You'll be good as new by morning."

"You can't blame a man for trying," he said. Her karate chops were awesome. He was feeling better already.

CHAPTER 13

"Six days you shall labor, but on the seventh day you shall rest; even during the plowing season and harvest you must rest."

- **Exodus 34:21 NIV**

Early Sunday morning found Rock putting the finishing touches on his sermon. He usually finished it up on Saturday, but what with decorating the church on Saturday morning and then going to the young adult Christmas party Saturday night, he was cutting it close.

Decorating the church for the Christmas season had always brought out a huge crowd of helpers. Jack Terry had brought his own seven foot ladder so they hadn't had to bother with the rickety one in the basement. They put greenery and large candles in all the windows, hung the Christmas tapestry that a former minister's aunt had woven, decorated the tree, and hung wreaths on the doors and between the windows. The church looked magnificent all decked out for Christmas and there was a lightheartedness and a feeling of camaraderie in the air. He had watched his congregants as they worked and chatted happily and could tell that there was no place they would rather be on a Saturday morning. It was a true blessing to have these people in his life. They had always treated him well and welcomed Liz, as his wife, into the congregation with open arms.

The Sunday School party had been a pleasant surprise. He found that he had been missing out on one of the most enjoyable aspects of a preacher's life - the social mingling with couples in the church. It had felt awkward while he was single, but he finally felt he was beginning to fit into the social circle with Liz by his side.

His sermon title this morning would be *The Unfolding Promise*. From the moment in the Garden of Eden when Adam and Eve had eaten the forbidden fruit, sin was destined to spread throughout the earth. But God was not going to sit by and let Satan take over. God unfolded a plan throughout the rest of the Old Testament that gave hope. A Messiah would come to cover the sin with His own blood. And finally, God fulfilled His promise by sending Jesus to earth from the womb of Mary.

As he finished up, he gathered his handwritten papers together and put them in a folder. He looked up as Liz walked into the room trying to button her skirt. "I'm going to have to break down and buy some new clothes," she said. "I can't get this skirt buttoned. Do you have a rubber band hidden anywhere? I've used mine all up." He pulled his briefcase out from under the armchair and snapped open one of the compartments. Here he kept paper clips, a stapler and a small package of rubber bands. He pulled one out.

"Here, let me help you," he said, pulling her over to him. "It's on the side where you can't reach it." He looped the rubber band through the buttonhole and pulled it across and twisted it around the button. The zipper wouldn't zip all the way, but the blazer she wore would cover it up so the opening wouldn't show.

"Thanks," she said. "You're getting to be an old pro at this. That's a pretty fancy loop."

"Boy Scouts finally paid off," he teased. "But you do

need some looser clothes. I don't like to think about you being uncomfortable. Let's go shopping this afternoon at the mall over in Sparta. We can stop by BJ's Diner and have lunch on the way."

"They're closed on Sunday, remember?" she asked. "Kit and BJ won't miss church and they don't have enough help to keep it open if they aren't there. Let's try the new Chinese buffet restaurant in the mall. I've been craving some Wonton soup."

Rock patted her stomach. "Well, we can't ignore those cravings, can we? I just hope they don't have squid on the buffet. I don't even like to look at it."

After the sermon, Liz was standing outside talking to some of the women as Rock shook hands with everyone filing out of the building. Kit Jones was the last one out and she pulled him aside.

"Rev Rock, if you get a chance, I want you to come out to the diner for breakfast one day this week. I want you to meet Maria, the young Hispanic girl we hired in the kitchen." When Rock looked at her expectantly, she continued. "I have a sneaking suspicion she's pregnant, and I'm pretty sure there's something not quite right about her home situation. She says her husband is with the bridge construction and they're living over at the state park in the campers they set up for the crew, but I noticed she walks in the opposite direction when she leaves. I'm beginning to think she's not living there, and wondering if she's homeless."

No wonder I'm always getting involved, he thought. People keep throwing me right smack in the middle of things and I fall for it every time. He sighed, then took a deep breath, trying to muster up a little courage. "I'm not sure when I'll have time, Kit. Maybe you should ask her and see if she has a church she attends. Is she Catholic?" When Kit nodded her head, Rock continued. "Try to pin her down for some answers and see if she's made friends with any of the crew member's wives. The few times I've encountered the Hispanic population in our area, I've noticed that they're very supportive of one another and are not exactly open to outside help."

"I hadn't thought of that," Kit said. "I'm going to try to watch to see where she goes tomorrow when she gets off. I'm just worried about her."

"I know you are, Kit. You have a heart of gold - you and BJ both."

"I just have a soft spot for girls that age," she said as her eyes filled with tears. Rock gave her a hug and she went to join BJ as he was talking to Maura and Danny.

Kit and BJ had lost their only daughter in a car accident two days before she was to graduate from high school. That had been eight or ten years ago, and Rock knew they would never fully recover from their broken hearts, but their faith had sustained them. They had become involved in volunteer activities at Beverly Hills Children's Home and had even provided foster care from time to time when Beverly Hills had been full.

As he looked at the two of them, he had a sinking feeling that he was going to get involved whether he wanted to or not. "Rats," he said under his breath, "there goes my resolve."

"What's that you're saying?" Liz asked as she walked over to him.

"I was just using my one offensive word," he said, and

smiled as he took her arm and walked down the path that led to their house. He knew she was curious and since their marriage, he had shared everything with her except for confidentialities. But he had to sort this out in his mind. He would tell her later. "Are you ready for some beef and broccoli and Wonton soup?"

CHAPTER 14

T he LORD *gives strength to his people; the* LORD *blesses his people with peace.*

- Psalm 29:11 NIV

"When is this warm spell gonna' end? It don't even feel like it's close to Christmas! It's hurtin' our sales." Junie had come back to his seat after ringing up the only customer he'd had all day. "Hammers and nails, that's all I've been selling. Why, we ain't sold nary a one of our little red wagons yet. Usually by now, they'd be flying off the floor."

"They're not living up to their name, are they?" Larry Braswell was grinning as he looked at Junie.

"What's that supposed to mean?" Junie asked.

"Radio Flyers. They're supposed to fly, aren't they?" The whole group laughed except for Junie. He looked serious, but then he smiled.

"I surely do wish they would fly. We've got a pretty penny tied up in our Christmas inventory. I tell Kathleen every day that we're gettin' too old for this, but she keeps saying, no, just a little bit longer. She's gonna take me to m' grave from right here in this store."

"I hope not," said Fred. "It'll be the four of us that'll have to carry you out of here."

"Well, I'm light as a feather - don't even weigh a hundred and forty-five pounds soakin' wet. But then again, all you little wimps, except for Rev Rock here, would have trouble picking me up, that's for sure."

A bell rang signaling that someone was coming in through the back entrance. They all looked up to see Kathleen walk in. She was carrying a big platter covered in aluminum foil. "Quit your Monday morning grumbling," she said as she walked over and held out the platter, taking the foil off. "I brought you a big plate of homemade chocolate chip cookies to brighten your day." Hands started reaching from all directions. "Whoa boys. One hand at a time. I'll start with the preacher."

Rock took two and held them up for the others to see. "See boys, being a preacher does have its fringe benefits." He took a bite. "M'mm m'mm, these are delicious, Kathleen."

Cap Price took one next. "I thought it was oldest first," he complained. "I think I'll go to seminary."

"Do you have any plans after school today?" Rock was sitting up in bed watching Liz scramble around getting ready for work.

"No, I should get home by four o'clock this afternoon," Liz said as she pulled on one of the oversized shirts they had found at the mall on Sunday. "Does this look okay with these pants?" She stood in front of the mirror for a moment and then turned to face Rock. "I feel like I have on granny pull-up pants," she said.

"You sure don't look like any granny I've ever seen," he said. He sat on the side of the bed and pulled on his bedroom slippers. "You look beautiful." He walked over to where she was again looking in the mirror. As his arms encircled her waist, then rested on her tummy, he stared at their reflection. Each time he felt the slight rounded belly with their baby growing inside, it gave him a sense of wonder and joy. A miracle - there was no other word for it, he thought. Their eyes met in the mirror. She put her hands over his and smiled.

"Any particular reason you wanted to know if I would be home on time today?" she asked.

"Only that you told me Sunday you had been craving pancakes, so I thought we could go over to the new Pancake House in Sparta and have breakfast for supper."

"Ah," she said. "Going out to eat on a Tuesday night.... You do know the way to a pregnant woman's heart is through her cravings, don't you? You've got yourself a date."

He put his arms down and moved away. "I'm holding you up - you're going to be late."

She slipped on her shoes and walked out of the bedroom. "Don't forget to get the leftover pasta out of the fridge for your lunch," he said.

"Got it," she said. "And I have a package to mail. It's sitting on your armchair in the living room. Do you mind taking it to the post office?"

"Got it! Love you...."

"Love you back." He loved saying and hearing those words. He hadn't known what he was missing all those years.

Walking back to the church from the post office, Rock noticed Holly and Maura sitting on the screened porch across the street.

"Morning Rev Rock," Maura called out. "It's an Indian Summer kind of day, isn't it? Only in the South can you sit on the porch in short sleeves in mid-December. Come join us for a cup of coffee."

Why not, thought Rock. He had a lot of work to get done, but it would wait for him. At least he didn't have any appointments on his calendar. He had intended to drop in to see Holly anyway. Instead of walking left to the office, he took a right and started up Danny and Maura's driveway. Maura got up. "You like your coffee black, don't you?"

"Yes ma'am, you know me well," he called back. By the time he had walked up their steep driveway, Maura was back on the porch with his coffee. He opened and closed the screen door and sat down at the wicker table beside Holly.

Maura sat across from them. "It's supposed to turn cold tomorrow," she said. "I don't expect we'll be sitting on the porch much more this winter."

"You never know about our weather," he said. "There's been plenty of times we've had 70 degree days in January." He turned to Holly. "This must be Abby's day for pre-school - I'm sure I would hear our little chatterbox if she was here." He took his first sip of coffee and put it back down on the table to cool.

"Be assured, she would be right out here in the thick of things if she wasn't at pre-school. She goes Tuesday and Thursday each week, and she's going to be mad when she finds out you visited while she was gone."

All the while Holly had been in the hospital in a coma, Rock had wondered what this young woman would be like. She had looked so vulnerable lying there with all the tubes and IV's. When she had come out of the coma and during her rehabilitation, she had seemed shy and unsure of herself. As she recovered, they had finally seen the real Holly. She was a confident young woman, and an excellent mother to Abby - thinking only of her needs. The brain tumor they had discovered had impaired her judgment leading up to the accident, but you would never know it now. The radiation had thinned her hair, but it was growing back fast and her new short style hid the toll the cancer had taken on her. Rock was thrilled to see her looking so well. Six months ago, she was fighting what they all thought was a losing battle. It was fair to say that they had all fought it for her, since she had lost her will to live. She was now cancer-free and her prognosis was good.

"I was glad to see Sonny home and at church Sunday."

"I'm so glad he's here for good now. We've got a lot of catching up to do, but you know, he and Abby are bridging the gap beautifully - especially for two people who didn't even know the other existed. They bonded right away because of my illness - they had something in common to worry about. If I had known how much Sonny had loved me and grieved over thinking he had lost me all those years, I would have been on the first plane to California. We wasted almost six years we could have had together, but we're not looking back. We're doing our best to make up for it."

"I'm glad to hear that, Holly. You've got the rest of your life to spend together and that's all that matters. Did you get a chance to talk with Jill Cooper yesterday about the pageant?"

Holly's eyes lit up. "Yes, we brainstormed quite a bit, but we decided we're going to do a traditional nativity program. We'll have Joseph, Mary and the baby Jesus in the stable. It's one of those things everyone enjoys, but now we have to come up with a real baby. Do you know anyone in the church who has a newborn?"

It was all Rock could do to keep from saying that maybe this time next year, their baby could be Baby Jesus. Let's see, he thought, she would be about five months old by Christmas... He realized Holly was watching him.

"Maybe little Grace, Miss Edie's great-granddaughter. She's not quite six months old and such a good natured baby."

"That's a good suggestion. I'll call her today."

Rock picked up his coffee cup and took another sip. Maura had been listening to the two of them as they talked. She was proud of her new daughter-in-law. She had helped to nurture Holly back to health, and they had created their own special bond. "Can I get you some more coffee?" she asked as he placed his cup back down on the table."

"No, thank you," he said and stood up. "I've got to get back to the office."

She got up from her chair and walked over to him so she could give him a hug. "Rock, I know we've told you this many times before, but I'll tell you again. If you hadn't been willing to get involved with Holly's situation, none of us would have been having this conversation today. Holly may have died without the proper medical care, and I would have never known that Abby was my granddaughter. We have so much to be thankful for."

Rock shook his head. "Maura, God had His hand in it from the very beginning. He just used me to bring it to fruition. It's amazing how it all turned out just as He planned it."

He thought about his conversation with Kit yesterday and how he told her he shouldn't get involved. "Thank you Maura, I needed to hear what you just said. I'm always getting myself head over heals in other people's problems, but that might just be where He wants me to be. Please pray that I'll be able to discern what He's calling me to do."

"It's an honor to be asked to pray for you Rock. Danny and I always do, but I'll make it more specific this time."

Their eyes met and they both smiled. He walked to the screen door. "Thank you for the coffee and the conversation, ladies. And don't forget, my calendar could use your prayers too. As always, I may be biting off more than I can chew this Christmas season."

Reva was waiting for him when he walked in the office. "I saw you walk across to Maura's and I didn't want to disturb you, but Jay Harvey came over here earlier looking for you. He's run into a problem under the sink. While they were changing the sink out, they noticed that there's been a leak between the cabinet and the floor. They'll have to tear the bottom of the cabinet out and some of the sub-flooring to get to it. He just wanted to let you know there was going to be a delay and a little extra cost to the job."

"Typical," Rock said. "You fix one thing and find another. Isn't that the way it always works? I'll go over and talk to him right now."

"Do I need to call the Session members for a meeting to approve the extra cost?"

"No, I don't think so. They gave us a generous budget to work with, and we've scaled back on some of the changes, so we we're way under budget. I'll run by to talk to him before I go home for lunch. Hold down the fort!"

"Fort? Hmph! It's more like a sinking ship with all I've got to do."

Rock didn't wait to hear her list of things she had to do. She would probably still be talking to herself when he got back from lunch.

Jay's white van was gone, but the door was open to the parsonage. Rock introduced himself to Ramon, the young man who was busy dismantling the faucet and spray nozzle from the sink. Ramon smiled and nodded while Rock was talking. He had asked him how long Jay would be gone, but it was clear that he didn't understand.

This was the first time he had been inside the house since his family left and he checked inside the laundry room to make sure there were no wet clothes in the washer. He opened up the washer and then the dryer. Even the lint basket had been emptied. He should have known his mother wouldn't have missed a thing. He decided to kill some time waiting for Jay. He didn't want to miss him when he came back. Absent-mindedly, he opened the refrigerator and then the freezer. Aha, more turkey - he was sick and tired of turkey. He had learned a few words in Spanish when he'd gone to Nicaragua and about the only one he remembered was 'eat'. What a surprise, he thought, and chuckled to himself. He pulled out a package of frozen turkey and left the freezer door open, then walked over to where Ramon was working.

"Ramon?" He looked up from the sink. Rock held up the turkey for him to see and then pointed to the refrigerator. "Comer?"

Rock could tell he was puzzled, but he smiled and nodded, "Si, Senor," and then went back to work under the sink. This was going nowhere. Maybe Ramon didn't like turkey either - he was gaining a whole new respect for the man.

After putting the turkey back in the freezer, he decided that while he was here, he would go up to the attic and get down the few Christmas ornaments to add to their tree. He walked upstairs. The access door that led to the attic was in one of the bedrooms. He pulled it down and climbed the steps. He got the old tree out - now was as good a time as any to take it to the curb since the garbage service ran on Tuesday afternoons. There was one lone box of Christmas decorations and another box marked 'Pyramid'. The tree was wrapped in a burlap bag so he pushed it down ahead of him and then backed down the steps with the boxes. After putting the stairway back up, he carried both down the stairs and laid the ornament box on the table and opened it up. It held the Christmas decorations of a bachelor - no more and no less than he remembered packing up last year. The nativity pyramid was wrapped in tissue at the bottom of the other box. He took them both and set them outside the kitchen door so he wouldn't forget them and came back inside. Now he needed to dispose of the tree - good riddance, he thought. Half the fake needles had disintegrated and fallen off over the years. It looked pitiful. He took it out to the road, burlap bag and all, and put it beside the garbage can. As he looked up, he saw a young Hispanic woman walking by the church. She looked as if she had planned to walk into the parking lot, but when she saw him, she hesitated for a moment, and instead kept walking toward him. She had two bags - one looked like it was filled with groceries and the other had what looked to be two styrofoam takeout boxes from a restaurant. Something about her looked familiar - he wondered for a moment if she was a friend of Ramon's bringing his lunch, but she kept going. He nodded and spoke to her, but then he had an idea. Maybe she would know how to communicate with Ramon.

"Senorita," he called out to her. He could tell it startled her. Maybe she was a Senora, or maybe she was insulted that he called out to her at all. Maybe I should just keep my mouth shut, he thought. For a moment she looked as if she would ignore him, but then she stopped and looked around. "I'm sorry if I frightened you," he said. "Do you speak English?"

She paused and then answered. "Yes."

He held out his hand, but she looked confused, so he put his hand back by his side. "I'm Rock Clark, it's nice to meet you."

"I am Maria." She said it almost in a monotone voice, with no feeling at all. She was still wary of him, he could see it in her eyes, but she was polite.

"I need someone to translate for just one quick moment. Do you mind helping me out? He's inside." He pointed to the house.

"I will help," she said and followed him inside. Ramon stopped what he was doing when he heard them come in. He smiled at the young woman and looked pleased to see her.

"Maria, this is Ramon. Would you ask him where his boss is and how long he will be gone?"

She spoke to the young man and he answered. She turned to Rock.

"He said that his boss went to Charlotte to pick up..." She hesitated for a moment searching for the word, and then patted the opening on the counter where Ramon had been working.

"A sink," Rock said, "he went to pick up a sink?"

"Yes, a sink, and other things. He thinks he will be gone a long time."

"Would you ask him if he'll tell him to come by and see me when he gets back? I'll eat lunch at my house and then I'll be waiting in my office." He pointed in the direction of the office.

She spoke a few words to Ramon, and also pointed. He grinned at her. "Si," he said, and nodded at Rock.

Rock turned back to Maria. "Thank you so much for your help. I hope your lunch didn't get cold," he said, pointing to her bag. She shook her head, no, and smiled.

Rock started walking out the door, but then remembered the turkey in the freezer. He opened the door and turned back to Maria. "I tried to tell Ramon that there's plenty of ham and turkey in here and if he gets hungry while he's here, he's welcome to it."

"I will tell him," she said, and started talking to Ramon in Spanish.

"I'm off to lunch. Thanks again," he said. He picked up the Christmas boxes by the door and waved over his shoulder as he walked quickly up the path to the house to eat lunch. He wondered why he was so hungry all the time now. You would think he was the one eating for two. He really needed to cut back, especially now that he was having to let his belt out a notch. Maybe after their pancake supper tonight...or better yet, after Christmas.

Maria hesitated a moment and then walked out the door behind the man who had called to her from the street. Maybe Ramon had not recognized her. He was the last person she had expected to see in this town she had come to for refuge.

"Maria?" Ramon called out to her as she walked away. She turned around. "Do you not know me?"

She had been shocked to see him, here of all places. He was from a neighboring village in Honduras, and the odds of him being here in the same town? But she would have known him anywhere - he had been a frequent visitor to her home as a friend of her brothers.

"Si, Ramon. It is good to see you," she said, and for the first time since she had left the apartment in Raleigh, she broke down and cried.

Ramon listened as Maria told him her plight. He was outraged at how she had been treated at the hands of the missionary's son. He had never liked Ernesto who had fancied himself a ladies' man, even after his engagement with Maria. Her brothers had tried to convince their father that it was not a good match, but Ernesto had put on quite a show to win her father's approval for Maria's hand in marriage.

"Where are you staying?" he asked, and then was apprehensive when she told him of her hiding place under the church. "You can't stay there," he said. "The weather is turning colder - you'll freeze."

He thought for a moment. "Let me ask around. There's no room for you in the apartment I'm living in - there are four men living there and it would not be good for you to live with us. One of them is a heavy drinker - not someone you would want to be around."

Sharing her situation with Ramon was comforting. To have him here was a connection to home and it made her happy.

She remembered her bags of food that she had put on the floor as she was talking to Rock - what a funny name, she thought.

"I have food from the restaurant," she told Ramon. "Can you take a break and eat with me? Do you think the man would mind if we eat at the table? He seemed very nice."

"I don't think he would mind," Ramon said, and they sat at the table eating the roast beef on Rye and french fries that BJ had packed in the styrofoam box, and discussed Maria's options. When they had finished, she cleaned the table carefully with paper towels. "I have the water turned off at the sink," he told her. We can wet the paper towel in the bathroom to wipe the table."

She came back into the kitchen with the wet towel. "Ah, warm water, she said. What I would give for a hot shower."

"That's it!" Ramon broke out into a big smile. "You can stay here at night. I will leave the key where you can find it and you can come back into the house tonight and sleep where it is warm. You will be gone to work by the time we get back in the mornings anyway."

"Oh, no Ramon, it is not yours to offer me." Ramon shrugged. Maria hesitated. She knew it was wrong to stay in someone's home without asking, but the thought of a warm place and a hot bath won her over. "Only for one night," she said. "I will bring over my sleeping bag," and it was settled.

At 2 pm, Jay was back at work. He was in Rock's office and they had just finished discussing the extra cost of the sink. "Ramon told me you had come by," he said. "How in the world did the two of you communicate?"

"Oh, I remember my Spanish," Rock said with a smug look.

"You do?"

"Si," he said, and rubbed his stomach. "Comer?"

Jay laughed as he put his hat and jacket back on. "Only you, Rev Rock. I'll bet the only two words you know are 'yes' and 'eat'."

Rock smiled. "You would be wrong, my friend," he said, opening the door and walking out into Reva's office. "Adios, au revoir, and goodbye."

Jay stopped at Reva's desk. "Reva, how do you put up with this man?"

She smiled and shook her head. "It's not easy, Jay, no it's not."

CHAPTER 15

"*S*peak to one another with psalms, hymns and spiritual songs. Sing and make music in your heart to the Lord.*"*

- Ephesians 5:19 NIV

"There's a cold front moving in today - better take a heavier jacket," Rock said as he finished packing a brown paper bag lunch for Liz with a chicken salad sandwich and an apple. "We've been spoiled with this warm spell."

She walked up behind him and hugged him. "You've been spoiling me a lot lately - pancake suppers, paper sack lunches.... I'm hoping this constant feeling of being tired all the time will go away soon."

"I think you need to call your doctor," he said, turning around to face her.

"I'm one step ahead of you," she said. "I called from work yesterday and he wrote me a prescription for some prenatal vitamins. I've been taking vitamins, but he says I need something more specialized... 'for my condition'." She dropped her voice a couple of octaves to mimic Dr. Alexander, and Rock laughed at her impersonation. "Do you mind going to the pharmacy and picking them up today? I had him call them into Carter's Drugstore on Main Street so you wouldn't have to drive out to the one in the mall. "

"Of course, I don't mind at all." He kissed her forehead and helped her put on her jacket. "I've got to go to the post office again anyway, so I'll swing by afterwards."

"And while you're there, see if they have a strand of lights like the ones on our tree. Humor me - I'm still concerned about that flickering strand.

"I'll check." He watched her walk out the door. He was worried about her, but she had assured him it was normal to be tired in the first trimester of her pregnancy. At least she was eating well. He smiled as he remembered how she had outeaten him at the Pancake House the night before.

The lone car in the parking lot belied the number of people gathered inside the post office. Betty was behind the counter weighing some packages that Hank Burns had brought in to mail. Betty Ann Williams, one of Rock's church members, and Hank were in an animated discussion when Rock walked in.

"Rev Rock, Hank and I were just discussing Wanda's book. Have you read it yet?"

"Liz is reading it now, but I plan to read it when she's finished. How is it?"

"I just can't believe it's her first book. I love it, and so does everyone else who's read it. Hank says she's having her first book signing in mid-January, so I'm going to get up a group from the Woman's Club to go. I'm trying to get the scoop on how her characters came into being. Some of them sound suspiciously like some of our townsfolk."

"I'm not telling," Hank said, "she made me swear to secrecy." Then he laughed, "Seriously, she doesn't need to model her characters after people she knows. She's got characters swimming around in her head day and night.

Sometimes she wakes me up in the middle of the night and says they're talking to her."

"A creative mind never stops," said Rock. "The characters won't leave her alone until she gets them on paper. I've heard of other authors who say the same thing. I have a friend who wrote a book and he told me that he keeps a pen and paper by his bed. When he wakes up in the middle of the night with thoughts and inspirations, he writes it down while it's still fresh on his mind or he'll forget."

"Yeah, she does that too. I'll wake up sometimes after midnight and she'll be in her office writing like she's demon possessed saying they won't leave her alone. I told her I was jealous about her sleeping with all these crazy people. If truth be known," he whispered, "she's a little on the wacky side herself."

"I wouldn't touch that with a ten foot pole," Rock said. He looked out the window. "Shh...she must be psychic too. Here she comes."

The outer door opened and Hank's wife, Wanda walked in. Betty Ann greeted her. "Guess who we were talking about?"

Wanda looked confused. "I don't know, who?"

"Well, you of course.... and this!" She pointed to the book on display on Betty's counter.

Wanda smiled, "Well, I did feel my ears burning."

Rock elbowed Hank and snickered. "Yeah, Hank's just been telling us how you like to write at night." Hank gave him an evil look.

She turned around. "Hank, I didn't know you were here. Where's your truck? It's not in the parking lot."

"Oh, I parked over behind Crowder's Feed and Seed.

I've gotta get some chicken scratch for your bantams."

Betty cleared her voice. "Hank! I told you that hidin' your truck behind the Feed 'n Seed wouldn't work. They were bound to catch you sneakin' in here like a fox in a hen house."

Rock had never seen Betty Ann Williams laugh so hard. Her laughter was contagious and Wanda joined in. All eyes were on Hank and he good-naturedly spoke up. "You're not supposed to give away our secrets, Betty. Now I'll have to find another parking place."

"Hey, I just came in for stamps," Rock said. "I didn't know I was getting in the middle of a soap opera."

Betty took his money and handed him the book of stamps and his change. "The Bold and the Beautiful," she said, "and I should get nominated for an Oscar."

Carter's Drug Store was across the street from May's Flower Shop. Rock looked at May's window as he walked by and noticed she had added more to her Christmas display. She must be feeling the competition from the antique shop window, he thought. The merchants would spruce up their windows nearly every day during the season trying to outdo each other for the Woman's Club 'Best Display' blue ribbon.

There was only one stoplight in town and it was on this corner. There had been a lot of controversy over adding a stoplight. The traffic had not been a problem since they added the new highway ten years before, but the town council thought that lowering the speed limit and adding a light would help the Main Street businesses. When people had to slow down and stop, they would naturally look into the store windows and see something they couldn't live without. It wasn't a bad idea, Rock thought. Before they had posted the 25 MPH speed limit, cars had zoomed by - one almost knocking Junie down last year at Christmas as he jaywalked from the Main Street Grill back to his store.

The wind had picked up and as he walked up to the front door of Carter's, a gust of air almost opened it for him. He had told Liz to wear a heavy jacket, but he didn't take his own advice. The temperature had been a balmy 58 degrees when he left home this morning, but the bank thermometer at 9:30 was blinking 44 degrees now, just two hours later. The weatherman had called for below freezing temps during the night.

The inside of the drugstore hadn't changed much since its humble beginnings. As you walked in the door, the cashier's counter was to the left. It was cold and flu season so remedies for those illnesses were front and center.

The flooring was the original wide pine boards except for the space on the right where the lunch counter and soda fountain were located. A strip of chrome flashing separated the wood floor from the colorful red and white checkerboard tiles covering the eating area. A smaller pattern of tile covered the countertop and the backsplash on the wall behind the counter. Six tall bar stools with chrome bases and red padded vinyl seats were in front of the counter. Two signs with the names and logos of popular cola brands were on the wall, along with a menu. An old lighted wall clock advertising NuGrape Soda hung beside a leftover 1950's sign showing that Hot Fudge Sundaes could be had for a mere 20 cents. When customers would ask Coy Baker, the soda jerk about buying a sundae for 20 cents, he would answer, "Sorry, we're fresh out of 20 cent sundaes. Would you like to buy one for $2?" Most everyone did.

Julius Carter had bought the building in 1948 right after World War II when businesses were beginning to thrive again. Through the economic ups and downs over the half century since, the family had managed to keep the pharmacy business going and the building maintained with only a few minor changes to the interior.

Rock walked to the back of the store to the pharmacy. Harry Carter had followed in his father's footsteps and was the town's only pharmacist. The threat of big chain drugstores came and went - they kept creeping a little closer, but the closest was inside the Harris Teeter in Sparta.

After chatting a few minutes, Harry rang up the prescription at the register and handed the white bag to Rock. "Do you have any questions about the prescription?" he asked. "The dosage is on the bottle and there's a drug interaction leaflet inside the bag."

"I don't think so - if Liz has any questions, I'll have her call you."

It was pretty obvious what the vitamins were for - the label was clearly marked as prenatal vitamins, but Rock knew that it would go no further than Harry, and he didn't speak of it now.

"I see you have the poles up for Lighting the Way - it's starting at 4:30 at your church Sunday, right?" he asked. Rock nodded. "Is your Park Place Tabernacle Choir going to perform this year? If so, I want a front row seat."

They both laughed. Rock was proud of the church

choir. Jenny Wilson, the music director and organist, worked hard each year to make the music for the Christmas season special. One of the liturgists, Jim Bowers, had been especially impressed with them one Sunday morning and had asked for a round of applause for the "Park Place Presbyterian Tabernacle Choir". Word had spread and the name stuck.

"Yes, they are," he said, "I've been hearing them practice and they're good."

"I'm sure they are - I always enjoy hearing them sing. We've got quite a treat at our church too." Harry belonged to the Methodist Church. "Our son will be singing a solo." His face beamed with pride.

"Now that will be a treat. It's been amazing watching him over the past years. I heard he won a scholarship to a music school in New York - is that right?"

"It is! He'll graduate from high school in May and then off he goes to New York. We'll miss him like crazy, but it's a great opportunity for him."

While Harry was talking, it again occurred to Rock that here they were, the same age, and Harry had an eighteen year old getting ready to go off to college. He mentally calculated how old he would be when their baby turned eighteen. Oh my stars, he thought. I'll be in my sixties! He didn't hear much else that Harry said, but said his goodbyes and walked back to the front of the store where the lunch crowd was beginning to fill up the stools at the counter. He saw the Christmas ornaments and lights on the other side of the store and started to walk over.

"Better gitch'a self a hot dog, Rev Rock," Coy called out from behind the counter. "Today's special - two dogs for $3, with a glass of tea thrown in for free. Can't resist that."

No he couldn't and he walked out twenty minutes later with indigestion and the smell of onions on his breath.

CHAPTER 16

An arctic blast of cold air had come in mid-week and parked itself right over Park Place. A fine mist had settled over the area on Wednesday night and the whole town awakened the next morning to a winter wonderland. The sun rose magnificently over the horizon and brought to life each glistening tree branch looking very much like the vintage silver tinseled aluminum tree that graced the display window of The Banty Hen Antique Shop on Main. It melted by mid-morning, but the cold air stayed behind and crept into damp basements and drafty attics all over town.

After Maria's talk with Ramon on Tuesday, he had moved the van to a position where it would be difficult for anyone from the little house or the office to spot her going back into the basement. When she went in, she wrapped her toiletries, her towel, a candle, flashlight and some clothing up in her sleeping bag and waited until nightfall to walk over to the parsonage. She left her other things in the far corner of the basement under the insulation. The key was where Ramon had left it and she walked in the back door. She used the flashlight to find her way to the stairway, and then made her way up the stairs in the dark by holding onto the banister. The glow of a streetlight helped guide her to the small bedroom at the end of the hallway, chosen earlier because it faced the street rather than the back where the preacher and his wife might spot her occasional use of the flashlight from their house. The chosen bedroom had only one window and the blinds were closed. A small windowless guest bathroom adjoined it and the first thing she did was light the candle and take a long, luxurious shower - the first real shower she'd had since she left Ernesto. The sponge baths had served their purpose, but the shower felt as if it had washed all her troubles away. She dried her hair with the small hair dryer in the drawer and then cleaned away any signs that she had been there. She walked back into the bedroom and spread the sleeping bag on the soft warm bed and drifted off into the deepest and most comfortable night of sleep she had ever had in her life.

She had intended to sleep only one night in the empty parsonage. She woke before dawn on Wednesday morning and put the key back where she found it. She took her possessions back into the basement and hid them in the corner, and then walked to the restaurant feeling better than she had felt since she had been in Park Place. A shower and a good night's sleep had worked wonders. She worked her five hours, stopping only when Kit locked up the thrift shop and came into the restaurant to relieve her. She insisted that Maria sit down in one of the booths to eat and brought vegetable soup and cornbread to the table.

"It'll stick to your ribs and keep you warm to boot," she had said, and refilled her bowl when she ran out. When she finished eating, Kit gave her the key to the thrift shop and told her to go find some warmer clothes.

She found a pair of leather boots in a boy's youth size that fit her small feet, along with some boy's wool socks. Then she spotted a fleece jogging suit that would normally be one size too big, but the pants and sweatshirt and jacket were now perfect for her growing middle. When Kit left the restaurant and came back to the shop,

Maria showed her what she had picked out.

"I'll take them out of your pay on Friday," she had said, and threw in a wool scarf and a pair of gloves. She had said the same thing last week when Maria had purchased a few items, but had not withheld anything on Friday.

"Don't forget - I still need to pay for what I bought last week, so take that from my pay also."

Kit was pleased that she had remembered. She liked the way Maria took responsibility for herself. She wasn't just out for a free ride. "I remember," she said. "It wasn't much, but we'll work it out."

Maria put on the socks and boots before she walked back to town, but by the time she got there, she had wished she had put on the sweatshirt too. Ernesto's coat had kept her warm up until now, but the cold wind blowing in from the North seemed to whip right through it.

Ramon had again parked the white van at such an angle that she could easily slip unseen into the basement. She pulled out her makeshift bed and wrapped up in the sleeping bag for warmth. She was exhausted and there was a dull, aching pain in her back. Even with the sleeping bag, she shivered and couldn't get comfortable - maybe it was because she had spent a night in the warmth of the small guest room.

Still shivering at 8 p.m., she gathered her things together, walked across the yard and let herself in the parsonage. Just one more night, she thought.

Saturday morning arrived and Maria had not been

able to bring herself to go back to the cold basement. She forced herself awake from a troubled night's sleep and was surprised that it was already daylight and even more surprised when the small clock beside the bed blinked 9 a.m. She jumped out of bed and gathered her things together. She had been wrapping everything in her sleeping bag in the mornings and stuffing it in the back corner of the closet. The closet held several long robes similar to what Father Thomas wore on Sundays back in her village in Honduras. The hanging robes provided a good hiding place for the bag. She smoothed out the bed and used the restroom, then thoroughly cleaned up after herself as she had done each day, making sure there were no signs she had ever been there. Her back was not hurting this morning - maybe the baby had just been changing positions - something that her own mother had complained of during her last pregnancy.

It was last Spring when she realized her periods had stopped. When her baby brother was born three years earlier, she had been fourteen at the time and the youngest child. She had two older brothers, sixteen and eighteen. A surprise, but a blessing her father had said of having a baby after fourteen years of thinking they were done with their family. Two young unmarried girls in the village had born children when they were not much older than Maria, so her mother had shared with her the stages of her pregnancy right up until the day Leon was born, hoping to deter her from being led astray by the passionate young Latino men who preyed upon the young girls swept away by their charm.

It had worked - the labor induced screams from her mother as the midwife delivered Leon were enough to make Maria vow to live a life of celibacy, but her fears were forgotten as she grew older and dreamed of marrying a handsome man, having children of their own, and living happily ever after. Those dreams had been dashed by Ernesto's cruel treatment, and when she found out she was pregnant with the child inside her, her tears had not been tears of joy.

The comfortable nights in the house had given her a chance to think about the baby. Since she left the apartment, she had been in survival mode with no time to think of anything except just getting by, but the last few nights she had lain in bed, placing her hands on her ever-growing belly and concentrated on every single movement the baby made. She had grown to love this baby inside her and last night as she felt it move in the comfort of the bed, for the first time she had felt hope and tenderness washing over her and a feeling that everything would be all right.

She walked to the stairway and listened. There were no sounds in the house. It had been her greatest fear all along that she would be found out and arrested for trespassing. She made her way down the stairs and walked into the kitchen. After the first night, she had pulled some of the turkey out of the freezer to thaw since the preacher had been so generous as to tell Ramon to eat it. She made turkey sandwiches each evening with the biscuits BJ continued to give her at the end of the breakfast shift. Her small amount of trash was emptied by Ramon when he came into the house to work.

She looked around the kitchen. The cabinet doors had been removed for painting and Ramon told her they were waiting for the new countertops to be installed before they could put the new sink in. The refrigerator was still plugged in, but had been moved out of the way of the cabinet working space. There was an empty spot where the stove should be. She couldn't understand why they were tearing things out of a perfectly good kitchen.

She looked in the pantry and found a box of Pop-Tarts. She felt bad about eating them without permission - just as she felt bad about using the house for shelter without permission, but her options were few. She would replace the Pop-Tarts and the jar of apple juice when she went back to the Dollar Store. She had popped a bag of microwave popcorn the night before. She took a mental inventory on what she would need to replace.

As she was putting her trash away, she suddenly heard strange sounds out front. It was a loud clanging and pounding noise, then the sound of musical instruments being played. It startled her and she hurried back up the stairs and opened one slat of the blinds to see what was happening. A large crowd had gathered in front of the church and it was a strange sight to behold. Little boys and girls in uniforms were marching down the street behind a fire truck. A marching band was right behind them with drums and flutes and trumpets, followed by young men and women in military clothes carrying flags. There were horses carrying riders with fancy hats, and small convertible cars with people smiling and waving. A shiny red tractor was carrying a wagon full of people who were throwing candy right and left to the children on the street. Several other vehicles pulling wagons decorated with ribbons and banners lined the street as far as she could see.

She knew she should move away from the window to keep from being seen, but she was mesmerized at what was happening on the street below. People had lined up on both sides of the streets to watch the spectacle. She looked around to see if she could spot the one who called himself Rock. Yes, there he was across the street with his pretty wife. As if the lady had a feeling someone was watching her, she looked up at the window where Maria was standing.

She panicked but had the presence of mind not to push the slat back down. Instead, she reached over and picked up a coin out of a bowl on the dresser and propped it open without moving it. She slipped away from the window and pulled her backpack from under the bed. She ran down the stairway to the back door. Thankfully everyone was out front watching the parade. She slipped out unnoticed and although she wanted to run, she walked casually, without drawing attention to herself, across the parking lot to the narrow street that ran behind the church. After stopping a moment to catch her breath, she walked over to the next street to the laundromat and put the few dirty clothes from her backpack into the washer and started the cycle. She breathed a sigh of relief. She must be more careful. She knew that staying in the house was too risky and she had been lucky not to have been caught. She had to find a place to live. The basement had become too damp and cold and what would happen if the baby came early. Ramon had told her there was a Catholic church on the east side of town - the only part of town she had not walked. She would go there tomorrow and talk to the priest.

CHAPTER 17

"**I** know I saw a movement behind those blinds." The parade was over and everyone had dispersed. Rock and Liz walked up the front steps of the parsonage. The Presbyterian Women had put a large evergreen wreath with a red velvet bow on the door to spruce it up for the parade. The participants had marched from Main Street, turning right on Church Street and finishing up in the parking lot of the Methodist Church on the next block.

"Liz, there's no one in this house - I promise you." Rock unlocked the door and stood back for Liz to go in.

"Su-re, make me walk in first you big brave man," she teased.

Rock laughed. "That was rather weak of me, wasn't it? Here, let me go get the broom."

That made Liz go into a fit of laughter. "So if we have an intruder, you're going to sweep him out?" she said.

Rock pretended to be offended. "Well, it's better than nothing. Maybe it's a mouse trying to watch the parade." He walked over to the stairway. "I'll go up first."

"I'll have your back," Liz said, trying to stifle a giggle.

Rock took one or two steps up and then with an exaggerated gesture, pretended to have a magnifying glass up to his eye, peering at the handrails and then furtively up the stairway. He motioned for Liz to follow. When she reached the step below him, he stopped and whispered, pointing up the stairway. She thought that he had heard something and was wary for a minute, until he whispered, "Inspector Jacque Couseau at your service, Ma'am" and started humming the 1960's cartoon theme song of the Pink Panther.

Liz had to sit down on the step to control her laughter, but he hushed her with a finger to his mouth. He was still playing his role of the bumbling detective, hoping to keep her entertained so she wouldn't worry about finding an intruder.

"You stay here Ma'am, while I go investigate."

"Oui, monsieur," she said, staying where she was on the stairway.

Rock walked down the hallway checking each bedroom and closet as he went. "All safe now," he said. "You can come up."

"I smell popcorn," Liz said as she joined him at the top of the stairs.

"So now our intruder is eating popcorn," he said. "At least he has good taste."

"I wish I'd thought to use my cell phone to record you," she said. "Your congregation would never believe that their handsome, sane and stable minister was role-playing the Pink Panther."

"You wouldn't dare?"

"Your secrets are safe with me - at least for now. Of course, someday I may have to testify when they come in their white coats and take you away."

"Ah, I don't think you can be forced to testify against your own husband." He kissed her full on the mouth. "Which room did you see the movement of the blind?" he asked.

"The one at the end of the hallway," and she walked ahead. "And I'm not sure I saw it move. It was propped open and I just sensed that there was someone behind it."

"There's nothing in here, but let me look under the bed just to reassure you." He got on his knees and looked. "Nothing. I'll check the closet." He opened the door. "Ahh, there's where all my extra robes are," he said. I'll need this white vestment for when we change liturgical colors at Christmas." He pulled it off the hanger and carefully folded it up, draped it across his arm and shut the closet door. Liz had walked over to the window.

"Look at this, Rock." He walked over to where she was standing and pointed to the blinds. A penny was holding one of the slats of the blind open on one corner. Rock pulled it out and the slat fell back in place. "Who would have done that?" she asked.

"The kids," he said. "Chase stayed in this room when the family was here and it's typical of something a little boy would do."

Liz was visibly relieved. "Let's go see what kind of progress they're making on the kitchen."

Rock was not quite as relieved. The penny thing would have gone unnoticed by most anyone, he thought. Anyone but his mom who had an obsession about such things. Each time they had visited him, one of the last things she would do was take a feather duster to the blinds and admonish him in her best motherly voice, "If you want to keep your allergies at bay Rock, always, and I mean always keep your blinds dusted." Oh well, he thought, even Mom can slip up once in a while. Maybe she was getting over her obsessions, he thought, and dismissed it from his mind.

The tempo around the church was picking up along with the temperature. Rock was helping the Presbyterian men put up the Nativity scene in the courtyard where Jack Terry had just announced that it was 64 degrees. "That's what the old blinker at Liberty Bank says anyways. From an arctic blast to a heat wave in three days," he said as he stepped back and looked at their work.

Lonnie Welch's EMS van had been in the parade and as he pulled out of the Methodist church driving up Church Street, he stopped his van and came up to help. He picked up the manger and placed it in front of Joseph and Mary. He commented on a motorcycle as it rode by. "Nice day for a ride."

"By the way, Rev Rock, do you know how to spot a happy motorcyclist in fair weather?"

"I can't say that I do, but I have no doubt that you'll tell me."

"He's got bugs all over his teeth." Rock didn't get it, but tried to look like he did. Lon went on - "You know, bugs all over his teeth...he's happy, don't you get it? Happy and grinning so when he rides he gets bugs on his teeth."

Jack looked over at him. "I hate to tell you this, Lonnie, but you're falling down on your joke material. You better go get you a good joke book."

"Y'all are just losin' your sense of humor, is all," he said as he moved Joseph over to the right.

"Oh, I get it now," Rock said.

"A day late and a dollar short," Lon said as he brushed some dust off the manger. He was trying to pout but it wasn't his nature. He laughed and patted Rock on the back. "Don't worry, I'll have a doozy for you next time." He walked back to his truck, got in and cranked it up. All of a sudden the air was filled with the blast of a siren, startling all the men. Lon rolled his window down and called out to them, "If I can't make you laugh, I'll scare you half to death." He waved and they could hear him laughing as he drove off down the street.

Rock watched as parents drove up and dropped their children off in the Fellowship Hall. Holly and Abby walked across the street and joined them. The Beverly Hills Children's Home van was pulling up and Rebecca got out and herded the children all in. It was time for the Christmas pageant practice and all the kids were excited about getting to try on their shepherd and wise men wardrobe.

The choir was practicing for their cantata and just beginning to crank up the volume. Walt Carrington's daughter told Jenny Wilson at church the next morning that her daddy had been driving by the church and said he could hear the angels sing. "Oh, how sweet of him to say that," Jenny had gushed.

"And he's stone deaf," Walt's daughter said.

Rock and Liz were relaxing by the fire. There had been no down time at all over the weekend, and Liz looked beat. First, the parade on Saturday morning - then the adult Sunday school class Christmas party that evening. It was held at Miss Edie's big house on the hill and again, Rock had enjoyed the social time with his congregation.

This evening, the Lighting the Way ceremony had

gone off without a hitch. Each of the four churches had a sweet service of music and the last one at the AME Zion church was the highlight of the whole night. The lively choir had everyone tapping their feet and swaying to the music and Terrence Mobley had brought the house down with his rendition of *Go Tell it on the Mountain*. It was a perfect way to end the evening, but now that they had time to take a breather, they both realized they were exhausted - both mentally and physically. Rock was sitting and Liz was half sitting - half lying against the arm of the sofa with her feet in Rock's lap.

Liz wiggled her toes as Rock began massaging one of her feet. "The Lighting the Way program went well, don't you think? It's my favorite event of the year."

"Mine too," he said. "Our choir sang their hearts out tonight - oh, and when Abby sang her solo, there was total and complete silence in the church as if they were all spellbound."

"Away in a Manger tends to do that to people," Liz said. "But her rendition with her crystal clear little voice was amazing."

Rock picked up the other foot and started massaging it gently. "Ah, much better," she said. "All of a sudden, all my shoes are too small. I suppose my feet are just swelling."

"Is that supposed to happen?" he said, with alarm.

She laughed. "Rock, you can't get all worried every time I tell you about the subtle little changes that are happening in my pregnancy. I'll just quit telling you if you do."

"No, please! I want you to tell me everything. I think I need to read the book."

"What book?" She looked at him curiously.

"The one I ordered last week on Amazon. It's called *The Expectant Father* and it's still sitting in my office. I thought that you and I could read it together, but it's been such a hectic week."

She was touched that he had bought a book to try to understand what she was going through. "Bring it home tomorrow, and we'll start reading."

"I'll do just that," he said and stood up. "Now let's get you off to bed. It's nine o'clock and we need our beauty sleep."

"What? So I need beauty sleep, do I?" she said.

"Nope, you're the most beautiful woman in the world," he said. "It's me that needs the beauty sleep." He held his hand out for her to hold on to as she got up off the couch.

"You're a slick one, all right, Rock Clark. You know all the right things to say." She stood in front of the fire for a moment gazing fondly at the Christmas tree. "Don't forget to turn off the lights," she said. "They were flickering again when I turned them on tonight which still worries me. Did Carter's not have the right kind of lights?"

"I totally forgot about them. I had a hotdog and it sort of took my mind off the lights. I'll try to run by there again tomorrow. We'll take the ornaments off the top and replace the strand." He turned off the gas logs and then unplugged the tree lights and they walked back to the bedroom. Theo was curled up right in the middle of the bed with no intentions of moving. She turned to Rock. "I guess you're going to have to sleep on your side tonight."

"Go get in your own bed, Theo," he said, but Theo

didn't budge.

"Hm," Liz said as they lay in the bed separated by the cat. "Theo's feet are much warmer than yours."

CHAPTER 18

Maria's visit with Father Nathaniel had not gone very well. She had told him the truth that she had run away from an abusive husband, but she couldn't bring herself to tell him she had been trespassing in the basement of a church and in the home of the minister of Park Place Presbyterian for the past two weeks. His solution was for her to go to the police and take out a restraining order to keep her husband from hurting her. She couldn't seem to make him understand that if Ernesto found her, he would probably kill her now that she had run away from him. When she told him her age, he told her of a children's home that would take her in if they had space.

"But I'm not a child," she had said.

He tried to reason with her. "You're just sixteen and in the eyes of the court system, you are still a child. It would only be until you are on your feet. When your baby is born, it can stay with you unless you want to give it up for adoption."

It was much too confusing for Maria, this talk of court and giving her baby away. She told him she would think about it and come back to see him, but she had no intention of doing so. Her thoughts went back to home.

Ernesto's mother had taken a special interest in Maria from the time she was a toddler. "This child has an exceptional intelligence and a naturally good heart," she had told her mother the year Maria had turned ten years old. "I would like to give her some extra tutoring. She seems to be a natural at learning languages." Her parents had not minded as long as it didn't interfere with her chores at home. Her spiritual quest for knowledge had deepened under the guidance of Senora Ann, and Maria had developed a deep-seated faith that God was in control and would take care of her no matter what the circumstances. It was that faith that had brought her this far, and she knew that He would give her the answers when she needed them. He had also given her a baby in her womb and she had no intention of giving it up for adoption.

As she walked down Church Street, she noticed that the church parking lots were still pretty full even though worship services were over. She had come to think of Park Place Presbyterian as her own since she had been living right underneath its sanctuary and it had become her safe haven. She was beginning to even recognize some of the members. The pretty lady with the black hair was the busiest one. Every time she was inside the building, beautiful music wafted through the walls, ceilings and floors. It was she who must play the organ, and the other ladies who appeared right behind her were the ones with the voices singing the songs of angels. The music was coming out of the church today, and Maria wanted so badly to go in and listen, but knew she should not attract attention to herself.

This was her first Christmas away from home where the holiday had been celebrated simply. A Christmas mass, a display of the nativity figures, and a small gift from her parents had been all it took to make a spiritual and meaningful day of celebrating the Lord Jesus' birth. Here, there was a sense of urgency that made her nervous. The faces she saw on the streets seemed to be preoccupied and people darted in and out of stores.

What she wanted more than anything was to take a nap, but there was no getting into the basement with all the activity around the building. Maybe a short walk would do her good. She had only eaten an apple for breakfast and suddenly she was starving. She remembered that she needed to replace some items from the parsonage refrigerator, so she set off in the direction of the Dollar Store near the diner.

"Getting breakfast for tomorrow morning?" It took a second for Maria to realize that the girl behind the counter was talking to her. "Pop-Tarts and apple juice," the girl said. "I just figured you were stocking up on breakfast items. I live on Pop-Tarts myself." Maria's cart held only the boxed pastries, microwave popcorn and apple juice, the things she had taken from the parsonage kitchen. She'd picked up an extra box of Pop-Tarts for herself.

"Oh...yes, breakfast," Maria said.

"I've seen you around here - you work at the diner, don't you?" Maria nodded. "Kit told me y'all were opening up tomorrow? Something about a men's breakfast club having a Christmas party. That's the first time I remember them opening on a Monday. I'm sure it'll help our business. We're always slow on Mondays - your breakfast and lunch crowd are some of our best customers."

Maria nodded. "Kit says the diner gets busy this time of year anyway. They asked me to work tomorrow."

"By the way, my name's Carmen." She started ringing up the groceries and putting them in bags. The girl was friendly and only a few years older than Maria. It would be nice to have a friend, she thought - someone she could confide in. It gave her a little more confidence.

Maria relaxed and smiled. "And I'm Maria."

"Hey, that's the first time I've seen you smile! You're always so serious looking - or maybe sad?" Maria didn't know what to say. Carmen had finished ringing up the groceries and Maria started fumbling in her bag for money. There was only one other person shopping in the store - an elderly woman who was taking her time looking down the candy aisle.

After she paid, she started to pick up her bags, but Carmen stopped her. "Maria, I hope I didn't hurt your feelings. I'd like to be your friend. I don't want to pry, but I've worried about you since the first day I saw you."

Maria blushed and stuttered. "Me? Uh, no, I'm fine."

Carmen stood her ground. "Look, Hon. I know the signs of being in a bad relationship - I've been there. I've had those same 'punches in the face' bruises that you had the first day you came in." She looked at the back of the store as if waiting for someone. "Look, I'm getting ready to take my break. My replacement just walked in the back door. Wait outside for me - please... I'll just be a minute. We need to talk."

Maria walked out the door. She was tempted to just keep walking, but something held her back. She'd never had anyone to show interest in her problems since she moved away from home. She knew that Kit cared and was concerned about her, but she was more like a mother figure.

Carmen hurried out the door. "I was afraid you'd run off."

Maria looked at her sheepishly. "I almost did," she admitted.

Carmen had been in her sophomore year of college when she met Mark. He had seemed perfect at first, she said - maybe a little possessive, but she had been flattered by all the attention he gave her. After a while, his jealousy became obsessive. Then came an occasional twist of the arm, and slaps on the face.

"He would be so apologetic, saying he would never do it again, and stupid me, I believed him. The finale came one night when I had been studying for exams with a friend and when I got home to my apartment, he was there waiting for me, claiming he had proof I had found another boyfriend. It took two surgeries to repair my broken jaw and I was black and blue for weeks. I took my exams from my hospital room and the only reason I got to finish out my sophomore year was because he was in jail. They let him out after three months and of course I didn't go back for my junior year. I still live my life wondering if he'll show up on my doorstep here someday, but at least my daddy and two brothers would beat the tar out of him if he did." She smiled and for the first time, Maria noticed that her smile was a little crooked. Carmen noticed. "Yep," she said. "They didn't quite get it straight," she said, rubbing her jaw.

Maria found herself sharing part of her own story. "I'm scared he'll find me," she said.

"You're pregnant, aren't you?"

Maria rubbed her stomach. "I'm afraid I can't hide it any longer," she said. "I don't know what I'm going to tell Kit and BJ. They may fire me when they find out. I need my job."

"Maria, you don't know them very well, if you think that. They're the type that would bend over backwards to help you. Please share what you've told me with Kit."

Maria looked uncertain. "And if you need anything at all, please let me know. If you need a place to stay... where are you staying?" She looked at her watch. "Oops, my fifteen minutes are up. Seriously, Maria - here's my phone number." She wrote her number on one of Maria's grocery bags with a pen she had in her pocket. "Promise you'll call."

Maria nodded. "I will." She breathed a sigh of relief, happy that Carmen was distracted from her questions. Her stomach was growling. She had not eaten since early morning. She held her mid-section and laughed. "My stomach is making noises. Is there any place to eat nearby?" she asked. "I'm starving."

"Not much," Carmen answered. "The convenience store between here and town has decent enough food I guess - if you just want a hot meal."

"I'll try it." she said, and waved goodbye. She was feeling better just for having talked with someone who understood.

As she passed by the diner, she noticed that BJ had replaced the *Closed Monday* sign on the door with a poster saying *Open Monday - December 15th.* She was ready to get back to work so she could eat a decent meal. She thought again how God had brought Kit and BJ into her life at just the right time and she was thankful, but she didn't want to burden them with her problems.

She carried her food to a small round table near the

window of the convenience store. She had ordered fried chicken and mashed potatoes. She was starving but she ate slowly, enjoying every bite. The clerk spoke to her as she started to leave. "Buenas noches."

He seemed surprised when she answered in English, "Good night to you also". She gathered her coat around her and set off in the direction of town, with the temperature dropping as the sun was slipping from the sky.

The chill in the night air seemed to permeate her thoughts as she walked back to town. Whereas she had been confident and hopeful earlier with Carmen, she now became despondent and fearful. Walking past the Catholic church, she decided to try one more time to talk to Father Nathaniel. He had done most of the talking earlier and she had left confused, forgetting to ask him if she could go to prison for running away from Ernesto. She should have asked Carmen, but she hadn't thought of it. She walked up the steps to the rectory door and knocked. She waited a while and knocked again, but there was no answer so she turned around and headed to the only place she had called home since coming to Park Place. Her nights of sleeping in the house had been comfortable and had given her time to think logically. The basement was no place for a baby, and she knew she couldn't handle childbirth alone. She was running out of options. Maybe she should consider the place Father Nathaniel had told her about. It was too risky to continue trespassing in the basement of the church.

Where the church parking lots had been full of cars earlier in the afternoon, now they were all empty - not a soul in sight. She made her way to the back of the church and waited until the last of the lights were turned off in the cottage. She walked across the yard, got the key out of its hiding place and once again ventured inside the house. She put the groceries she had borrowed back in the pantry. She retrieved her sleeping bag from the closet, hid the key again and went back to the church basement. A feeling of defeat was descending upon her. A dog was barking nearby and even though she was exhausted, each time she drifted off to sleep, the dog would start up again.

Rock couldn't sleep. Irma Rembert's dog, Oscar, was at it again. He finally gave up and grumbling out loud, he pulled the covers back and sat up on the side of the bed. The dog hadn't bothered Liz - she was sleeping soundly. His eyes had adjusted to the dark. He watched her for a while and envied her ability to sleep through anything. He felt for his slippers under the bed and put them on. Theo watched him but stayed where he was, guarding his position between the two of them.

He walked into the living room, opened the front door and looked out into the night. Things had been peaceful for a while with Irma's dog. He had a feeling she had heard through the grapevine about his ongoing joke of spraying the squeaky wheel - the dog, with WD-40. The next thing he knew, she had bought a bark collar. He felt a little sorry for the poor dog the first few times he tried to bark after Irma put it on him. He would start to bark and then stop immediately and look around. Irma said it was electronic and interrupted his bark by transmitting a low voltage shock. Even after she took it off, he apparently thought it was still on, and had only recently realized that it was gone. It seemed strange to hear him again. At least they'd had a little peace and quiet for a while.

Rock peered into the darkness. The church was visible from the cottage, but several large oak trees separated the two yards. He thought he saw something walk around the side of the church, but the largest tree was in his line of vision. He had seen deer on the property quite a few times. The oak trees were a magnet for them - they thrived on the acorns during the winter months. They were getting braver -even coming right up to the back steps of the cottage now and then. He loved how graceful they were and he could coexist with them peacefully, as long as they left the rhododendrons alone. He didn't know exactly what he would do if they did dine on his rhododendrons, but he would think of something - maybe he could send Theo out to attack them. The thought made him smile. Oscar had different barks for different occasions and apparently this was his deer bark, he thought, and walked to the kitchen. He got a glass of water from the spigot and went back to bed. He seemed to be the only one in the room having trouble sleeping. He tried to nudge Theo over a little bit with his feet without waking him up, but out of nowhere, a front paw appeared like a snake and attacked his foot through the covers. "Ouch," he said out loud, and thought seriously about kicking him out of bed, but when he looked again, Theo was innocently curled up in a ball. He grumbled a little and pulled the cover up to his chin. "Sleep well while you can, Theo," he said. "Tomorrow night is another story."

Sometime after midnight, Maria finally slept and didn't wake until she heard the slamming of the door to the construction van early on Monday morning. Oh no, I'm late, she thought as she scurried around in the dark basement trying to brush her teeth and put on a clean shirt and pants. The weather was supposed to be warmer today so she grabbed the fleece jacket she had bought at the thrift shop instead of the heavy coat. Opening the vent, she looked out and saw Jay and Ramon walk into the big house so she slipped out the door and quickly set off to work. She pulled the hood of her jacket over her head and was walking at a brisk pace when she got to the convenience store on her left. As she passed it, she saw a car pull away from the gas pump and slowly enter the road in the direction she was going. The car was familiar and when she saw the North Carolina license plate surrounded by a bracket stamped with the name of a Honda dealership in Raleigh, she panicked. The car slowed down as it passed her, but sped up again as a truck came up behind it. The truck passed her too, but slowed down and backed up. There was no place to hide.

CHAPTER 19

"Order up," Kit shouted from the kitchen. Becky grabbed the scrambled egg and country ham plate and started towards table number three where Red Bivens was sitting alone. "No sign of Maria yet?" BJ asked. She had seemed excited about getting an extra day's work in, so he knew she couldn't have forgotten they were open today to serve the men's Christmas brunch.

"Nope, and it's not like her," Becky said, stopping for a moment to answer. She had been waiting tables at full speed all morning. BJ regretted that he hadn't thought to hire some temporary wait staff during the Christmas rush. He was concerned about Maria - she had not been late a single time since she started her job. When they had first met her, she had bruises consistent with spousal abuse, but there had been no more bruises since she started work. He called Kit from his cell phone and asked her to drive over to the State Park where the bridge construction workers were staying in campers and see if she could find her.

"Now how am I going to find her in all those trailers?" she asked. "It'll be like huntin' a needle in a haystack. What am I going to do - knock on doors?" She was trying to sound like her normal flippant self, but he could hear the worry in her voice. "It's not like her to be late though. I'll drive over that way now. Maybe I'll meet her on the way."

Thirty minutes later, she drove into the restaurant parking lot without Maria. "I knocked on every door," she said. "There's at least twenty campers in there and not a single person came to the door except one angry young woman carrying a baby. I couldn't understand a word she was saying, but her expression said it all. I'm sure I woke her and the baby with my loud knocking. I asked her the best I could if she knew Maria and she shook her head and closed the door in my face."

She had just finished getting the words out of her mouth when a truck drove into the parking lot and Maria got out of the passenger side. "Why that's Rev Rock's truck," Kit exclaimed. She didn't see the small white car that had pulled in and parked a short distance away.

Rock got out of the truck and walked in with the young girl. Maria's face was flushed and she was out of breath.

"Look who I ran into. I think she needs to sit down for a minute. She's a little out of breath," Rock said, leading her over to one of the booths. "Someone's having fun," he said, pointing to the back room where the men's breakfast club was gaining steam.

"That's a rowdy bunch," Kit said laughing. "There's not a man in there under sixty-five and everyone of 'em's hard of hearing. They try to compete to see who can talk the loudest." She sat down at the booth facing Maria. "Are you okay, Honey?" Maria nodded. Kit looked at Rock waiting for an explanation.

"I was headed over here for breakfast so that I could meet this Maria you mentioned at church last week and I saw this young girl just standing next to the highway. She looked confused and I thought she was lost. I'd met her last week near the parsonage so I stopped to offer her a ride. I didn't know she was your Maria until she told me where she was headed." He didn't tell them that the car in front of him had slowed down as if to pick Maria up. The reason he had stopped was to make sure she was okay - the car's actions were suspicious. The car had pulled to a stop and waited until Rock's truck passed it. As he had driven, he thought he saw the car following them from a distance, but he couldn't be sure. He was glad he had come along when he did. Maria's small size made her vulnerable to the sort of people who preyed upon young women.

BJ came back from the kitchen with a glass of water and a wet paper towel. "Use this to wipe your face, Maria," he said. "Take a few deep breaths and drink the water. It'll help you settle down." Maria looked both frightened and embarrassed as she sat in the booth. "I'm feeling fine now," she said. "I just slept late and was trying to get here as fast as I could. I'm so sorry I'm late."

"That's okay," Kit said. "You've never been late before - BJ was just worried about you. I went by the park but couldn't find where you live." Kit waited for an explanation, but when Maria didn't offer one, she asked, "That is where you're staying, isn't it?"

Maria looked down at her hands and then back up at Kit. She could not tell a lie to this woman who had been so kind to her. "No... I'm staying... well...," she paused trying to find the words. "I'm not with my husband anymore." Tears started rolling down her face.

"Maria! Why didn't you tell us?" As usual, Kit's voice stood out in the crowd. Red Bivens was still eating and four construction foremen had just given Becky their order. At Kit's outburst, the room was suddenly quiet. Kit looked around. "Sorry folks," she said good-naturedly. "Just a little diner drama here." The men laughed and went back to their conversation.

"Let's go over to the consignment store so we can have some privacy," she said. She reached out and took Maria by the hand. "Maria, Honey - we'll work it out."

Rock followed them out the door. BJ watched them and smiled as he saw his wife lead the parade. Becky brought a tea pitcher back to the counter to re-fill and stood there with him for a moment. "There ain't no problem too big for that woman to fix," she said.

"Yep," he puffed up, visibly proud of his wife. "That's my little fireball. She tries to solve everyone's problems." He sighed as he thought of all the times Kit had gotten involved in one thing or another. There's no telling what she's getting us into, he thought. He filled the pitcher for Becky and she started back towards the private dining room.

"I don't think you're ever gonna' get these old men out of here," she said, pointing to the back room. "Better make another batch of tea."

"Oh, they'll leave when their Lasix starts kickin' in," he said. "We only have one mens' restroom."

Kit unlocked the door and led Maria and Rock to the back of the store, picking up a folding chair along the way. "I don't usually have guests back here, so there's nowhere to sit. Rev Rock, you sit behind the desk and Maria will sit in this chair." Rock felt like a kid in school again with the teacher telling him what to do. He dutifully took the seat he was assigned and as Maria sat on the folding chair, Kit got down on the floor beside her. "Now, why don't you start from the beginning?"

Maria looked at Rock, then back at Kit. Her eyes were still red rimmed but her tears were gone. Rock watched as she composed herself, first pushing herself up in the seat and then squaring her shoulders. The fear and confusion in those childlike eyes belied the brave persona she was trying to portray. Then she slumped in her seat as if giving up.

"I don't know where to start," she said, and then slipped out of her seat on to the floor like a limp rag doll.

The emergency room was crowded, but when Rock strode in with Maria in his arms and shouted, "She's about to have a baby!" everyone scurried around and within minutes, they had her on a gurney wheeling her back to an examining room. Kit was allowed to go into the examining room but Rock stayed behind in the waiting room and prayed. He had no idea why he had shouted - the words had just come out. He did know without a doubt that she was very pregnant. As he carried her out of the restaurant, her pregnancy was much more pronounced as he held her in his arms. The baggy shirts she wore may have hidden the rounded belly to the outside world, but as his hands had encircled her stomach to lift her up, there was no doubt that she was very near her due date. The book he and Liz had been reading each night had taught him a lot about the different stages of pregnancy. And as Park Place Presbyterian's pastor, he'd had the pleasure of counseling couples as they married and rejoiced with them as they started their families. He had visited young mothers in the hospital as they were about to give birth. He had even assisted in the delivery of Ruthie Cuthbertson's baby when her water broke in the choir loft one Sunday after church services were over. Little Tabitha was born amongst ten or so choir robes laid upon the floor because there was no time to even get her over to the parsonage. He had been relieved when someone ran out to the parking lot and flagged down Jessica Mills, one of the church members who was a delivery nurse at the hospital. The delivery had gone off without a hitch, but the EMS workers took Rock along for the ride to the hospital, because in Lonnie's words, "the snow-white choir robes were a darker shade than Rev Rock's face when we got there." Anyway, he knew what full-term pregnancies looked like, and Maria was getting pretty close in his opinion.

As soon as the nurse had taken control in the examining room, Kit slipped back out to the waiting room to ask Rock if he would call Liz and get the phone number for her gynecologist.

"My old Dr. Perkins retired and I haven't found a new one yet," Kit told him. "I know Liz must have one. The emergency room doctors are fine for emergencies, but I think Maria will be better off with an ob/gyn."

He waited until Kit walked away, then found Dr. Alexander in his phone contacts. He didn't have to call Liz - he was one step ahead of the game. He had entered the good doctor's number as soon as they had their first prenatal visit. You could never take any chances when your wife was pregnant. He was relieved when the office said that the doctor was already at the hospital and they would get in touch with him to see Maria. He settled down in the waiting room with a second hand newspaper and Elvis Presley's *I'll be Home for Christmas* being streamed into the emergency waiting room and unconsciously started humming along.

Kit scanned the examining room while she and Maria were waiting for the doctor to come in. A metal examining bed right in the center of the room was the main focal point and Maria was lying on it in a reclining position. She was covered with a white sheet up to her chin and a blue hospital blanket was spread across her feet. A metal table beside the bed was almost hidden under a monitoring system with numbers alternately changing on the screen - blood pressure 140 / 80, heart rate 84.

A metal cabinet with drawers underneath and a blue countertop full of medical instruments butted up against a stainless steel sink and spanned one whole wall of the room.

Kit grabbed a tissue from a complimentary tissue box on the counter with an advertisement for a pharmaceutical company imprinted on the side. There was one lone chair beside the bed and she sat down in it.

She reached for Maria's hand. Her eyes were like saucers in her petite face and her dark olive complexion was now pale and sallow.

The nurse walked back in. "Your blood pressure and heart rate are a touch on the high side," she told Maria. "But that's not so unusual. Some people have white coat syndrome when they come into the hospital. The stress

causes the numbers to be elevated. Are you nervous?"
Maria nodded.

Kit squeezed her hand. "Everything will be fine,
honey - just relax."

Maria's fright was evident and Kit's heart went out to
her. She looked from Kit to the nurse. "My baby?"

"We'll know in a little while when the doctor comes
in and does a full examination. From my quick exam just
now, it looks like you're going to be fine. Just stay calm - it
will lower your blood pressure."

Kit spoke up. "Maria, we'll pray that God will take
good care of you and the baby. Do you believe in God?"

"Si," she said, slipping back for a moment to her
native language. "He has been with me all along." She
closed her eyes.

A man, larger than life, appeared in the doorway. His
size was in sharp contrast to the soft gray hair and
twinkling blue eyes Kit saw as she studied his features.
She saw his expression soften as he looked at the
frightened young girl on the bed. He strode across the
room and with his long stride, it took him only a couple
of steps to get to Maria's bedside. He held out his large
hand, and Maria, as if mesmerized, put her small hand in
his.

"Maria, do you speak English?"

"Yes." Her answer was weak and timid.

"Good, I'm Dr. Alexander and I'm an ob/gyn doctor.
Do you know what that means?" Maria shook her head
no. "Well, in your case, it means that I specialize in
pregnancies and births, and something tells me you might
need my services." He smiled at her tenderly. Maria
nodded again. "Have you seen a doctor during your

pregnancy?"

"No." Maria answered hesitantly. Had she done something wrong, she wondered.

"Do you know when you had your last menstrual period?"

Maria thought for a moment. "I think it was in April."

Kit was flabbergasted and started ticking off the months on her fingers. Dr. Alexander turned to her.

"Do you know this young lady?"

Kit stood up. "Yes, Dr. Alexander, I'm Kit Jones, and Maria works in our restaurant."

The doctor looked at her with consternation. "How long has she worked for you, and did you know she was pregnant."

Kit knew he was just being thorough, but she couldn't help but feel guilty. She had suspected Maria was pregnant but had never talked to her about it. She's just a child, she thought. Why have I not talked to her?

"I did suspect that she was pregnant, but since she didn't confide in me, I didn't think it was any of my business. I've only known her for a few weeks. I felt that when the time was right, she would tell me."

Dr. Alexander turned back to the patient. "I'm going to move you up to the ob/gyn floor, Maria. We may keep you overnight since you haven't been receiving prenatal care. We'll do a complete exam and then an ultrasound today. Do you have someone you need to call to let them know you'll be staying in the hospital? They can take you home in the morning."

Maria looked at Kit and then looked away. "No, I have no one," she answered. "And I have no home to go to."

Kit was expecting her answer. "And I didn't know that until today, Dr. Alexander. We were just having this conversation when Maria fainted and we brought her here."

Maria looked uncomfortable and hesitated before saying, "I'm sorry. I didn't mean to tell a lie. I was afraid that if I said I was alone, you wouldn't hire me."

Kit walked over to the bed and leaned down and kissed her on the cheek. "Oh, Maria. Just the opposite. If I had known you were alone, I would have..."

Dr. Alexander interrupted. "We'll have time for more questions later. Let's get this young lady moved upstairs. Maria, we'll get your paperwork filled out after your examination. I want to find out what's going on with you. Mrs. Jones is welcome to go to the waiting room on the 3rd floor." He turned to Kit.

"Dr. Alexander, you can call me Kit. And yes, I'll wait, but first I need to go tell Rev Rock what we're doing so he can go home."

She found Rock right where she'd left him in the waiting room, but this time he was holding hands and praying with a young family. When he finished, he saw Kit waiting for him. He shook hands with the father, and briefly hugged the mother and said his goodbyes. She thought he looked troubled as she walked across the room towards him. We're two peas in a pod, she thought, taking on the burdens of others.

"That family needs our prayers, Kit," he said quietly. "Their six year old boy was hit on the head by a falling tree limb on the playground at school today. He was knocked out and hasn't regained consciousness yet." His eyes were filled with compassion and she felt proud to know him.

She looked at the family sitting huddled in the corner. The mother was crying freely and the father was wringing his hands, but the twelve-year old was sitting quietly with a serene expression on her face. She took her dad's hand in hers and Kit heard her say, "Stay calm Daddy. Remember what the preacher said - God's in control."

Oh, to have the faith of a child, Kit thought. She remembered how she had unleashed her fury on God when Lindsey had died. It had been Rock who comforted them even when they had resisted being comforted. His words had reached into the hard shell of her broken heart. The drunk driver who had hit Lindsey head-on had died instantly just as Lindsey had. Rock had been with them at the hospital. "Kit," he had said, "Since the beginning of time, man has had the freedom to make choices. The man who caused the accident made an awfully poor choice - a choice that leaves us all broken-hearted. God didn't promise us that we would not suffer from broken bodies and broken hearts. But He did promise by sending his own Son to suffer and die on the cross that He would be here to comfort us in our grief. His Holy Spirit lives within us. Sometimes He's right there on the surface ready to embrace us, but other times our own spirit is so broken that we need to reach down in the far recesses of our hearts to find Him. He is there, I promise you, Kit. Just reach deep and bring the Holy Spirit forth and He will be right beside you in your grief."

The scripture he had quoted afterwards was from Psalm, 91:4. "He will cover you with his feathers, and under his wings you will find refuge."

Even after seventeen years, the heartache was still there, but the difference had been that she and BJ had been covered with the wings of the Holy Spirit during it all. She wondered how people made it out of the dark places in their lives without God. Who or what do they have to give them comfort?

When she looked up, Rock was watching her. "You're remembering this emergency room, aren't you?" he said with compassion.

"Yes," she said, "and I'm remembering the words of the man who helped pull us out of the depths of despair."

"Not my words," he said modestly. "It was His words."

"Yeah," she said. "But sometimes He needs a messenger."

"I get paid to do that," he said with a grin.

She laughed. "And you're well worth the ten percent we put in the collection plate each Sunday." The somber mood was broken.

"You can leave, Rev Rock. They're keeping her overnight. I'll stay here the rest of the day, and then come back in the morning to pick her up. I'll call you in the morning. I have something I want to discuss with you about Maria."

Rock nodded. They prayed one more time for Maria and he left through the exit door of the emergency room.

Kit knew she needed to talk to BJ. He needed to be in agreement with the plans that were taking shape in her mind. Maria would need somewhere to go.

CHAPTER 20

D r. Alexander had just finished washing up and came to Maria's bedside where Kit was waiting to hear the results of the examination. Maria had told them the circumstances of her leaving Ernesto and about the beatings she had suffered at his hands.

"The ultrasound results show that the baby is moving about normally and appears to be fine. It's a good thing your abusive husband didn't aim for the stomach. In some situations it can cause uterine separation or blunt force trauma, but you don't have to worry about that." Maria and Kit both let out a collective sigh of relief. Dr. Alexander had performed the ultrasound, bypassing the technician. He had been anxious to see things for himself since the young woman had not received any prenatal care. He waited for a moment before announcing, "And by the way, it's a girl," and then smiled as he watched the reaction of the two women in front of him.

"She's tiny - just about a six pounder, but Maria, you're small so it's normal for the baby to be small. It's remarkable that the baby appears so healthy, especially after what you've been through and the fact that you've been virtually homeless for the last few weeks."

During their questioning, they had pressed her on where she had been staying and she clammed up. "Here and there," she had answered. "I moved around a lot." It was true but somewhat deceptive. They both assumed she had been moving around staying with different friends. She was still not ready to reveal that she had been trespassing on church property. She was sure she would be in trouble if they knew.

She'd considered telling Kit about seeing Ernesto's car pulling out from the gas pumps, but now she wondered if it was really his car. Many cars came from that dealership - how could she be sure it was his - she wasn't that familiar with makes and models and there were more white cars than any other color. She wished she'd been able to see the people inside. The windows were tinted like his car and she could tell there were two, but neither seemed quite as tall as Ernesto. She was glad she hadn't been wearing Ernesto's jacket. That would have been a dead giveaway if it was him and he had seen her. There was no use to worry Kit about it. She herself had been enough trouble to Kit and BJ already. She watched now as Kit and Dr. Alexander continued their conversation.

"Why did she faint, Dr. Alexander?" Kit asked.

"We'll probably never know. She had been walking unusually fast, out of breath and it was cold - a lack of oxygen perhaps. Or it could have been a combination of things - anxiety and stress can cause dizziness. The important thing is that she gets rest tonight." He turned to Maria. "Please try to get some rest, Maria. If you need anything, use the button here to call a nurse. Don't be shy about making your needs known. We want to help you." He moved the cord that held the call button so she could reach it easily. "Promise me you'll use it if you need something. We've ordered your dinner and it will be here shortly." Maria nodded.

Kit looked at her watch and couldn't believe it was almost 4:30. She wondered how BJ had made out in the diner without anyone but Becky helping. Dr. Alexander motioned for her to follow him. "We're going to leave you alone now so you can rest. I'll be back in the morning to check on you and if all goes well, Kit will take you home."

Maria sighed. Kit could tell she was worried about where she would be going. "I'll see you tomorrow, Hon," she said. "Don't worry about a thing. Like I told you this morning, we'll get it all worked out."

Dr. Alexander closed the door behind them. When they reached the nurses station, he turned to Kit. "Kit, I'm facing a dilemma here." She looked at him expectantly. "This child is under seventeen and if she doesn't have a home to go to when she's released, by law I'm supposed to contact Social Services."

Kit started to protest. "Let me finish, Kit. I've worked closely with Rebecca at Beverly Hills Children's Home before, and if they have room, I'm sure we could get her placed there. I know she seems a little old for that, but she's had cases that were older than Maria."

Kit tried to raise her 5' 2" frame a little higher, and there was nothing little about her voice and attitude as she spoke to him.

"Dr. Alexander, there's no need for that. I'm going home right now and fix up a bedroom in our house for Maria. We want her there. BJ and I have grown to love and care for her," she said with conviction. She would have time to sort it out with BJ when she got home, but she knew that with his kind heart, he would not hesitate at all.

"Do you know what a big responsibility you're taking on?"

"I know full well what I'm getting myself into, and there's no use trying to talk me out of it. If Maria agrees, I'll take her to our house tomorrow."

Dr. Alexander chuckled as the petite redhead with a big heart walked away. If he was a gambling man, he would have bet money on Kit's response. But he had thought to give her another option so she wouldn't feel pressured. Maria had seen some hard times, but in his opinion, right now she was one lucky girl.

Rock watched Liz as she sat at the table. He had picked up a rotisserie chicken and the makings of a fresh salad at the Piggly Wiggly on his way back from the hospital. He had finished slicing the chicken and was putting the finishing touches on the salad. "Do you want onions on your salad?" he asked.

"Heavens yes, but they don't want me," she answered. "I would be up all night with heartburn, so leave them off mine."

"In that case, I'll leave them off mine too. They've never bothered you before."

"I was never pregnant before," she laughed.

"Speaking of pregnant, I'll have to tell you about my day," he said as he pulled the salad dressing out of the refrigerator.

"Hmm - this should be interesting," she said. "Is someone else pregnant?"

"Take your vitamin before you eat and I'll tell you during dinner." He was glad to see her looking so much better. She was no longer falling asleep as soon as supper was over and she actually seemed to have a spring in her step again. He had been worried - she had only been taking the vitamins for a few days, but apparently they were already doing the trick.

"So this young girl that you've seen around the church is the same girl Kit had asked you to come by and see at the restaurant?"

"Yes, she happened to be walking by the parsonage on a day I was having trouble communicating with Ramon, so I asked her if she would mind coming in and interpreting."

"Rock, you don't just pull a complete stranger off the street just because she looks to be Hispanic and ask her to interpret. That's racial profiling."

"It is?" he said, looking at Liz with his mouth open. "I didn't think about that. She didn't seem to mind."

Liz laughed. "That's what I love about you, Rock. Sometimes you're just so naive and innocent. How could anyone mind doing anything you ask when you're so doggoned sweet about it?"

He looked relieved. "So I won't get in trouble with the racial profiling police," he teased.

"Not this time," she said. "But next time they'll be watching."

He finished telling her the events of the day, leaving nothing out.

"So Dr. Alexander saw her?" she asked. "What did he determine?"

"I didn't talk to him after he saw her. Kit came out for a few minutes and said they would be keeping her overnight and releasing her tomorrow. She promised to call me in the morning to fill me in." He stopped talking and looked up at Liz.

"See, I get involved without even trying. Here I am right in the middle again."

"Well, you did stop and pick her up," she said. "But I'm glad you did. Just think what could have happened to her if you hadn't come along! She could have fainted on the road. All I can say is, if God leads you to it, do it. You may have saved her life."

When they had put up the last of the supper dishes, they settled in their respective chairs in the living room - Rock in his armchair, and Liz at the small oak desk.

"Look at this stack of Christmas cards! It seems to grow higher and higher." One side of the desk held the cards that had come and the other side held the ones she was sending out.

"Liz, there comes a point when you can't keep adding people to your list just because they sent us a card."

"I think you're right. How did you get so smart?"

"I'm not sure, but I think it skipped a few generations and was handed down to me from my great, great Uncle Alexander. Did I ever tell you he invented penicillin?"

Liz rolled her eyes. "I should have said how did you get so smart-alecky? You know your great, great uncle didn't invent penicillin!"

"Oh, maybe I got it mixed up with somebody else's great, great Uncle Alexander. That's a relief - it's not easy having a famous relative."

Liz grinned. "When you stop trying to figure out your family genealogy, how about helping me address these Christmas cards."

"Oh, I've got time tomorrow. I'll do them all for you."

"Wow! Thanks - I was really dreading this. I've done all our personal ones, but I couldn't find the address book for the church members. That'll help me a lot."

"Anything to help," he quipped. He didn't mention that he would ask Reva to run a set of address labels so he could stick them on and drop them off at the post office - and it's a good thing he didn't. He knew she had wanted to make an impression her first Christmas as the pastor's wife by having them all handwritten. He felt a little guilty, but not enough to spend all night writing addresses on Christmas cards. He had never sent cards before anyway so they should be happy just to get one.

He picked up his calendar from the side table. "Good grief, Liz! Did you know that Christmas is just a week away?"

"Yes, my dear. I do keep up with these things you know."

"Well, why didn't you tell me?"

Liz shook her head. "How in the world did you ever get through Christmas before?" she asked.

"By the skin of my teeth," he said. And he was dead serious.

CHAPTER 21

Reva was on the phone when Rock walked in the office. "Good morning!" he said as he hung his coat on the peg near the door. She put her hand over the phone speaker and shushed him.

"Two centimeters? Well, I don't know. I would say it could be anywhere between two days and two weeks. Yes Ma'am, I know that's not much help. Oh, wait, here he is now." She motioned for Rock to get the phone. "It's Kit Jones - for you." He took the phone from Reva's hand and sat down in the chair beside her desk as he talked.

Kit had just brought Maria home from the hospital and Rock wasn't a bit surprised that she and BJ had taken her in. "We've put Maria in our guest room and when the baby comes, we'll fix up a nursery in Lindsey's room. That room will hold a little bit of happiness again."

"Are you sure you're up for this, Kit? You barely know the girl. There's always Beverly Hills."

He grinned when he heard the Kit Jones temper showing through on the other end. "You and that dad-blamed doctor are trying to ship her off to the children's home. I know what I'm doing, thank you sir!" There was a pause at the other end. "Oh no! I'm sorry Rev Rock. I didn't mean to go off on you. I'm just trying to do what's best for Maria, and everybody's second guessing me."

"Don't give it another thought Kit - I know you are, and it's a generous thing you're doing. How does BJ feel about it?"

"It's funny that you asked that Rev Rock. I haven't

seen the man this happy since...., well, you know. It's like he's got a purpose now. I've got a baby crib in the thrift shop with all the accessories and he's going to bring it home tonight, just in case she goes into labor right away. You know, Rev Rock - that child wanted to go back to work today! I said, 'no way, Jose' - oops, I guess I shouldn't be saying that, should I?"

Rock wasn't sure how to reply. Her excitement was contagious, but he hoped she wasn't setting herself up for disappointment. There were a lot of unanswered questions about this girl. If her papers weren't in order, she could be deported and Kit and BJ would be heartbroken. But then again, he didn't want to discourage their generous spirit.

"I know exactly what you're thinking, Rev Rock. And yes, we did pray about it. We got on our hands and knees right there in our Lindsey's room. You know, we never go in there together and I don't rightly know why. Last night there were tears of grief and of joy as we knelt beside the bed that hasn't been slept in since that horrible night ten years ago. We both felt it at the same time - just a peaceful feeling came over us that we were being given another chance. We've been so closed up all these years and it's time to open up our hearts to another child. It doesn't matter what comes of it - if she needs us for just a month or for a year, we're content to let God work out the details."

Rock felt a mixture of happiness and relief. "Then go for it. Here I am trying to meddle, when you've already got God in on the plans. How did the ultrasound and examination go?"

"That's the best part! It's a girl, and she's already

dilated two centimeters. I think that means it won't be long! Hey, I gotta go. I forgot - she hasn't had breakfast yet."

Rock laughed as a dial tone sounded in his ear. Reva heard the dial tone too. "I guess you got put in your place, yes you did," she said and hung up the phone.

He scooped up the handful of Christmas cards he had dropped on Reva's desk when she handed him the phone. "Reva, can you run labels for all the church members so I can mail these cards today. I promised Liz I would get them mailed."

"Hmph! And I'll bet you told her you would hand address them too, didn't you?" She looked at him suspiciously.

"Well, I didn't exactly tell her that." He looked sheepishly at Reva.

"Well, you didn't exactly tell her you were going to run labels either, did you?"

"Alright, you win. What is it about women and Christmas cards?" He picked up her good writing pen and stomped off to his office. She chased after him.

"Don't you go takin' my good pen," she said. "You've probably got fifteen of my pens in your office now." She walked over to the pen holder on his desk and took five just like the one he was holding. He stood in the middle of the room and watched her take the pens with his mouth wide open.

"And where's your spirit of Christmas?" he said.

"Bah humbug," she said, and with the pens in her hand, she marched back to her office.

The door opened to the outer office. "Knock, knock!" Wanda Burns walked in. "I'm here to spread some

Christmas cheer and see if I can help y'all do anything. I know it's a busy time of year!" She looked from one of them to the other. "Uh, oh, did I come at a bad time?"

Rock rushed out to meet her. "Wanda, am I ever glad to see you. You came at just the perfect time."

"Oh, I'm so glad. It looked like the two of you were arguing."

"Oh, no. I was just telling Reva here, that I wished that someone would walk right in that door and help me address these Christmas cards. You see, I promised Liz...."

Wanda's smile got bigger. "Oh, that's just what I like to do. Anyway, I need to practice my handwriting for all those books I'm going to be signing!"

Reva shook her head and walked back to her desk talking to herself. "Lord," she said. "You knew he needed a blonde to walk in right now. But for all his deceivin' ways, don't strike him dead," she said. "Park Place wouldn't be the same without him. Amen."

There wasn't an empty space in the post office parking lot. Rock drove down Main Street trying to find a parking space but everything was taken. There were two or three that he could possibly squeeze into if he tried, but he always ending up being embarrassed over his parallel parking skills, especially when so many people were in town. He knew he should have walked.

Wanda Burns was right in front of him and looking for a space too. She had left his office ahead of him after hand addressing all the Christmas cards. She had knocked them out faster than Reva could have printed out labels and put them on. She had saved his bacon.

Reva was right - if Liz had got wind of him slapping labels on the envelopes of the cards she had taken such care to personalize, she wouldn't have been happy. He watched Wanda pull her big SUV up to an empty parking space. She put her right turn signal on and looked as if she were assessing the space.

"Whoa Wanda, you can't do that," he said aloud even though she couldn't hear him. "I wouldn't even attempt to park there - it's too tight." He looked on in amazement as she pulled up almost even with the car in front, shifted into reverse, turned the steering wheel hard to the right and then straightened up. She shifted back into drive, pulled up and made a perfect parallel park that would have made a driving instructor envious. He sighed and shook his head. "How did she do that?"

He pulled up beside her and rolled down his window as she was opening the door to get out. "Good job," he said. "You made it look easy."

"Oh, it is easy," she said. "I learned how to do that when I got my driver's license back in 1965." She closed her car door. "I've got to run," she said. "Junie's holding a bike for me and I promised I would pick it up this morning. It's the last blue one he's got and little Jackson would scream bloody murder if Santa didn't bring him a blue one."

Rock waved her off. He fumed a little bit inside. He'd learned how to park too, but hadn't tried it in so long, he knew he was rusty. He sure couldn't practice here with everyone on Main Street watching him. He made a resolution to go over to Rock Hill sometime and practice his parallel parking on East Main where no one would know him.

Betty took a look at his Christmas cards as he plopped them on the counter. "You gonna have to separate them into zip codes," she said and plopped them back in his direction.

"For heaven's sake, Betty, they're members of our church and they all have the same zip code."

"No, they don't. Look, this one is to Ruthie Oliver up in Asheville, and this one is to Billy Henderson in Charlotte, and this one...."

Rock pulled them back away from her. "Oh," he said, looking at them carefully. "Liz sent them to all our inactive members too." He was proud of his wife, but he felt a little guilty that he had never sent a single Christmas card. He started sorting them by zip.

As if reading his mind and feeding on his guilt, Betty piped in. "Hmph! I've never seen you send Christmas cards except to your mother and sisters," she said. "And they're lucky if they get one."

Larry Braswell was waiting in line with his stack of cards. "Don't worry Rev. Rock. People don't expect it of us men. We're not thoughtful like that. The people on Jenny's list would fall over dead if they saw my handwriting on one of these Christmas cards."

"Thank you Larry," he said. "You're a good man."

"Any time. We men got to stick together. Next thing you know we'll be expected to wrap the gifts and tie pretty little bows."

"I'd be the one to fall over dead if I saw you tying a pretty little bow," said Betty. "By the way Larry, what are you getting me for Christmas"?

"Well, I guess a big old can of popcorn, like always."

"I'm getting sick and tired of popcorn. Do you know how many cans of popcorn I get every year? How about some homemade cookies instead?"

"Alright, I'll tell Jenny. As long as I don't have to bake 'em. You'd sure get sick and tired if I made 'em."

"Or a teapot. I've started collecting teapots, ya know!"

Rock looked down at the Note app on his phone where he kept his small Christmas gift list. He hit the backspace button on 'popcorn' beside Betty's name and replaced it with 'cookies or teapot'.

Gingerbread and Elvis Presley, in that order, assaulted his senses as he walked in the door. Cookies and Elvis - they show up everywhere I go, he thought. Yesterday it was *I'll be Home for Christmas* at the hospital and today it was *Silent Night*. Elvis sounded so much better today though, especially since there was an angelic female voice accompaniment in the kitchen. The sweet soprano was Liz, and he stood in the hallway listening, not wanting to break the spell. His heart was full as he watched her take the cookies out of the oven while singing his favorite Christmas hymn. This is what Christmases should be like, he thought. No puttering about, going from one large room to another. The strange thing was, he hadn't realized he had been lonely. A new dimension, like an additional layer of happiness had transformed him from mere existence to a rich and full life.

"Ouch!" The pan slammed against the inside of the oven door. It rattled, but much to Rock's relief, it didn't turn over. It perched there precariously until Rock ran over and grabbed the oven mitt and righted it. He took it off the oven door and put it on the stovetop.

Liz was running her hand under cold water. "Are you okay"? he asked.

"I think so. I used a flimsy little pot holder instead of the mitt." She looked at him and smiled. "I didn't know you had come in."

"I just got here. I'll get you some ice." He put a piece of ice from the refrigerator in a paper towel and handed it to her. "How did you manage to get off work early?"

"I don't know how I got so lucky," she said. "Our director called from Central Office and said all the guidance counselors that went to the conference in October have two and a half days comp time to use before December 31st. So here I am! I don't have to go back to work until after New Years!"

"I'm not complaining. Every man would be thrilled to come home to a wife baking cookies and crooning to Elvis." He lifted the cold paper towel up and looked at her fingers. "Good as new. They're not even red anymore." His eyes were pulled back to the cookies. "How did you know gingerbread was my favorite?"

She took the spatula and scooped a few on a saucer. "Because you've told me about four hundred times in the last few days." She smiled and held one up to his lips. He started to take a bite and she pulled it away.

"Not until I've had a kiss," she said.

"But kisses are so much better with gingerbread on our breath," he said. The cookies were chilled considerably when he finally got to take a bite.

CHAPTER 22

"Maura McCarthy, you don't know how much I've been craving something sweet today. I just told Walter this morning that now he's a diabetic, I won't be baking any Christmas cookies. He would die for one of these, but what he don't know, won't hurt 'im, will it?"

"Oh, Reva! I didn't know he was a diabetic. You better leave them here then - I don't want to be responsible for making him go into a diabetic coma! Here's another plate for Rock - I'll set them on the counter."

"I won't take them home. I'll keep them here at the office and share them with visitors. Of course, I'll have to hide the plate from Rev Rock because when he eats his all up, he'll be expecting to eat mine too. I do appreciate all the trouble you went to baking for us - and I know Rock will feel the same when he gets back. You know how that man likes to eat."

"They're still warm from the oven," Maura said to Reva just as she popped a gooey chocolate chip cookie in her mouth. "Well, you just found that out," she said laughing. "Here, let me pour you a cup of coffee - cream and sugar?"

"Neither one, I drink it black. Laud a'mercy, I'm not used to somebody waiting on me hand and foot, Maura. I can get it myself."

"You stay put. I've got it." She poured a cup from the Bunn coffee maker, and brought it, along with a paper plate and napkin to Reva's desk. She poured herself a cup and sat down.

"Delicious - your cookies put mine to shame, yes they do." She took another bite and finished it off, leaving a big smudge of chocolate on her chin. "The taste is....I can't quite figure it out." She picked up another cookie. Maura handed her a napkin and pointed to her own chin indicating that Reva needed to wipe the chocolate off hers. It came close to blending in with the warm chocolate of Reva's complexion. She dabbed at her chin with the napkin. "Did I get it?" she asked. Maura nodded. "What's different about your cookies - or is it a secret?"

Maura laughed. "I have no secrets," she said. "I took Martha Stewart's advice and sprinkled a little sea salt across the top of the cookies before I put them in the oven. It brings out the flavor of the chocolate. Oh, I almost forgot - I used dark chocolate chips instead of the milk chocolate and two tablespoons of almond butter."

"I knew there was something." Reva put the foil back on the platter and stood up. "I better put these away or I'll eat half of 'em just sittin' here. I'll empty them in a paper plate and wash your pretty platter so you can take it back with you." It was a Christmas platter and had a blue border dotted with large white snowflakes.

"No Reva, the platter's yours too. I pick up pretty plates at yard sales when I can find them for a dollar. I use them for taking food when there's a sickness or death in the family. I just put stickers on the bottom saying not to return the plate. It's such an aggravation for a family already suffering for one thing or another to have to return dishes."

"I would'a never thought of doing that. I might just pass it on by doing the same for somebody else the next time I bake." She went to the sink and washed her coffee cup. A small black tape player that her husband had given her was on the counter beside the refrigerator and Reva popped open the deck and chose a tape from the stack beside it. Let's get some Christmas music going. Do you like Elvis?"

"Ooh, Elvis!" Maura pretended to swoon as she had done during her teen years over her favorite singer. "Blue Christmas is on there, I hope?"

"As a matter of fact, it is." She put the cassette in the deck. "Walter gave me this cassette player and the cassette for Christmas back in the '80's. About the only time I get the thing out is at Christmas. You can't even buy cassettes anymore. When this one wears out, I'll be in trouble. I guess I'll just have to buy me a CD player or maybe one of those little thingamabobs that my grandson clips onto his belt and puts little buds in his ears."

The thought of Reva with earbuds made Maura smile while Elvis' voice filled the room.

After closing the tape deck, Reva turned back to Maura. "Have you been cookin' all morning?"

"No, just making some goodies to give to the neighbors. I will be cooking this afternoon though. Sonny Haywood is coming over for dinner tonight. You know he and our Sonny and Holly have gotten to be good friends."

"How in the world can you keep their names straight when they're in the same room together? I'll bet they both look up when you call their name."

"Well, it helps that our Sonny was using his given name while in California. He wants us to use it, but it sure is hard for me and Danny to get used to. His workplace and all his friends in California know him as Dan. Holly has picked it up easily, and Lord knows I've tried, but I've called him Sonny all his life and I'm having a tough time changing. It would be like if you were all of a sudden trying to call Walter another name - like George."

Reva laughed at the idea. "I've called him worse."

"I've really enjoyed getting to know Sonny Haywood, Reva. There's nothing fake or phony about him."

"Me too - I liked him from that first day I met him - or at least after I got to talkin' to him. He was right scary at first, but underneath all those tattoos is a heart of gold. How did he come to be friends with Sonny and Holly?"

"I think he feels a special connection with our family since Rock hunted him down as one of the Sonny's last year in his attempt to find Holly's family. It was like hunting a needle in a haystack, wasn't it? The only clue they had was the only word Holly spoke before she lost consciousness after her car accident. *Sonny*, and at first they thought she said *sunny*, like the weather forecast. Two long months that girl lay there in a coma - bless her heart."

"Seems like yesterday, doesn't it Maura? And then finding out Abby was your own granddaughter with your Sonny being her Daddy. Like they say, it's a small world."

Maura smiled. "And what a blessing that turned out to be, finding out I had a granddaughter I never knew about."

"And neither did Sonny," Reva said. "I just shudder to think what would have happened if that accident had happened anywhere but here in Park Place. Holly might have died from cancer and no one would have made the connection. You would'a never known you had a granddaughter."

"Yes, Reva, God was very much at work in that situation. I don't understand how anyone can doubt God's plan in our lives. And it helped that He had a determined preacher as His servant. I'll never be able to thank Rock enough for his persistence in finding Sonny and in getting the proper medical care for Holly."

Reva chuckled. "I still get to hootin' and hollerin' everytime I try to imagine Rock's face when Sonny Haywood walked into this very office with his grandpa's shotgun. He said it pretty near gave him a heart attack."

"Well, you were a sight to behold yourself, dear girl. Running through the parking lot with your shoes off, flagging down Jess Hamilton thinking poor Rock was about to meet his maker."

Rock walked in just as they had broken into a fit of laughter. "I have a feeling this discussion is about me," he said.

"It is, dear man, yes it is," Reva managed to get the words out, and then handed him his plate of cookies.

"Wow," he said, looking at the cookies. "Well, at least I can eat myself into oblivion while I'm the butt of your jokes." He walked into his office with nothing on his mind except chocolate chips. Elvis' slightly risque *Blue Christmas* was playing in the background. Elvis again, he thought.

"Hey ladies," he said. "Did you know that Elvis is alive and well in Park Place this year?"

They looked at each other and then at him and shook their heads. "Really, he is," he said. "I've heard him in my house, at the hospital, and now he's here. Mark my words,

Elvis is in the house." He lowered his voice about two octaves and started singing along with the music. It was so out of character for him that Reva and Maura covered their mouths with their hands and giggled like two school girls. He walked in his office still singing. "Who is this man?" Maura asked, and her question set them off laughing again.

The potatoes were peeled and the tea was steeping. While Maura was preparing the salad, the pork tenderloin was marinating in a bold berry vinaigrette in the refrigerator waiting to be cooked to tender perfection. The fresh apple pie was cooling on the counter and all that was left to do was to turn the burners on to cook the potatoes and green beans about an hour before dinner and put the angel rolls that were rising on the windowsill in the oven as soon as their guest arrived.

Maura took a cup of coffee and walked out onto the screened porch to wait for Abby's bus. The weather was nice - highs were forecast to be in the mid-60's over the next couple of days. Then, what they called a winter blast, was said to be coming through on Christmas day.

Abby was excited about Sonny's visit. While they were eating, she was trying to get his attention and called him Mr. Sonny.

"We're going to have to come up with something better than that," he said. "What if I started calling you Miss Abigail?"

Abby laughed. "I wouldn't like that. I like being called just plain Abby."

"Mr. Sonny sounds so grown up and sophisticated. Do I look like a Mr. Sonny to you?"

Abby giggled again. "Not really. Can I call you Uncle Sonny - like I call Aunt Laura's husband?" She loved Laura and Nicole, her daddy's sisters and their husbands. It was an instant family, where she'd had no family before.

Sonny looked up at Holly and Dan and they both nodded. "Uncle Sonny it is! I like that. I've never been an uncle before. Now what were you going to ask me?"

Abby answered. "I wanted to ask you if I could go coon huntin' with you sometime. I think Fluffy's going to make a good coon dog." Everyone at the table broke into laughter.

Maura watched as her granddaughter chatted animatedly with the adults and was amazed at how she had become a little Southerner in just a few short months. She was already beginning to acquire the Southern drawl just from being around her South Carolina family and her friends at school. Why, just a minute ago, she had pronounced dog as dawg. It made Maura smile. Danny had noticed it too. She looked up at him and their eyes locked. He smiled at her and winked - she could tell he was enjoying having a full house again just as much as she was. She took a good long look at her husband of forty-five years. It was an effort for him to put on a good show in front of the kids. His lungs had improved somewhat since the doctors had put him on a new drug last summer, but he still couldn't go very long at a time without his oxygen tank. She was just thankful for everyday she had with him. They had gone through some scary moments last year when pneumonia had filled his already damaged lungs, but he had recovered and for that she was grateful.

They had finished dinner and she got up from the table to get the dessert. Holly followed her into the kitchen with the dinner plates from the table. "What can I help you do, Maura?" she asked.

"I'll serve up the pie - would you mind asking everyone what they want to drink with their dessert? We have cold milk or hot coffee. Tell them it's decaf."

Over dessert, the conversation turned to work. Sonny had moved back in with his grandparents, Eva and Jack Haywood, who lived a few miles north of town. Since he had found salvation, he had felt his calling in the large non-denominational church in Sparta that had nurtured him through his newfound Christianity. He had witnessed to people in biker bars and on the streets, blending right in with his tattoos and piercings. The church had finally hired him on in a new position they created especially for him. His job was to go out in the mission field, but the mission field was to be the streets and bars - just as he had been doing, only this time in a paid position. He was able to quit his job at the livestock auction, but still worked part time in a bike shop during the morning hours.

Looking at the two Sonnys together, Maura thought what an unlikely friendship they shared. They were as different as night and day, but seemed to really enjoy each other's company. Their common bond was that they both loved the Lord - and motorcycles - in that order, she thought. Dan's mode of transportation in Los Angeles had been a bike and he'd had it shipped home when he moved back for good. Their bikes were both Honda Gold Wings and as Sonny got up from the table to say goodnight, they made plans to ride over the weekend.

"Now that Holly enjoys riding, you'll have to start looking for a bike for her," Sonny said.

"I don't think so. Not unless she really wants a bike of her own." He turned to look at Holly. She smiled and shook her head. "We like riding together," Dan said. "We were separated for much too long. It's too much fun having her behind me holding on to me for dear life."

Maura's heart sang as she watched her son take his wife's hand and pull her beside him in an embrace. It does a mama's heart good, she thought.

CHAPTER 23

W*hoever listens to me will live in safety and be at ease, without fear of harm.*

- Proverbs 1:33 NIV

Maria had grown restless. Kit had insisted that she stay in bed, and she did go back to sleep when Kit left, but woke up with her back hurting a short time later. She tried changing positions, but the longer she lay, the more it hurt. She finally got up and dressed in the freshly laundered clothing she had worn the day before. She had slept in one of BJ's long t-shirts and now folded it up and put it on the bed. She was worried. Except for her backpack, all of her things were still in the church basement. It was just a matter of time until someone found them and she wondered if they would arrest her for trespassing.

In the kitchen she found a note from Kit telling her to reheat some sausage biscuits in the microwave for breakfast. She had also put out two kinds of cereal and a bowl on the kitchen table with another note telling her there was plenty of milk in the refrigerator. She decided on the biscuits and after warming them, she took them, along with a glass of milk, into the large den. The room was warm and inviting. The gas logs were burning, so she eased herself down into the comfortable arm chair near the fireplace and munched on a biscuit.

The house seemed huge to Maria. The studio

apartment she and Ernesto had lived in was tiny and cramped and had only one bedroom. As she looked up at the high vaulted ceiling, she had a thought that their entire apartment would have fit into this one room. She finished eating and put her glass and saucer on the lamp table beside the chair. The warmth from the fire was making her sleepy and she found herself nodding off. She pulled a warm knitted throw blanket off the ottoman and cuddled into the chair. She was soon fast asleep.

Kit spotted Jess Hamilton when he walked in the door of the diner. She had asked him to come at 9:30 when the breakfast crowd had thinned and he was right on the button. "What'll you have, Jess? It's on the house."

"Just a cup of coffee for me, Kit. I've already had breakfast."

She brought two mugs and a carafe of coffee over to the corner booth where he had taken a seat. She poured a cup for each of them and sat down. "I'll get right down to business Jess. I know you've got things to do and I need to open the thrift shop at 10."

She looked at her old friend sitting across from her. She had known Jess all his life - had even done some babysitting for the Hamilton boys during summer break one year when she was a teen and Jess and his younger brother were about eight and ten. As the years passed, she and BJ became good friends with Jess and Rebecca. Rebecca and Kit had a lot in common - both were running businesses and both loved children. Kit had spent many hours volunteering at the Beverly Hills Children's Home where Rebecca was the director and she and Jess resided. Her volunteer work kept her busy after Lindsey's death and Kit credited Rebecca with helping her regain her sanity during those grief stricken years.

"Whatcha got on your mind?" Jess said, as he lifted the cup to his mouth. He gave her a look of concern. She had sounded both worried and distracted when she called him at the office.

She handed him Maria's immigration papers. "I have this young woman living in my house right now," she said. "She's been working here at the restaurant for the past few weeks and I've just now found out that she's very much pregnant and homeless. Can you take a look at these papers and make sure she's legally here in the states?"

Jess looked them over. "Can you tell if she's the girl in this photo?" he asked.

"Yes, there's no doubt."

"The papers look legit. There's no signs of erasures, white-out, or cut and paste. The only problem I see is that her residence shows she lives in Raleigh. She's crossed the state line, but that's a pretty easy fix. She should have reported it to immigration, but she has a full month to report a change of address. It says here that she's married. Where's her husband?"

Kit's face took on a menacing look. "That's where we have a problem," she said. "When she showed up at our restaurant the first time, it was apparent she had been beaten. Her face was black and blue and one eye stayed puffy for days. She's just now confiding in us - I don't know how the poor girl is alive - and it's a miracle that the baby is. I'd like to kick his tail from here to China!"

"Well, she can certainly have the guy arrested for

assault and battery. That's also a good excuse for not reporting her move - it'll go in her favor." He studied the paperwork. "He's a US citizen. Apparently one of his parents is American. Hmm...Ernesto Ramirez - I'll see what I can find out. I may need to talk to her."

Kit fidgeted in her seat. "I can't let you do that right now."

"Why not?"

"She's scared to death of law officers. Apparently Ernesto told her that if she filed a complaint, she would be arrested and spend months in jail. She's not concerned about getting deported. I think she would love to go back to her parents in Honduras, but she's terrified of being in jail. So far I haven't been able to convince her that it won't happen. And she's gonna have that baby any day. She doesn't need any more stress right now."

"Okay Kit. First I'll check this Ernesto creep out. But if she's been here since the first of December, she's going to have to file a change of residency soon, and if she wants to press charges on this guy, I'll have to talk to her."

"Fair enough," she said. "Just please wait until after she has the baby."

BJ walked out of the kitchen. "You look beat," Jess said, as he looked at his friend.

"You don't know the half of it. Kit has stolen my little kitchen helper away from me." He and Kit exchanged a smile. "You don't know anyone who needs a job, do you?"

"They would have the best boss in the world to work for," Kit teased. "He only turns into a grumpy bear when he doesn't have any help."

"Hmm - I may just know someone," Jess said. "She

worked at the ice cream shop on Main Street last summer, so she's got a little bit of experience. Her name is Cheyenne. She's one of the two older girls at the children's home and since she just turned eighteen, she'll be aging out. She's been with us since she was thirteen. It makes us sick when they have to do that. It's a rule, but it sure feels like we're throwing her out to fend for herself. She did an early graduation from high school this week, but she can stay with us until the end of the school year in May. She's getting some financial aid to go to the community college next fall, but for now, she'll need a job so she can ready herself to be on her own."

"I'm willing to give her a try," said Kit. "I know you wouldn't recommend her unless you thought she could do the job."

"She'll be thrilled," said Jess. "I'm sure she'll like the job - I know you're good to your employees."

"Yes, so good in fact, this last one somehow ended up living in our house." He nodded his head toward Kit. "It's her fault."

"Oh yeah, it's always my fault," Kit said. "And with all the bravado and bluff this big guy tries to portray, his heart is made of marshmallows. And hey, we wouldn't be mad if Cheyenne could start tomorrow. She could earn a little Christmas money."

"Maria, I have your lunch." Kit put her keys on the counter as she set the styrofoam box down too. "Maria?" She walked to the bedroom that Maria was using but she wasn't there. "Maria. Honey, where are you?"

She walked through the house and into the den.

Maria was sound asleep on the chair near the hearth. A blue and white knitted throw was spread across her shoulders. It was the throw that BJ's mother had helped Lindsey make when she had expressed an interest in knitting during her sophomore year of high school. She wondered how long she had been asleep. She saw an empty glass and a saucer on the table so she knew she hadn't eaten much for breakfast. "She lifted the throw back and gently tried to awaken her. "Maria, I brought your lunch. You should eat now."

Maria was startled for a moment but smiled when she saw it was Kit. "I'm sorry that I slept so long she said. Is it lunch time already?"

"You don't have to apologize. The doctor wants you to rest. How are you feeling?"

"My back has been hurting, but I'm better now. Right here," she said, putting her right hand on her lower back.

"It could be false labor pains," Kit said. "But call me if it gets worse. She wrote down her cell number and the number for the thrift store. "Promise me you'll call if it starts hurting bad."

"I will," she said. She stretched and walked into the kitchen behind Kit. She filled a glass of water from the sink and opened the lunch box. Roast beef, mashed potatoes with gravy, lima beans and a slice of cornbread filled the container in front of her. She looked at Kit and smiled. "Are you eating with me? There's enough here for both of us."

"No, I've already eaten - I need to get back and unlock the store. There are a lot of people in and out today." She was glad to see Maria looking so refreshed after her nap. Today, for the first time since she'd met her, there were no dark circles under her eyes and her complexion was glowing.

"Oh, by the way, Carmen from the Dollar Store came by today asking about you. I didn't realize you were friends. I told her you were staying with me and she looked relieved - said she may come by to see you." Maria looked pleased. "I've got to get back to work! I'm closing early so I can go to the mall in Sparta and pick up some decent clothes for you to wear. You'll need some gowns too. I'll be home by 5:30."

"Kit?" Maria had called out to her as she headed toward the door. She turned back to her.

"Yes, do you need something before I go?"

"No, I have all I need. Please let me go back to work tomorrow. I want to pay you for the things you've been buying me."

"Pshaw child! Your smiling face is payment enough for us. We just want you to deliver a healthy baby, and from that glow on your face, I don't think it's going to be long."

"Kit?" She paused for a moment. "I'm scared."

Kit walked back and put her arms around this young woman who should be enjoying the carefree days of high school, not delivering a baby.

"Don't you worry 'bout a thing, child! Kit's going to be right here with you all the way."

Kit turned away and walked out before Maria could see the tears streaming down her face. When she stepped out on the porch, she offered up a silent prayer. "God, watch over her and be with her and the baby she's carrying during the days ahead. And God...thank you for bringing her into our lives." What the next few weeks would hold, Kit did not know, but she knew one thing - it would be hard letting go of this child she had grown to love. "And God," she prayed. "I know it's selfish to ask, but if it is your will, please find a way to let her stay with us."

Maria had come close to telling her what she was afraid of, but stopped short. Maybe she was imagining it. Surely Ernesto couldn't have found her in Park Place.

CHAPTER 24

"This is nice. It's not everyday we get to have lunch together." Liz finished off the last bite of pecan pie and sat back at the table. "Whew, if I keep eating like this I'll be big as a house when the baby gets here."

"Are you announcing it to the world now?" Rock teased. They were sitting in BJ's diner. The busiest time was over, but there were still a few booths and tables filled.

"Oops, I didn't mean to say it so loud. It won't be long before we'll be spilling the beans though. I can't wait to see the reaction of our church members. You'll have to announce it during one of the joy sharing times."

"Good idea," he said. "After we've heard all the joys of the congregation, I'll invite you up and we can watch all the jaws drop."

"I think I would rather watch from the pews, thank you. I don't feel comfortable in the spotlight."

"Would you care for more tea?" Rock and Liz had talked to Cheyenne when she first came to take their order. They both knew her - Rock by way of the Children's home and Liz had guided her in her decision to graduate early since she had all the credits she needed to receive her high school diploma.

"No thank you," Liz said. "You've done a great job waiting our table."

"Thank you, Mrs. Clark. I was lucky to get a part-time job so soon. I think I'm going to like it - it's busy but the owners are super nice."

Liz smiled at her enthusiasm. Cheyenne always had a

good attitude and she had lots of friends. She was also smart and would do well in college. "You couldn't find better people to work for," she told her. "Do you have our tab ready?" Cheyenne tore it off the pad and gave it to Rock.

"It's been nice seeing y'all again," she said. "I've got to get busy with this tea pitcher." She hurried away to the next table.

Liz picked up her purse and jacket. "Are we ready to go?" she asked Rock.

"Any time," he answered. "What do you want to do now? I think Reva can handle things at the office this afternoon."

"Really? Let's go shopping on Main Street then. I haven't had a chance to do any Christmas shopping yet other than the few things I bought online for Gillian, Chase and Rachel. I still have to shop for your sisters and our parents."

"What about Ron's mom?" Rock asked gently. He knew that Liz hadn't seen Ron's family since the summer before when she had attended his father's funeral in Atlanta. "I know you stayed active in their lives long after Ron's death, and I don't want to be the reason for you to stop. Your closeness to his family is natural after all the years you two were married and I understand completely."

She reached for his hand as they walked to the cash register. "I've taken care of that," she said. "I sent her a nice card telling her that we had started our new life together as husband and wife, but if she ever needed anything to feel free to call. I have new in-laws now that I need to spend time with."

He reached over and gave her a quick kiss at just the same moment BJ walked to the register from the kitchen. "Nothin' better than a little kiss to start the afternoon, huh Rev Rock?" Rock handed him a $20 bill and BJ was making change.

"Hmm, I don't know, let me check." Rock said. He reached over and kissed Liz full on the lips and lingered a while. "Just what I thought," he said. "The only thing better than a little kiss is a big one." BJ stood there speechless - this was certainly out of character for their reserved preacher. Rock reached over and took the change out of BJ's hand. "Let's get out of here Liz, before we make the big guy blush." Liz laughed. She was loving this new side of her husband.

Liz looped her hand through Rock's arm as they walked down Main Street. She shivered. "Are you cold," he asked. "I can go home and get you a heavier jacket while you shop," he offered.

"No, it's just the excitement of being here on Main Street shopping with you," she said. "I love the hustle and bustle of Christmas. I can't believe how many people are out today."

"It's because all you school employees are off and are just now getting your shopping done," he said.

Liz wanted to look in every shop window. Main Street was just so quaint. This should be on a Christmas card, she thought.

"Has the Park Place Woman's Club picked winners yet for the windows?" he asked.

"They should have, but I haven't heard. The Beautification Committee was in charge. Oh, look! I see a

ribbon in Junie and Kathleen's window." They stopped
and looked together. A white ribbon was tied to the
handle of the Radio Flyer Wagon and on it was printed
Honorable Mention.

"Junie is gonna be fit to be tied," Rock said. "I can
just hear him now saying 'if I can't win a blue ribbon, I
don't want no ribbon at all'."

"Oh, I'm sure he'll be proud of his ribbon. Everybody
can't win first place."

Junie saw them walking by and ran out the front door
to speak to them. "Nice ribbon," Rock said.

"Dad blame-it. Look at this window - it's got all those
pretty little horses and an old timey wagon. Even a Red
Ryder BB gun, for heaven's sake. We should'a done better
in the prize department. If I can't win a blue ribbon, I
don't want no ribbon at all," he said.

"I think you did pretty well, myself," said Rock. "You
had some stiff competition."

"Oh Junie, think positive! Only four of the window
displays in town got a ribbon - and yours was one of them.
Twelve windows didn't get a ribbon at all. And look at it!
No one else has 'Honorable' on theirs. It's an honor to
have an honorable ribbon."

As Liz bragged about his ribbon, Rock saw Junie
visibly perk up. She could easily win a first place ribbon if
they had a category for making people happy - himself
included.

"Well, I hadn't thought about it thataway," Junie said.
Kathleen was wheeling another bike in the window to
keep the pink one company since Wanda Burns had
bought the blue one. Junie knocked on the glass to get
her attention. "Look Kathleen! Ours is the only ribbon

that says honorable on it. Ain't that somethin'?"

Junie was speaking so loud, Rock knew Kathleen could easily hear him through the window, and he had no doubt that the people shopping inside Carter's Drug Store at the end of the next block could hear every word he said.

"That's good" mouthed Kathleen and winked at Liz and did a thumbs up sign with her free hand.

Liz hadn't had an opportunity to walk down Main Street during the Christmas season yet. She stopped in front of all the stores, oohing and aahing over their displays. May was behind the counter at the flower shop and she waved as they passed by. A steady stream of customers were walking out her door with shopping bags and flowers.

"Uh oh." Rock stopped in his tracks.

"What's wrong?"

"There's a red ribbon in her window. She's won 1st place three years running and that's a second place ribbon."

"Oh, she'll be fine," Liz said. "Knowing May, she was probably feeling uncomfortable winning it all the time. I'm sure she'll be happy that someone else won it. It's good to spread the joy."

"Not everyone is as generous and willing to spread the joy as you are, Liz. That's one of the many things I love about you."

"Well, May certainly is. She spreads her joy all over town with her flowers. Let's stop after we finish shopping and get one of those pink poinsettias," she said. Rock immediately felt guilty. He hadn't sent any flowers to her since the red poinsettia the weekend after Thanksgiving. Maybe he should by two to make up for his lack of attention in the flower department.

"Let's get two."

"We don't have room for two in that small little house," she said. "But why don't we go in and order two nice poinsettias to be wired to our mothers since we won't be seeing them until after Christmas."

"Good idea, but the shop is full of customers right now. Maybe it'll be cleared out some when we walk back this way." He would order a dozen pale pink roses to be delivered on Christmas Eve. That should do the trick. He had picked up a pamphlet in May's shop a while back telling the significance of colors. *Pale pink roses connote grace and gentleness along with love, admiration and happiness,* it had read. He was feeling a little smug. A man should know what color roses to send, he thought. He couldn't wait - she would be impressed. He started whistling one of the Christmas carols from Reva's tape deck. "Remind me to get Reva some new Christmas music," he said to Liz. "I'm sick of Elvis."

"We'll look in Hathaways on our way back to the flower shop. They'll have a good selection." A Girl Scout troop was selling baked goods and hot chocolate outside Hathaway's Music Store where a soft mix of Christmas music was coming from their sound system. She looked up at Rock. "Main Street has never looked so good. All we need is a good snow." Rock took in their surroundings and decided the reason it looked so good was because she was there in the middle of it.

"Want some hot chocolate?" Rock asked.

"Do you have to ask?" Liz stopped in front of the

stand and as Rock talked to the girl scouts, she noticed a new seasonal toy store had set up shop in the empty Belk Department Store building.

"Who's in here now?" she asked Rock as he offered her the steaming cup. They sat on a park bench and she pointed to the toy store.

"If we're to believe Junie, they're 'fly-by-nighters'." He chuckled as he recounted Junie's description of the store owners.

"Here today and gone tomorrow," Junie had complained at their Monday morning meeting. "They won't be around to warranty nothin'. You just wait and see - on Christmas day they'll pull out faster than that Wily Coyote feller chasing that tricky roadrunner. I'll guarantee it."

Liz laughed. "Poor Junie. He's afraid he'll lose some business, I suppose."

"I don't think he has much to worry about," said Rock. "Junie's customers are loyal." They got up from the bench and started walking again.

"Ah, here it is!" Liz pointed to the window at Banty Hen Antiques. A large blue ribbon with a certificate that announced *Best Display* was tied to the Flexible Flyer sled leaning against the window. "Oh, they won the blue ribbon! Valerie is a good friend, Rock. We were in the same circle at church. I heard she and Sam had opened this shop. Have you met them?"

"I know Sam pretty well," he said, "and I've met Valerie through him. They're nice people. I saw their display a while back. I knew it would give May's window some competition. It's brilliant though. They deserve to win it."

"It's the nostalgia that gives it a magic touch," Liz said. "It reminds me of Nana Ruth and all the fun things she had in her attic." She paused when she saw the train going around the track circling the Christmas tree. "Oh Rock! That train - it's just like the one Grandpa had under their tree every year!"

Rock watched as her eyes followed the train around the tree, and the look of pure joy on her face was touching. He reached down with his thumb and wiped away a few tears that had settled under her eyes, caressing her cheek as he did. She hugged him. "Sweet memories," she said.

Hmm, he thought. It was like someone ringing a bell right in his ear. He'd have to talk to Sam in private. He had been racking his brain to find a gift - something to make their first Christmas together special. During her Thanksgiving visit, his mother had brought with her an antique pearl necklace that had belonged to her mother. She gave it to him to give to Liz for Christmas. Liz would love it, but it wasn't a personal gift from him.

"Let's go see what's inside," she said.

"Yes, let's do," and he guided her in the door all the while keeping his eye on the train set. "Maybe we can find a gift for Betty in here. She's started collecting teapots."

"Well, you're in luck. There are usually teapots galore in antique stores. Liz browsed through the store finding treasures along the way. "Ask Valerie to start me a stash," she said, thrusting several items at him. "I think I can do all my shopping in here."

"Uh oh," he said. "You've got that glazed look of a rabid shopper - do I dare turn you loose in here?"

"Can you find a place to put all this?" he asked Valerie as he emptied his arms on the counter. "I don't think that's the end of it either."

"Nope. I've been shopping with Liz. She's on a roll," Valerie teased.

After several trips back and forth to the counter, he finally cornered Sam who had been busy helping a customer pick out a cameo from the locked jewelry counter. He pulled him aside where Liz couldn't hear.

"Sam, is the train in the window for sale?" He looked hopefully at his friend.

Sam paused. "Who is it for?" he asked.

"I want to get it for Liz. She was so touched by it, she was teary eyed - it reminds her of the one her grandfather had under his tree each year."

"I've had several people want it, but I didn't want to sell it to just anyone," Sam said. "It has a lot of sentimental value to me, but Valerie and I have decided to start letting go of our collections that are just sitting around gathering dust. That train hasn't been out of our attic since the boys left home. I've asked both of them if they want it, but they're not like me and Valerie. They're minimalists at best." He paused and gave out a collective sigh. "I would love to see someone who would value it and use it," he said. "I'll sell it to you."

"How much?" He was almost afraid to ask - he knew the old Lionel train sets were valuable.

"For you my friend, $100. I've been offered much more."

"Let's do it!" Rock said, much louder than he intended.

"If you're wanting to keep it a secret, you'd best lower

your voice," Sam whispered.

"I'll pay you now, and come get it on Christmas Eve if that's okay."

"How about I just deliver it. That way she won't be wondering where you're going on Christmas Eve."

Rock shook his hand. "You've made my day," he said.

"I think someone's trying to get your attention." Sam pointed to where Liz was trying to wave him over.

"What do you think, Rock"? she said when he walked up beside her. "Which of these teapots would Betty like?" The cupboard beside her held a variety of teapots in all shapes and sizes.

"I like this one," he said, picking up one that had purple and yellow pansies all over it. "She likes purple."

"I like it too! You've got good taste, I might add." She turned it over. "Fine bone china. She'll love it." She handed it to him. "One more thing," she said. "Follow me."

They walked together across the aisle. She picked up a porcelain music box and when she wound it up, the music was just as beautiful as the figural piece itself. The tune was *Ava Maria*, and the pure, sweet notes were loud and clear and wafted through the room. "Let's get this for the children's home. See, it's Mary and the Christ child. And the music! It's perfect, don't you think?"

"Perfect," he said. He stood back and watched as Liz wound it up again and thought how thoughtful and kind she was. She had taught him more about love and generosity in the few months they had been married than he had learned on his own in a lifetime.

The counter of The Banty Hen Antique store was

loaded with their packages. Liz was looking through the glass on the counter at the jewelry below. "We have some nice estate jewelry," Valerie said. "If you see anything you like, I'll pull it out for you."

"I love that ring - and the charm bracelet. Can I see both of them?" She tried the ring and it was a perfect fit, but she took it back off. "Too much bling," she said. "It's just not my personality, and the charm bracelet is too heavy. Oh well, I'll look again sometime."

Just then she spotted a necklace with a cross pendant. "Oh Valerie," she said. "Where did you get that? It's exquisite!"

Valerie pulled the necklace out from under the counter. Her eyes lit up as she held it up to show Liz. "It is beautiful, isn't it?" She fingered it and handed it to Liz. It's a mid-nineteenth century European cross. It's more than likely Italian and made of 24 karat sheet gold, wire, and seed pearls. It's so delicate, it's a wonder how it ever survived all these years."

It was apparent that Liz was taken with it. Rock stood behind her and got Valerie's attention. "I'll take it," he mouthed. She winked.

Liz looked up at Valerie. "I'm afraid to ask you how much it is. Is it outrageous?"

"Well, it's a little outrageous," she said, and laughed. "But it's not available. I'm holding it for someone."

Liz sighed. "Well, it's just not meant to be, I guess. But if you ever see a similar one, let me have the first chance to purchase it."

Rock walked home and drove back to the store with his truck. He loaded the packages in the small back seat. "Where are we going to put them"? he asked, as they pulled into the driveway.

"Let's unload them in the parsonage," she said. "We'll put them upstairs in one of the bedrooms and I'll bring my wrapping paper over. It'll be much easier since we can spread everything out."

Rock backed up, then pulled into the parsonage garage. They carried the packages through the entrance that led to the utility room.

"We went a little overboard, didn't we"? They were making their second trip upstairs with the bags.

"Maybe," he said, "but it was our first Christmas shopping together."

"And you had fun...come on admit it," she teased.

He laughed. "I never thought I'd see the day when I'd have fun shopping, but yes, I did, and it was because I was with you."

They walked back down the stairs hand in hand.

"I can't believe this kitchen. It's only been a week since we were over here and it was a mess. Look at it!" She waved her arm to encompass the whole kitchen. "It seems to have transformed overnight."

"Just like you planned it," he said. "Jay told me yesterday the only thing holding them up now is the range we ordered. Since it was an odd size, it's not stocked locally and it could be at least two weeks before it comes in. But now they'll start on the bedroom and bath. That won't take nearly as long as the kitchen."

"We could move in right after the new year if you want," she said, hopefully. "We could use one of the bedrooms upstairs until they finish yours."

"Ours," he said. "Don't forget it's your bedroom too. But let's don't rush to move in - let's wait until they're finished."

She was looking at him, trying to read his expression. He knew she didn't understand his reluctance.

"You'd still rather live in the cottage, wouldn't you?"

He sensed her disappointment. "I would," he said, "but I'm beginning to see that the coziness of it comes with a price. It's just not going to be big enough for a family of three." He pointed upstairs. "Especially if we keep going on shopping trips."

She laughed. "This will all be going back out at Christmas," she said, "but we'll be shopping for the baby soon, and baby stuff takes up a lot of room."

"I was lonely in this big old house," he said. "But somehow it doesn't seem so cold and impersonal anymore, now that you'll be in it. I like what you've done."

"Jay's done a good job! I love it already. I'm ready for a change of scenery!"

"Once it's ready, we'll move right in," he said. "I promise I won't hold things up any longer."

They left the truck parked in the garage and walked back to the cottage.

CHAPTER 25

"*E*very good thing given and every perfect gift is from above, coming down from the Father of lights, with whom there is no variation or shifting shadow.*"

- James 1:17 NASB

Reva looked up when he walked in the office. "Where's your truck?"

"I left it in the garage of the parsonage last night. We unloaded our Christmas presents in the house."

"Good... I didn't see it parked here or at the cottage and was hoping no one had stolen it in the middle of the night."

"No one would steal that old truck," he said. "They go for the newer cars."

"I don't know. There was a white Honda with North Carolina license plates yesterday checking it out pretty good."

"Where?"

"Out in the parking lot. You and Liz had gone shopping. I have a good view of the parking lot here, you know."

"How well I remember," he snickered, recalling last year when he had watched Sonny Haywood walk across the parking lot carrying a gun on his shoulders. He had rushed to lock the door, but he was too late - Sonny got there before him and rushed on in.

"I just happened to be looking out the window and this car comes creeping into the parking lot like they were up to no good. They parked for a few minutes just checking your truck out. Then they saw me through the window checking them out and they backed out of there like a bat out of Cuba."

"Cuba?"

"Well I can't very well say a bat out of hello while I'm on church property, can I? But that's beside the point. Somebody was trying to steal your truck, I tell you."

"They were probably just lost. You said *they* - was there more than one person?"

"I could see two people in the front seat but I only got a good look at the passenger. The rear glass was tinted but I don't think there was anyone in the back seat. The passenger side window was down. He wasn't from around here."

Rock laughed. Most Southerners used that expression to describe the different dialect of transplanted Northerners - he'd even used it himself a time or two, and it usually came out "*you ain't from around here, are you*"?

"How could you tell they were Northerners, Reva? Could you hear their dialect all the way from the parking lot," he teased.

She gave him an annoyed look. "Of course not! I could see one of 'em well enough to know they weren't Yankees. Anyway, if I could have heard 'em talking, they would'a been speaking Spanish."

Rock shook his head and walked in his office. "I'll be working on my sermon if you need me. Since the truck's locked in the garage, they may try to steal your car."

She ran to the window and pulled the curtains all the way back. "Not on my watch, they won't."

He chuckled as he closed the door. The office would

be so boring without Reva.

Maria and Kit were setting the table when BJ opened the kitchen door. "Ho, ho, ho," he said while dragging in a large Fraser fir tree. He had found a tree stand in the garage and had already attached it to the bottom of the tree.

Kit's eyes filled with tears, and Maria clapped her hands and gave a squeal of delight. "A tree!" she said. "I've never had a Christmas tree." It had been ten years since Kit and BJ had put up a tree. She had mixed emotions when she first saw it, but quickly dispensed with them when she saw the joy it brought to Maria. "Well, I can see what we'll be doing after supper," she said. "Do you know where the decorations are?" she asked her husband.

BJ walked over and cupped her chin in his large hand. She met his gaze and he smiled. "In the left hand corner of the attic," he said, "where they've been for far too long."

Kit and BJ lay in their bed recounting the events of the day. "We've been ten years without a Christmas, Kit," he said as he pulled her closer into the fold of his arm. "I hope it hasn't made you too sad."

"Just the opposite," she said as she snuggled closer. "It's brought some much needed joy back into our house. We've managed to get through each Christmas, which I'm not sure we could have done without each other to lean on, but seeing the childlike wonder on Maria's face unwrapping the ornaments and placing them so carefully on the tree made me see Christmas through the eyes of a child again. Did you see her eyes when you plugged it in and all the lights came on?" BJ nodded and smiled just thinking about it.

"BJ?" she asked as she turned over to face him. "I'm worried. What will happen to her - and to us, for that matter, when she leaves us? It's only a matter of time, you know."

"There's no use worrying about it right now, Kit. We'll take it one day at a time and do everything in our power to help her. Let's pray about it." He used his free arm to reach over and turn the bedside lamp off, then held her close. "God in heaven," he prayed, "we can't begin to know your plans for Maria, but protect this young woman child and her baby yet to come - especially from the baby's father who doesn't deserve to be a father at all. Her richest blessing will be You, Lord - her Heavenly Father. Kit and I are your servants - use us as you will. It is in the name of your Son, from the manger to the cross, Jesus Christ that we pray. Amen."

Kit held him tight. She loved this man she had promised in front of God to cherish and obey, in sickness and in health, 'til death they would part.

As Maria was washing her face and brushing her teeth in the bathroom at the end of the hallway, she said a prayer of gratitude that God had brought her to this place. She was no longer cold, hungry and uncomfortable on the hard floor in the basement of the church. God had brought her into the path of angels and they had taken her into their home.

She thought again of the tree and how pretty it was

with all the lights and ornaments. The three of them had lingered in front of the fireplace taking it all in. Kit had told her about Lindsey and how Christmas was her favorite time of the year. She pointed out some of the handmade ornaments Lindsey had made over the years and wondered aloud why they had locked them away for so long. They sat in silence for a while, lost in their own thoughts.

Kit had pulled out stockings from one of the boxes. One of them had Lindsey's name embroidered across the top. She set it gingerly aside and found one without a name on it. "This one can be yours, Maria," she had said. Maria looked at it curiously, then tried to put it on her right foot, wondering where the match to it was. Kit and BJ had doubled over laughing and then told her that the stocking was for little gifts left by Santa. Maria laughed now as she thought about it. She had then told them of the custom in her family of putting out earthenware bowls for Santa to fill with fruit and candy. She and her brothers had fought over who would get the biggest, but no matter what size bowl they had, Santa always left equal amounts for each of them. For the first time since she'd left Honduras, she felt loved. She knew now that Ernesto could only love himself.

She pulled the spread and top sheet back. Kit had put a mattress protector under the bottom sheet and it crinkled at her touch, but she marvelled at how soft the bed felt as she got in and pulled the sheet and spread up under her chin. She tried lying on her back for a while and then turned on to her side. The dull ache in her back was still there but she had no trouble falling asleep. She dreamed of good things - her little brother's laughter, the tinkling of wind chimes and fairy lights on Christmas trees.

Maria awoke with a sharp pain in her side and turned on the light. It was just past midnight. Her sleep had been deep, but the dull ache had grown into painful cramping. She lay back on the pillow thinking if she ignored the cramps maybe they would go away. She finally drifted off into a light sleep but awoke suddenly again, this time feeling a strange sensation. A gush of warm water had wet her pajamas and sheets. She jumped up quickly and pulled the sheets off the bed. The doctor and Kit had told her that this could happen. Trying hard not to panic, she quickly changed clothes and put on a pad. She took the wet pants and sheets to the laundry room and after starting the load of clothes, she sat down on one of the kitchen chairs. Be calm, Maria, she told herself. The next pain that hit bent her double and she cried out. When it subsided, she walked to BJ and Kit's bedroom door and knocked.

"What is it, Honey?" She could hear Kit scrambling out of bed. She came to the door and opened it, and after taking one look at Maria, she turned around and shouted for BJ to get up and get dressed.

"My water broke," Maria said, then doubled over with pain again.

Kit put her arm around her shoulder. "Take a deep breath, Maria," and then yelled back into the bedroom, "Get a move on BJ. We're fixin' to have a baby!"

They met no resistance to being admitted when they got to the hospital. Kit went in first, leaving BJ and Maria parked outside the emergency room door. She started giving orders immediately. "We need a wheelchair and we need someone to call Dr. Alexander. Tell him Maria's water broke and her labor pains are three minutes apart."

The waiting room was empty so it was less than a minute before an intern came wheeling through the double doors with a gurney. Kit was in a take charge mode and everyone was listening. She pointed outside, "In the car, right outside the door," then her sense of humor kicked in. "It's the woman in the back seat. Lawd a'mercy, don't get the man in the driver's seat even though he may look like he's pregnant. I'd never hear the end of it." The intern smiled and pushed the gurney outside.

The receptionist put down the phone. "You're in luck. Dr. Alexander is here. He's already had one delivery tonight and hasn't left yet."

Maria looked so small on the big gurney as they wheeled her in. She saw Kit and begged, "Please go with me. Don't leave me alone."

"You can bet your bottom dollar I'll be with you - holding your hand every step of the way." She looked relieved, but then another contraction hit and she moaned with pain.

Dr. Alexander was already in the labor room on the third floor when they got there. He washed his hands and put on sterile gloves. The intern was still in the room and when Dr. Alexander finished the exam, he turned to him. "Get her in the delivery room, STAT. The baby's already crowning - she's in a hurry to meet her Mama."

Rock got off the elevator on the third floor of the hospital. As he rounded the corner, the baby viewing area was straight ahead. He peeked in the window and it was easy to spot Maria's baby. There were five babies lined up in a row in small baby beds. He noticed that all the beds were new and looked a little bit like grocery carts with clear plastic cradles sitting on top. There was just one baby with a pink cap amongst the other four in blue. A young woman was standing at the window with her nose almost up to the glass. She turned when she heard Rock come up behind her, and motioned him over.

"I'm sorry - I was blocking the view of the window. Aren't they adorable?" she said. "Which one are you here to see? Is one of them yours?"

Rock laughed. "Heavens no," he said. It was a natural reaction from someone who had thought his chances of being a father were over, but then he realized that next summer, he would be standing at this same spot looking in on his own baby. It was mind boggling. "I'm here to see the little girl. Her mother is a friend of mine."

"Oh, me too!" she said and held out her hand. "I'm Carmen - I work at the Dollar Store near BJ's Diner. Maria and I have recently become friends. I was excited when Kit called me this morning. I thought I'd stop by before work. Isn't she adorable?" They chatted a while, pointing out different features of the babies. "I've already been in to see Maria. She's going to be a great little mother." She looked at her watch. "Oops, gotta get to work. It was nice meeting you."

Carrie Miller was wheeling another baby down the corridor in their direction. She waved at Rock and stopped to talk to him before she took the baby back in the nursery. "Good morning, Rev Rock."

"Good morning, Carrie." He waited until she pulled up beside him and looked inside the cradle. "What have you got here?"

"Well, it's not a puppy," she said laughing. The baby was sound asleep and was swathed in a blanket looking much like a cocoon. His cheeks were chubby and rose colored and his eyes were wide open.

"This little fella' is on his way out this morning. After he has a final weigh-in, he'll be heading home with his parents." She followed his eyes as he glanced back through the window in front of them. She looked too.

"We've had a run on baby boys as you can see, so we were excited to see this little girl arrive last night. Which one are you here to see?"

"I'm here to see Maria, the little girl's mother. She lives with one of our church members, Kit Jones. You know Kit, don't you? She and BJ run the diner."

"Oh yes - I know Kit and BJ. Their daughter Lindsey and I were friends in high school. Kit's with Maria right now - been here all night from what I hear. I've only been on my shift for an hour, but I heard from the night shift that Maria was a little trooper from start to finish. Of course, it helped that her labor didn't last long."

"That's what Kit told me when she called this morning. She said the baby was delivered no more than thirty minutes after they arrived."

"That's amazing for her first time," she said. She started rolling the baby cart on down the hall. "It's time for me to wheel her baby down to the room - you want to come with me?" Rock nodded. "I'll just hand this little guy over to Darlene to weigh and I'll be right back."

Carrie walked ahead of Rock into Maria's room. All eyes were on the baby so Rock stayed in the background watching as the women in the room oohed and aahed over the pink clad infant. This is what Liz and I will be doing in less than six months, he thought. He had been in rooms with mothers and newborns in the past, but knowing that they would soon be going through the same thing made it so much more personal and he got emotional just watching as the nurse lay the baby on Maria's chest.

"Maria, you have a visitor," she said. Kit turned towards the door.

"Rev Rock, it's good to see you." She jumped up and led Rock over to the bed. "Look what we have here. Five pounds, ten ounces soaking wet," she said. "And they're both doing so well, we can go home late this afternoon just as soon as Dr. Alexander comes in and discharges us."

"You're putting 'us' in the equation. Did they admit you too," he teased.

"Might as well have - I've camped out here all night."

Maria sat up in the bed, still holding the baby. She touched her little fingers and toes with wonder. Kit sat back down beside her, then looked back at Rock. "Just look at that," she said, "she's perfect - from the hair on her head to the bottom of her toes. And look, Rock. It's amazing that she has blue eyes. Maria's are so dark."

Rock smiled and quoted his favorite Bible verse, "Every good thing given and every perfect gift is from above, coming down from the Father of lights, with whom there is no variation or shifting shadow."

Maria looked up. "That's from the first chapter of

James, isn't it?"

Rock was surprised. "It is, Maria. The seventeenth verse. Does that verse have special meaning for you?"

Maria was quiet for a moment. "Ernesto's mother is a missionary in Honduras. She tutored me in English and the Bible. She's a good woman." She looked lost in her thoughts, then smiled and said, "And both she and Ernesto have blue eyes."

He pulled back the blanket and looked at the sweet little face. "She's beautiful, Maria. Do you mind if we say a prayer of praise and thanksgiving for her?"

"That would be nice." Kit took the baby out of Maria's arms and laid her gently back in the cradle. They joined hands and Rock's heartfelt prayer was heard on High by the powerful Presence that gives life.

CHAPTER 26

Rock rushed into the post office. The fire truck was in the parking lot and the room was full of firemen gathering around the Christmas tree when he walked in. "Whew!," he said to Betty as she looked up. "I thought for a minute the post office was on fire. There are never this many people here on Saturday morning."

"We're getting ready to deliver the gifts from the angel tree," she said. "You know good 'n well we always use the fire truck for Santa's sleigh." She pointed to the fire truck from the window. "Did you not notice Ralph Carpenter sittin' up in the captain's seat with his red Santa suit on?" Ralph saw them looking out the window and waved. Betty handed Rock some packages. "Here, you can help us load the packages in the truck. That's what everybody's doing in here - loading packages. We had a right generous turn out of Christmas gifts this year."

Rock's arms were full as he walked out to the fire truck. Doug Evans, the fire chief, took the packages from him and loaded them in the cab. It took several trips to the truck to empty the packages from under the tree. When he walked back in, Betty had her key in the door. "It's closing time and I'm going to help deliver these packages. I wouldn't miss it for the world - seein' all those little faces light up when Ralph walks up to the door, Ho Ho Ho'in. It's the highlight of my Christmas season. Do you need anything before I lock the door?"

"No, I just came to get the mail out of my box. You go ahead and have fun." He smiled. He had been on the gift delivering committee for a couple of years and he understood her excitement. Instead of picking a name from the tree each year, he gave money to buy gifts for the last minute names that got added to the tree, but next year, he thought, it might be fun going Christmas shopping with Liz for one of the "angels" on the tree.

Betty finished locking up. "We had three names added at the last minute," she said. "Your money came in handy. We got everything we needed. I can't wait to see the smile on the face of the Newton family. Their house was broken into last week and the thieves took everything they could find - even the presents from under the tree. Now that's just plain sorry, don't you think, Rev Rock? Stealing a kid's Christmas presents."

"Yes Betty," he said. "It is just plain sorry." He couldn't for the life of him comprehend someone stealing a child's presents. "Plain sorry," he said again to himself as he got the mail from his box.

Main Street was alive with shoppers. He headed down to the Banty Hen. Valerie had called him this morning. She had the necklace she was holding for him wrapped and ready for him to pick up. As Valerie had said, the price was a little outrageous, but it was their first Christmas together. He would have to find a place to hide it - maybe the garage.

He crossed the street and started walking down Church Street toward the church office. Reva would be gone by now, but he would put the mail on her desk. As he looked down the street towards the church he saw a small white car pull up to the curb in front of the parsonage. Something looked familiar about the car. Come to think of it, Reva had mentioned a car that seemed to be stalking the parking lot. As he got closer, he could see a woman in the driver's seat and a man on the passenger side. They were looking toward the parking lot. They didn't see him until he got closer and when they did, the woman quickly drove away. He tried to get the license tag number, but could only read the first two letters. He knew where he had seen the car before - it was time to pay a visit to Jess Hamilton.

He had called ahead and Jess was waiting for him in the outer office when he arrived at the police station. "Have some punch and cookies," he said, pointing to the table laden with food behind the receptionist's desk. "I always put on five pounds the week of Christmas." Jess already had his plate rounded over with food.

"Looks like I picked a good time to come by," Rock said, picking up a plate and fork from the end of the table. "Who puts on this spread?"

"Everybody in the office pitches in - even the people in the community," he said. "But I'll give you three guesses on who sends the pecan pies."

"Estelle's pies! My mouth is already watering."

"She just sent a fresh batch. We'd better hurry and get a piece or they'll be gone as soon as word gets out. You should take a piece for Liz."

Rock didn't need to be coerced. He scooped two pieces on his plate and helped himself to a chicken salad sandwich and a few carrots from a vegetable tray.

"Save some room. Wanda Burns just called. She's bringing her Orange Slice Candy Cake - it's an old family recipe, she says."

"I've had that cake," Rock said. "It looks like a fruitcake, but it's almost the best dessert I've ever put in my mouth. In fact, it runs neck and neck with Estelle's pies."

They finished filling their plates. "Let's go on back to my office," Jess said, leading the way. "Heather said you had something you wanted to talk to me about."

"It's a white Honda - maybe five or six years old," Rock said, "with North Carolina license plates. I couldn't read it all, but it was three letters and three numbers. It started off with GR."

"GRW-116," Jess offered.

"What? How do you know that?"

"Because it's sitting right here on my desk, staring me in the face." Jess seemed to be as surprised as Rock. "You weren't far off on the year model either. 2007 Honda Accord - white with silver trim. Small plate above bumper advertising the dealership it came from, Cramer's Jeep and Honda, Raleigh, North Carolina." He put the paper back on his desk and looked up at Rock. "It turns out that your neighbor, Danny McCarthy would make an excellent detective. He's noticed the car several times during the last week hanging around the church. His camera has a high powered lens and he took this photo." He handed the picture to Rock. It was the same car he had just seen.

"I've already run the tag and guess who it's registered to?"

"I think I already know the answer, but tell me anyway."

"Yep, Ernesto Ramirez."

"How old is this Ernesto anyway"? Rock asked. "There was a woman driving the car this morning and a man in the passenger seat. He looked a lot older than Maria."

"From what Kit told me last week, Rock, it was an arranged marriage, and Ernesto is older. I just don't know how much older. I've got some calls in to Raleigh. While she's with Kit and BJ, I'm not worried about her. From what you're saying, the people in the car last saw her in your truck, so they may think she's with you. But now that they know you've spotted them, maybe they'll stay away. I'm going to have the officers on duty to be on the watch for the car - you'll probably see them riding by the church over the next few days."

"Are you going to warn Maria?"

"As soon as I get more information, I'm going to talk to Kit, BJ and Maria."

Rock stood up to leave. He picked his plate up off the desk. He had eaten his sandwich while they talked, but he still had the two pieces of pecan pie on his plate.

"Get Heather to wrap that in foil for you," Jess said, "then call Liz and tell her to put the coffee on. It's better when you savor every bite. And see if Wanda's brought that cake by before you go. You don't want to miss out on it. If she has, get two pieces of it to go along with the pie."

"You don't have to tell me twice," he said. He picked up his cell phone and dialed home.

CHAPTER 27

The church was full for the Sunday morning worship service. Many out of town guests had arrived early for the holidays and were sitting in the pews with their moms and dads, grandparents, aunts and uncles. The Sunday before Christmas and Easter Sunday were the most well attended services of the year. The choir had been practicing for weeks and they sang like a chorus of angels announcing the Christ Child's birth.

Rock's sermon was titled *What Child is This?* He talked of the Jewish infant who became the King of the Jews - not an heir to a throne on earth like some had imagined, but now, Lord of Lords, sitting on the right hand side of His Father, God.

"Imagine," he said, "a newborn baby causing such a stir in those who heard the announcement and saw the star over the stable. I wonder what the good citizens of Bethlehem thought about the star hanging over their town. Did they know from whence it came or its object of attention? No, the babe in the manger was brought into the world without much fanfare. He was just another child to the innkeeper and the census taker. God only revealed the holy birth to a chosen few that were present that night - Mary and Joseph, the shepherds, and later, the wise men. People far and wide saw the star, but didn't know what it signified. If the world had known the identity of the baby in the manger, Jesus would have grown up being treated like a celebrity, or worse - scrutinized and hindered every step of the way. I wonder how His childhood would have unfolded with so much attention surrounding Him. He wouldn't have had time to listen and learn. No, He was raised as just a man, fully human to the outside world. Only when He started teaching and performing miracles did they get a glimpse of who He was - this was God's own son!"

As the people filed out of the church and shook hands with Rock, some of them gave him their Christmas greetings, but most of them indicated they would be back for the night's activities - the children's Christmas pageant and the soup and chili supper.

Wonderful smells were coming from the kitchen and Rock's stomach was growling as he slipped his feet into a pair of black loafers. He had laid out a blue shirt and tie along with his navy sports coat. He fingered the tie in his hand. Grumbling a little bit to himself, he hung it back on the tie rack in the closet. He pulled out a turtleneck. Theo was on the bed watching every move he made. "I'm sick of ties, Theo. What do you think, old boy?" Theo swatted at the turtleneck as he laid it on the bed. "Somehow I knew you'd feel that way. You have no sense of style."

He always looked forward to the children's Christmas pageant and an added bonus was the soup and chili supper in the fellowship hall. The worship committee had discussed doing just desserts this year, but he nixed that idea quickly. Some traditions you just shouldn't mess with, especially when they involved food.

He gave his hair an absent-minded comb through and then walked out of the bedroom. He could see the living room from the hallway. The Christmas tree lights were on. It was beautiful but looked a little empty with no presents under it - he thought of the unwrapped gifts that they'd put upstairs in the parsonage with the intention of wrapping them long before now.

Liz had added a few things under the tree - two stuffed bears and a small antique rocking horse she had bought at the Banty Hen kept it from looking bare. She'd also found a red and green plaid quilt that her mother had given her in the attic and had thrown it across the back of the sofa along with some decorative Christmas pillows. It all looked so festive. He couldn't wait to surprise her with the antique train set he'd bought from the Banty Hen. He had worked it out with Sam to deliver it on Christmas Eve. What was missing? Oh, yeah - Christmas music. I'll make my own, he thought and started singing Johnny Mathis' *It's Beginning To Look a Lot Like Christmas*. He was glad he had Elvis off his mind.

"I'm starving," he said as he entered the kitchen and eyed the cookies on the counter. "What are you cooking?"

"Vegetable soup in the crock pot and cookies that just came out of the oven. Here, have one." Liz handed him a chocolate chip cookie that was still warm and gooey. He popped it in his mouth and held out his hand for more. She gave him another one and this time he savored each bite.

"Delicious. Oops, look behind you, Liz."

Liz turned just in time to see Theo leap up on the counter. "Theo, for the last time - get down from there!" She swatted Theo on the backside with a dishtowel and he jumped from the counter, turned around and stared her down. "Rock, please do something about your crazy cat. I've got all these cookies on the counter cooling."

"You call him my cat when he gets into something, but he's our cat when he's being cuddly," he paused, "which is almost never." Theo was standing by the doorway watching them. "I think he understands us," he said. "It's creepy. We'll lock him in the laundry room while we're at church."

"No, I've got two cakes in there. He'll knock them off for sure."

"Cakes? Who are they for?" He looked hopeful.

"I made a fresh coconut and a Red Velvet. I was planning to take one to Cap and Madge. Which do you like best?"

He grinned. "Both."

"Okay, I'll cut them in half and take half of each one to the Prices. Is that fair?"

"Fair enough. Can we cut one now?"

"Rock, for heaven's sake - we'll be having dessert at church after our soup and chili. It won't hurt you to wait an hour."

"You can't blame me for trying," he said, pulling her close. "This is the first Christmas I've had someone to bake in my kitchen since I moved away from home."

She laughed. "Don't give me that. They may not have baked in your kitchen, but every single woman in Park Place has baked cookies and cakes for you ever since I've known you. You were spoiled rotten when I married you."

"Hmm... So that's why I've not been getting cakes this year - I'm married. If I'd known that...."

"You would've married me anyway. That's why I've been baking so much - I was feeling sorry for you." She pecked him on the cheek. "Now, let's decide what to do with this cat."

"We'll lock him in one of the bedrooms."

"Nope, that won't work either. I just got your black overcoat and my red coat from the cleaners. Yours is hanging on the closet door in our bedroom and mine is draped across the bed in the guestroom. I took them to be cleaned because they had cat hair all over them. I thought we were going to keep Theo out of our bedroom."

"That was our plan, wasn't it? What happened?"

She laughed. "Who can keep up with Theo? He slips in between your feet and you never know he's there."

"We can fix that. We'll just close off the kitchen and bedroom doors and he'll have free rein of the living room where he can bat all the ornaments off the tree."

"It's better than him nibbling cookies and turning over the cakes, I suppose." She took off her apron and hung it on the back of a kitchen chair. "I'm ready except for brushing my teeth. If you'll get Theo out of here, I'll finish up and close the bedroom door on my way out. Oh, and don't forget to bring the crock pot."

"How could I forget - its smell is tempting me." He picked up the crock pot, herded the cat from the kitchen and closed the door behind him.

Liz walked out of the bedroom with a tube of lipstick in her hand. "I didn't realize it was so late," she said as she pushed the door closed with her foot.

Rock thought she looked striking in her red sweater and black pants. The baby bulge was there, but the sweater was hiding it well. "People will only notice how beautiful you look tonight, Mrs. Clark," he said. "They won't even care that we're late."

Liz was the last one out the door and pulled it closed behind her without locking it. Rock had the crock pot in his hand, but he turned around to get a glimpse of the cottage all lit up. It looked like a postcard with the lighted tree glowing through the window and Theo perched up on the windowsill looking out into the night. He loved Liz, he loved the cottage, and he loved the Christmas season. All's right with the world, he thought.

"No worries"! Holly was in the choir room as Rock and Liz rushed in apologizing after dropping off the soup in the kitchen. "Remember," she said, "we're operating on Park Place time. I've learned that if the bulletin says a meeting starts at 6 pm, you're considered early if you walk in at 6:05. Anyway, the bus from the Children's Home is just now getting here and we're also minus Mary and Baby Jesus. Maura ran back to the house to get one of Abby's dolls."

I thought Miss Edie's granddaughter, Jessica and her baby, Gracie were playing Mary and Jesus," Rock said.

"They were, but little Gracie has an ear infection. Jessica called to say she's been crying all day. They've taken her over to the health clinic hoping to get some relief for the pain."

Rebecca walked in with the children who were making a mad dash to get around her and start putting on their costumes. It was chaotic. Rock looked at Liz and she grinned. "Yes," she whispered, "there'll be ear infections, teething, colic and all kinds of fun stuff."

"Just so you'll know upfront," he said teasingly. "I'll probably be a floor pacer."

"I'll be joining you," she said.

"Why are we whispering?" he asked.

"Because no one knows yet," she answered.

"We could be shouting with all this noise," he said, "and they still wouldn't know." He pulled her closer to his side.

"Okay, enough of the mushy stuff." Rock looked up to find Kit, BJ, Maria and the baby in front of them. Rock's smile deepened as he saw Maria and he turned to Holly as she was giving final instructions to the children in their costumes.

"Holly, the Good Lord sent us a Mary and a Baby Jesus."

"Praise the Lord!" she said. Rock and Liz laughed. She was beginning to sound more like a Southerner every day.

Kit fussed over little Angelina, getting her blanket out from the diaper bag and doing the best job she could of swaddling her tightly as Mary must have done with Jesus when she put Him in the manger in the stable. "I'm glad we brought the white blanket," she said, "even if it does have a yellow duck on it. I doubt seriously Jesus ever wore pink."

"I don't think he wore yellow ducks either," Holly said, "but I could be wrong."

Maria was excited about portraying Mary. In her home church, the Vicar's daughter had always played the part of Mary in their live nativity scene each Christmas. She had been envious, but now she would have her turn. She tied the cord of the white robe loosely around her waist. Angelina was only three days old, but it was hard to tell that Maria had just given birth.

Holly held the baby while Maria got ready. "Maria, she's precious," she said while cuddling her closer in her arms. "She looks so fragile." When Maria finished dressing, Holly carefully handed her back over.

Betty Ann's fifteen year old grandson was playing the part of Joseph and he looked down at the baby. He held out the palms of his hands and backed slowly away. "Huh, uh!" he said. "Don't ask me to hold no baby. She looks like she'll break."

The pageant was one of the few times Rock could just sit back and enjoy a service in the church without having an active part. He and Liz sat on the front pew together and watched as Sonny Watson narrated the program. Holly had recruited him because of his stature and his booming voice. The story was told from the viewpoint of a shepherd and Sonny was dressed the part in a large brown robe which Maura had to make special to fit him. He was holding a shepherd's crook and despite his size, his appearance was humble. The lectern had been moved and a large curtained frame had been constructed to keep the manger scene hidden during the narration. The shepherds had been visited by an angel, and Shirley Campbell, looking ethereal in her white garments delighted the audience with her part. Shirley had studied dance in New York City in the early 1950's and she delivered her lines with grace and flair. Then the lights were dimmed and scurrying footsteps were heard in the quietness. There was a sound of curtains being pulled back and suddenly a spotlight illumined the manger scene. Gasps from the audience were heard as they looked on at the serene scene before them. Holly had done wonders with the set design. It looked so much like a stable that Rock wouldn't have been surprised to see real donkeys and cows grazing on the hay. And Maria - Rock fully expected to see a halo surrounding her head at any moment. The crowd was in awe at the tender smile on the Virgin Mary's face as she looked down upon her baby and then lifted her from the manger and held her up for all to see.

Tears sprang to Rock's eyes as he watched. The miracle of the babe in the manger, the Son of God who was the reason they were all in church tonight. The child who grew to manhood teaching man to be kind to others, and to observe the new laws that were established when He died on the cross.

He heard Liz sniffling and he handed her the fresh handkerchief from his pocket. When the lights came back on, the younger children started singing *Away in a Manger* as Jenny Wilson played the piano.

Rock thought Holly had done a splendid job, apparently spending many hours of planning and rehearsal time to make it all come together. The audience clapped and the children all held hands and curtsied. Maria stayed in her seat holding the baby. She was smiling, but suddenly her expression changed. She's afraid of something, Rock thought. She had looked so serene earlier, surely she couldn't be getting stage fright at the end of the program. Poor child, he thought - she had just given birth a few days ago. Maybe the noise from the audience was too much for her.

Maria had enjoyed her role as Mary. Angelina had

slept the entire time and as she watched her sleeping, a love like nothing she had ever experienced washed over her. During her difficult days after leaving Ernesto, she had briefly thought of giving the baby up for adoption, but as she grew inside her and the fight for survival became her focus, she became more determined than ever to keep her.

Now as the children sang, she looked out over the audience. She saw Rev Rock and his pretty wife on the front row. The rest of the people were strangers except for Kit and BJ who were looking at her and smiling. Kit gave her a thumbs up sign and she smiled back at her. Just then, she saw a figure walk through the double doors leading into the sanctuary. He took off his hat and looked around. Maria tried to make herself look smaller as she sat lower in her seat, but finally his eyes stopped searching when they settled on her.

"Dear God in Heaven," she prayed silently. "Help me find a hiding place. Show me the way." Her first reaction was to run out of the church but that would be too obvious, so she stayed where she was through the song and waited while the audience clapped for their performance. She watched Rev Rock get up and congratulate Holly and the children. He then said the blessing for the food they were about to eat and invited everyone back to the kitchen for soup and chili.

As soon as the crowd started surging forward, Maria rushed out ahead of them. She found the diaper bag that she'd left in the choir room and slipped out the back door unnoticed carrying the tiny baby wrapped in swaddling clothes.

"This is the biggest crowd we've ever had for the pageant," Rock told Liz as they made their way slowly to the kitchen. The crowd had created a bottleneck in the small hallway that led to the fellowship hall. He watched as they inched forward. "I should have dismissed them one aisle at a time."

"It wouldn't have worked," she said. "When you mention food to this crowd, it's a free for all!"

"Yeah, about like I am when you mention cookies."

"Exactly," she said. "I'm glad we're tall - at least we can see over the crowd."

"Unlike Shirley over there," he said. "She looks lost." He stepped closer to Shirley and grabbed her elbow, leading her through the crowd. She was still in costume and had been looking everywhere for her husband, John, in the crowd. Rock could see John ahead of them looking for Shirley. He waved and got his attention. "Here's your angel," he shouted above the crowd. "Wait up and I'll deliver her to you."

John's look of relief when Shirley was delivered to him spoke volumes. They had been married for almost sixty years and rarely left each other's side. Everyone knew that John loved and cherished his petite wife as she danced through life as gracefully as a butterfly.

She took off her halo and handed it to Rock. "Here, you wear it for a while," she said. "I feel like I'm wearing an antenna." Rock laughed. The crowd was finally thinning as some of the people who had come only for the program left by the side door.

Kit and BJ were just ahead of them and when Kit

spotted Rock, she grabbed BJ's arm and they waited until they caught up. "Wasn't that the best pageant we've ever had?" Kit's voice was full of excitement.

"It was great," Rock said. "I was worried when Jill came down with pneumonia and turned the program over to Holly. I shouldn't have been - she did a great job." He turned to Kit. "But I think you're just a little bit biased because of Mary and Baby Jesus," he teased. "Where are they anyway?" he asked as he looked around for Maria.

"Probably getting out of costume," BJ said. "I hope she doesn't overdo it. We'll head on home as soon as we eat."

Jess Hamilton walked up behind them as they waited in line to get their plates. "Hey, no breaking in line - even if you are the Chief of Police," Kit said.

"The only place I would break in line for food would be at your restaurant," he teased back. "BJ makes the best hamburgers in South Carolina," he told the people around them.

"Only in South Carolina?" BJ asked.

Jess laughed. "I don't know. I don't get out of Park Place much - maybe North Carolina too." He looked at the table laden with food. "I hadn't planned to eat, but since we're so close to the food now, I may as well get a bowl of soup. It's supposed to turn cold again. I just heard the forecast and they're calling for a chance of snow on Christmas Day."

"I'll believe that when I see it," said Kit. "We've never had snow this early."

Jess turned to Kit. "I really just came by to talk to the two of you about Maria, but we can talk over a bowl of soup."

Rock was dipping soup out of Liz's crockpot into his bowl. He picked up a cornbread muffin to eat with it. "We'll let you guys talk. We'll go over and sit with Maura and Danny."

"No," said Kit. "If it involves Maria, we want you and Liz with us."

The five of them sat down to eat. "I would invite Rebecca to eat with us," said Kit, "but she looks pretty busy with the kids."

"We have a new one at the home and Rebecca's had to spend a lot of time with her today. She just came in this morning. The child's mother left her in a car up in Charlotte last night while she went into a bar to drink. Just six years old and here it is just a few days before Christmas. It always amazes me what some people put their kids through."

"Me too," said Kit. "If they only knew...." She looked sad for a moment, but then turned back to Jess. "What is it you wanted to talk to us about?"

"I want to get more information from Maria. Ernesto's car has been spotted here in town - in fact, right here in front of the church. Rock has even seen it."

"Oh no!" Kit said. "What will happen if he's come to find her?"

"Excuse me, Rev Rock." They all turned as they heard the small voice. Rock turned to find Abby and the twins, Ava and Emma standing beside his chair. They were fidgeting from one foot to the other.

"What is it Abby"? he asked.

"Mama said to tell you that Baby Jesus is missing!"

CHAPTER 28

Maria lit a candle and looked around at her bleak little corner where she had lived for nearly a month. She remembered how thankful she had been when she first walked down those steps through the narrow door to find a hideaway - a shelter from the cold and more importantly from Ernesto. Her few meager possessions were still tucked away behind the concrete support column - a sleeping bag, a pillow and some well-worn clothes. Two cans of Spam, an empty box of Pop-Tarts, and an unopened bottle of grape juice were stacked neatly behind the insulation. It had been her emergency stash for when the diner was closed. She remembered her first few days in Park Place eating discarded food from a garbage bag. She remembered it proudly, knowing she had done the best she could do under the circumstances and now she had a sweet, healthy baby to show for it.

She had survived! But she had been alone then. Looking at Angelina, she knew she could not subject her child to those conditions, but she was determined she would never go back to Ernesto - that much she was sure of. She was not the same timid and browbeaten girl that had walked into Park Place on Thanksgiving Day. She had friends now who cared about her. Kit, with her soft heart but fiery temper would help protect her from Ernesto. She would love to stay on with Kit and BJ and raise her daughter with the opportunities she would have here, but she couldn't impose on their generosity. She would be content just to go home to Honduras to her madre and padre and her brothers.

Angelina stirred in her arms and made a sucking motion with her lips letting Maria know she was hungry. A tiny cry came from her lips and Maria crooned softly, "Hush Bebe."

With a new determination and fresh resolve, she blew out the candle and opened the door to leave. She could no longer hide. Like the candles that had given light to help her find her way in the dark basement, she realized God had been lighting the way for her since she had arrived in Park Place. It was no accident she was here. It was time to tell the truth and face whatever came her way.

As she closed the door behind her and walked up the concrete steps, she smelled smoke. It had turned colder and the wind was beginning to blow from the North. She looked in the direction of the cottage and seeing a bright orange glow in the window, she let out a scream. "Fire!"

She would later tell Kit that she must have sprouted the wings of an angel to have reached the door of the fellowship hall so quickly. Just as she put her hand on the handle, the door opened and she was relieved to see Kit, BJ, Rev Rock and the police officer coming out in just as big a hurry as she was going in. She didn't know they were looking for her.

"Fire!" she screamed to them. "There's a fire in the little white house."

"Liz, call the fire department," Rock shouted over his shoulder, and Jess Hamilton talked frantically into the radio he took from the holster on his side.

The fire truck arrived only seconds after Jess and Rock climbed up the porch steps and were behind them as they rushed in the front door. Pungent smoke filled the air and the orange glow was coming from the smoldering Christmas tree.

"Those dratted lights," Rock said aloud. "And Liz was depending on me to replace them."

"Get out!" one of the firemen behind him shouted, pulling a mask down over his face. "The chemicals in artificial trees are dangerous to inhale."

"Oh no!" Rock said. "Where's Theo?" He looked pleadingly at the fireman. "My cat - I have to find my cat." He started for the hallway and the fireman grabbed his arm.

"Sir, you can't stay in here. It's an electrical fire and dangerous. Where's the breaker box?"

Rock told him and backed out the door just as Lonnie came running up the steps. "Anybody hurt?" he asked. Rock was glad to see him - he had never seen him so serious.

"Lonnie, it's Theo. He's in there somewhere."

Lonnie grabbed a mask from the fire equipment on the porch. "Lord 'a mercy," he said. "That poor cat's already used up who knows how many lives. I'll find him." He put on the mask, turned his flashlight on high beam, and rushed down the hallway.

Rock was on the porch praying. "Please Lord, don't let my carelessness kill poor Theo."

In less than a minute, Lonnie had come out of the house with Theo, who was not making a move or a sound in his arms. "He has a pulse," he said. He shouted to Doug Evans, the fire chief. "We need oxygen over here."

"Five more minutes in there and your cat would'a

been a goner." Lonnie was pushing air out of Theo's lungs and then hooking him back up to the oxygen. Theo had recovered enough to know that he didn't like it and was trying his best to escape Lonnie's grasp. "Ouch!" he exclaimed. "You don't know what's good for you, do you old boy?" He handed the cat over for Rock to hold. "See, he'll be fine, but he's got some vicious claws," he said, wiping the blood off his hand that Theo had swiped.

"Tell me about it," Rock said.

Lonnie donned a pair of rubber gloves and took Theo back. Theo nuzzled against his neck and started purring. "Aw, you're not such a bad kitty after all." Rock couldn't believe it. Theo was not a nuzzler.

"Why, I've never seen such a sight!" Doug was pointing to the parking lot. "Look at that!" he said in amazement.

Rock and Lonnie looked up. It seemed as if half the people in Park Place were in the church parking lot. They had formed a circle and were praying. It was the most heartwarming scene Rock had ever witnessed. He bowed his head until he heard a loud *amen*. A single tear made its way down his cheek and fell on a tattered and singed angel that he was cradling in his arms. One wing was askew, and he wondered how in the world it had made its way down off the tree to the floor in front of the door. He felt an arm slip around him and a voice near his ear. It was Liz. She took the angel from his hand and looked it over.

"Never underestimate the power of angels," Liz teased. She was trying to put up a brave front, but Rock saw the tears welling up.

"Liz, I'm so sorry..."

"Shush," she said, hugging him tighter.

"But it could have been prevented if I had changed out the lights. It's all my fault."

"We don't know that for certain," she said.

Rock held her and they rocked back and forth. After a moment she seemed more composed and broke their embrace. She smiled up at him and started talking again.

"It appears our wonder cat has survived once again," she said. "We have so much to be thankful for. And the house will be okay. I talked to Doug and he said that a good restoration company can have it back in order in no time at all."

"At least we have a place to live," he said. "The remodeling is almost finished in the parsonage - enough for us to live in it, at least. But you won't be able to cook yet. The new stove hasn't come in."

"And that's a problem?"

He was glad to see Liz smiling. "I don't see you complaining," he teased. "We'll be gone to visit our parents after Christmas anyway. If it's not in by the time we get back, we'll use the microwave or pilfer off the neighbors."

"I've been ready to move in," she said. She reached up and kissed him on the nose. "Doug said that having the doors shut off to the rest of the house likely saved having to replace a lot of things. These old doors are good and tight and very little smoke reached the kitchen or bedrooms."

"So I can still eat the cookies in the kitchen?" he asked hopefully.

She laughed. "And you can have your cake and eat it too." The tension they both had been feeling was suddenly relieved by their infectious laughter.

Both his arms encircled her waist. "I will thank God every day of my life that He brought us together. I love you, Liz."

The fire trucks were packing up their hoses which they hadn't needed after all. Rock and Liz walked off the porch and started back toward the church. "I hope and pray that Theo will be okay," she said.

"I'm just glad Eileen was willing to open her office to check him out. She's going to keep him overnight."

"Lonnie was wonderful - he saved Theo's life, you know?"

Rock laughed. "And now he thinks he has some sort of bond with him. He insisted on taking him to the clinic, much to Doug's dismay. I think Doug was hoping for an excuse to see Eileen. I've heard through the grapevine that there's a spark there. They're both still single and they were high school sweethearts."

"Aha," she said. "A little romance between the fire chief and the veterinarian!"

"Remind you of anything?" he asked.

"I suppose so," she said sheepishly. "Last summer they were saying the same thing about the preacher and the high school guidance counselor."

He held her tighter. "That didn't turn out so bad, did it?"

A half dozen of the Presbyterian Women were cleaning the kitchen as BJ, Jess Hamilton and Maria sat down at one of the tables. Holly carried Angelina to the nursery to feed her a bottle. Kit took a seat beside Maria at the table.

"Maria, this is Jess Hamilton. He's the police chief and a good friend of ours." Maria nodded to Jess. Kit reached out and took her by the hand. "We were worried about you," she said. "We were on our way out to try to find you when you came in the door." Her voice was not quite a reprimand, but it made Maria fidget in her chair.

She hung her head for a moment, but then lifted her shoulders and looked up. She turned her eyes towards Kit. "I must tell you all the truth." She turned around and faced Jess. "I saw you walk into the church while the children were singing and I thought you had come for me. I thought my husband Ernesto had sent you after me for leaving him. My first thought was to run away so I took Angelina with me so we could hide. We went down to the church basement."

She looked down at Kit's hand touching hers and it bolstered her confidence. She looked back at Jess. "You see, I knew where the basement was - I had been there before."

Jess didn't say anything - he let her continue talking. "I didn't know what to do, but I finally decided I was going to have to face up to my problems. I can't go on hiding from Ernesto for the rest of my life - I have a baby to think of now."

They listened spellbound as she told them about hiding in the basement and how she had survived the cold, the hunger and worst of all, the fear of being found out. She told them of staying in the house for a few nights during the extreme cold weather, but she didn't implicate Ramon - she just told them she saw him hiding the key.

Kit's mouth had dropped open and stayed that way throughout Maria's confession. She tightened her hold on Maria's hand trying to convey her support to the young, frightened girl. When she finished telling her story, Kit hugged her and turned to Jess. "Will she get in trouble for trespassing?"

"I don't know," said Jess. "The officers of the church will have to decide if they want to press charges, but truthfully, I don't see that happening.

Kit looked at the Christmas tree glowing warmly beside the large arched window in the room. Large gold ornaments, feathers and garland filled the white snowy branches creating a shimmering iridescence. It was so brilliantly decorated that it was named appropriately, The Glory Tree. The cold, dark basement underneath all this beauty had been the only home Maria had known since Thanksgiving. When all of Park Place had been snuggling in their warm beds at night, this child had struggled to stay warm. When they had taken for granted their family members and friends, Maria had felt all alone. The joys and abundance of the Christmas season had been all around them, and the young pregnant girl had wondered where her next meal was coming from. The thought brought tears to her eyes.

Jess' next words brought Kit out of her thoughts. "Maria, I wish you had confided in someone. Park Place is filled with warm and caring people. We would have made sure you received help. But this is not what I had planned to discuss with you. It's about Ernesto. We have reason to believe he may be in Park Place."

Hearing her husband's name sent shivers down her spine. She had not eaten since lunch and she suddenly felt sick. Kit noticed the odd pallor of her skin.

"Good grief," she said, and rushed to her side. "What was I thinking? This poor child hasn't even had dinner and she just had a baby three days ago! Jess, can't this wait until morning? She can't handle another thing tonight. BJ, please carry the leftover soup to the car and let's get this child home. Jess, go ask Holly to bring the baby and then come back in here and help me get Maria to the car."

The conversation had been quiet until Kit sprang into action. Wanda Burns was watching from the kitchen. She would go home and tell her husband that the scene had reminded her of the E. F. Hutton commercial on TV. "When Kit Jones speaks, people listen."

"They do, don't they?" Hank had said.

"Yeah, and she packs more punch in that tiny little frame than... well, than Baby Ruth's bat."

"Honey, that's BABE Ruth's bat."

"Oh, whatever," she said. "Babe... Baby... I didn't know there were two of 'em - It doesn't matter which one's bat it is! You know what I mean."

Hank rolled his eyes. It was just too much trouble to explain. "Yes, Dear, I know what you mean."

CHAPTER 29

Maria had been dreaming of a white car. In her dream she was walking down the road with the baby in her arms and the white car was following silently behind, not even a sound came from the motor. When she stopped, the car would stop. When she picked up her pace, the car sped up. She finally started running and the car sped up and came along beside her. The passenger window rolled down and she saw Ernesto's face and heard him laugh as he reached his hand out the window. She woke with a start, trembling all over. The clock on her bedside table was blinking 6:03 am. She shook her head in disbelief. Angelina had been on a three hour feeding schedule and her last feeding had been at midnight. Her feet hit the floor and she hurried over to lift her out of the cradle. The abruptness of the move startled the baby out of her sleep, and she cried. The sweet newborn cry was music to Maria's ears. She laughed, then crooned as she cradled her in her arms.

"Oh, my sweet girl! You slept so long and your mommy was worried." The sound of Maria's voice soothed her for a moment, but she soon started crying again. "You're hungry, aren't you?" she cooed. She walked with her over to the small antique rocking chair and settled her in a nursing position. Her milk had been slow to come in and each time she had tried, they both became frustrated so she had been supplementing with a bottle. Kit had encouraged her to keep trying, if for nothing else but the bonding experience, but this time the baby latched on greedily and seemed to be getting enough to satisfy her hunger.

As she nursed, her mind drifted to her dream. She remembered the car that had pulled alongside her the day Rev Rock gave her a ride. She had been sure it was Ernesto's car, but what would he be doing in Park Place? She had covered her tracks carefully. Could it just be by chance that he was here? What if Ernesto tried to take Angelina away from her? She shuddered at the thought. No, she was no longer afraid of him. She had friends now. She was through running and through hiding. Kit had told her last night that Ernesto could go to prison for the abuse if she testified against him - not the other way around. And to think, she had been so terrified that she would go to prison.

There was a knock on the door. "Come in," she called out. Kit walked in carrying a cup of coffee in one hand and a glass of juice in the other. Her bright red pajamas clashed with her fiery red hair and Maria couldn't help but laugh when she looked down at her bedroom slippers.

"What?" Kit said, following her gaze to her feet. "Have you never seen penguins before?"

"Yes, but they're on the wrong feet." The penguins looked as if they were running away from each other and it struck Maria as funny. Kit joined in the laughter and changed them around.

"Well, I was in a hurry. I heard you stirring about and couldn't wait to get in here and get some baby cuddling in. Oh, Maria, you're nursing and she's not crying!"

"I know, I finally have enough milk, I think," she said proudly. She had nursed from both breasts and Angelina was perfectly content.

"Aw, she's asleep again." Maria saw that Kit looked

disappointed that she wouldn't be able to feed her a bottle.

"She does need a diaper change," she said, as she repositioned her nursing gown.

"Oh, I'll do it for you!" Kit gently lifted her out of Maria's arms and took her to the changing table, cooing all the while. "Come on little munchkin - Nana Kit will fix you right up." She pulled a diaper out of the package and opened it up. As she was taking off the wet diaper, she looked back at Maria. "Did she sleep all night? I didn't hear a peep out of her after midnight."

"Yes, and it worried me when I woke up and she was still sleeping."

"Knock, knock." The door was partially open and Maria turned around as BJ entered the room. He walked over to the changing table. "Are you going to hog her all for yourself?" he asked Kit.

Maria watched the two of them make silly faces as they cleaned Angelina up and changed her diaper. Her first thoughts were how lucky she was to have Kit and BJ and how they genuinely cared about her and the baby. Then she thought back to Ernesto's mother's words. During their tutoring sessions, when Maria would mention anything about good luck, she would say, "It isn't luck, my dear. It's all part of God's plan." She wished she could think of his mother without it bringing Ernesto to the forefront of her mind again.

"I want to go to the police station today," she announced in a voice louder than she normally spoke. She saw the surprise that registered on their faces simultaneously.

"Are you sure?" BJ asked.

"Yes." She paused. "I need to get this over with."

BJ picked the freshly bathed and diapered baby up and put her tiny face up to his shoulder and started patting her on the back. "Well, let's do it," he said. "You ladies fix us some breakfast and I'll burp the baby - then we'll be on our way."

They both looked at him in surprise.

"Y'all look like you've never seen anyone burp a baby before," he said, all the while patting her back.

They hesitated before they started for the door. "Don't forget to lay her on her back - not her stomach," Kit called out.

"Don't worry," he said. "I know a thing or two about babies. Just go on and start breakfast. I'm starved."

Maria and Kit looked at each other and shook their heads, then giggled as they made their way to the kitchen.

After breakfast, BJ insisted on washing the dishes. "I'll take over from here ladies. You two can go take your showers. When I finish the dishes, I'll call Jess and tell him we're on our way."

While they were in the shower, BJ called the police station.

"He took the day off, BJ," Heather told him. "He and Rebecca went up to Charlotte to go Christmas shopping. Otherwise, old Santa Claus was going to skip clean over the orphanage. If he gets back in the office today, I'll have him call you. Hope y'all have a Merry Christmas out your way."

"Merry Christmas to you Heather." He hung up and walked back to the bedroom. "Kit," he called through the bathroom door. "Y'all may as well just settle in today. Jess has gone to Charlotte."

CHAPTER 30

Rock loaded another box in his truck and headed back inside the house. He and Liz had been boxing up the things they would need in the parsonage from behind closed doors in the bedroom. There was still a chemical smell in the living room from the burned artificial tree so Rock had declared the room off limits to her. He quickly opened and closed the door again as he went back into the bedroom one more time. Liz was tying a scarf around her nose and mouth.

"You look like you're planning to rob a bank," he said. "Which one do you have in mind and I'll drive you over in the getaway car."

She laughed. "Maybe we should try the credit union," she said. "It's more isolated than the others."

"Good plan."

"No banks today," she said. "I thought I'd slip this on and make a mad dash to the kitchen to pack up a few things in there."

"I've already taken the cookies and cakes to the parsonage."

"I should have guessed," she said, eyes twinkling. "How many did you eat?"

"Let's just say I've worked up an appetite."

She was having trouble getting the scarf to stay on. "Turn around," he said. She turned her head away from him and he finished tying the knot. "There, that should stay put."

"You've got it over my eyes," she said. She pulled it down and led the way into the kitchen with Rock following close behind.

"Be sure to keep the door closed while you're in there. I'll drive the truck around to the kitchen door."

He walked back through the living room and took a last look around. The doors and windows to the outside were open and the smell was finally beginning to dissipate. The insurance company had given him a list of house restoration people. He had called Hart's Restoration in Charlotte and made an appointment for them to come out and give an estimate. It would be the first week of January before they could start.

He stood in the middle of the living room and took in the scene before him. The walls were dingy from the smoke. The rug was ruined where the tree had smoldered. Some sort of gooey substance had bled onto it, and when he tried to pull back the rug, it was stuck hard to the old pine floor. He stepped over broken ornaments and shards of glass from the window until he reached his arm chair. His Bible lay on the table where he had left it the day before. It didn't appear to be hurt, but he picked it up and the chemical smell clung to it. Maybe a good airing out would help it, he thought. He couldn't bear to part with it. It had been his constant companion throughout his years of preaching in Park Place. It was like an old glove that fit perfectly - filled with bookmarks and notes - even a dog ear or two to mark the place of some of his favorite passages.

What bothered him most was seeing the broken ornaments scattered all across the floor. They were the only Christmas keepsakes Liz had to show for all the Christmases she had spent with Ron. And all because of his carelessness! He had promised her he would replace the strand of lights that kept flickering on and off...

"I thought you were bringing the truck around."

He hadn't heard Liz walk up behind him. He turned around. His face was filled with remorse as he looked into her eyes.

She stepped closer to him and took his hand. "Rock, when are you going to stop beating yourself up over this? The fire was an accident."

His voice faltered as he spoke. "But look at this," he said, pointing to the mess on the floor. "All of your Christmas memories with Ron - all crushed to pieces and it's my fault. You know I loved Ron like a brother," he said. "I wanted his memory kept alive for both of us."

"Rock, get this through your head. Ron's memories will stay alive in our heads and our hearts, not in material things. And remember, this is our first Christmas together. We're making our own Christmas memories now. We don't want to remember it as a placing the blame kind of Christmas."

"How did you get so wise?" he said. "We do have our own memories to make, don't we?"

"Yes, and please quit dallying around and bring the truck around to the kitchen door so we can get busy making those memories. I'm ready to get into that big old house you always complained about."

He laughed, "Are you calling me a whiner?"

"If the shoe fits," she said.

Doug Evans walked in from the open front door and greeted them. "You don't mind if I take a look around, do you? I've got to finish filling out my report."

"Help yourself, we're just leaving," Rock said.

On their way out, he noticed a small box near the hall tree. It was marked "Pyramid" on the outside of the box, and he remembered that he had brought the box containing his grandmother's German pyramid and his few ornaments to the cottage over a week ago with plans of putting them out with the other decorations. He grabbed it up, grateful that it had not been anywhere near the tree, but feeling somewhat guilty that his own decorations had survived.

Rock spent the rest of the morning carrying boxes and suitcases into the parsonage. Two of Betty Ann's teenage grandsons were on Christmas break from school and volunteered to help. They made light of the work, carrying two boxes at a time up the stairs to the bedroom Rock and Liz had picked out to use until the master bath remodeling was finished.

"They don't even have to hold on to the rails," Rock told Liz as they were eating lunch in the dining room. "I was huffing and puffing up the stairs and they passed me going up and then coming back down. I wish I had their energy."

"Well, you're not an old man, Rock Clark," she said. "You've got plenty of energy for me."

"I think it's all those cookies I've been eating, and I told you Reva thinks I'm getting fat."

"Don't worry - I think my belly's going to be outgrowing yours by leaps and bounds over the next few months." She put her hand over her tummy and felt a slight movement. Her face registered her surprise. "Oh Rock! She moved! Come feel it!"

Rock jumped up and put his hand over her stomach

as she sat at the table. A tiny little flutter stirred on the inside of his palm as he held it still. His heart was filled with the awe and wonder of the special moment. "This is the best Christmas memory I could ask for," he said and gave her a gentle kiss.

"I was hoping she would move before Christmas," she said. "Now I can rest easier knowing she's moving."

"Now you're the one saying *she*," he said.

"I know, I just can't help myself. It's just a feeling I have. I'll be happy no matter what the gender, but for some reason, I just keep thinking of it as a girl."

There was a knock on the door and Rock went to answer it. It was Holly. "Come on in, Holly. Can I get you some coffee?"

"Thank you Rev Rock, but I can't stay. Maura said to tell you to plan on eating dinner at our house tonight. Your kitchen isn't functional yet and she's already started a huge meal. She said she doesn't want any excuses!"

"Well, how could we refuse an offer like that?" Liz said. "Tell her we gladly accept! What time?"

"Six o'clock," she said. "See you then!" She turned and walked out the kitchen door.

Rock picked his car keys up from the counter. "I'm going to see if Eileen will let me bring Theo home," he said. "You want to ride with me?"

"No, I'll stay here and get organized. You go ahead."

Rock opened the garage door and started backing out. Doug's truck was parking in front of the office, but when he saw Rock in the driveway, he got out of his truck and walked up to the driver's side window. "Faulty wiring," he said. "The flickering lights were just a coincidence. It wouldn't have mattered if you had changed them."

Rock felt a sudden unburdening. "Will you go inside with me to tell Liz"?

Just then, May drove up in her floral delivery van. She got out and walked back to the rear door.

"Do you think this will do?" She was holding a large vase with at least two dozen pink roses. Rock had never seen such a pretty arrangement. He had almost forgotten he ordered them. "Wow," he said.

"Wow!" Doug looked on in amazement. "You're going to make the rest of us men in town look like cheapskates," he said. "That must have set you back a pretty penny!"

Rock didn't care how much it set him back. They couldn't have come at a better time.

May laughed. "Don't panic," she said. "I know you just ordered a dozen, but I had twenty-three total of the pink ones. No one orders anything for at least a week after Christmas, so I always close for a few days. I couldn't bear to have these just sitting in the flower shop with no-one to enjoy them. Besides, Liz needs a little pick-me-up after all you two have been through."

"Well, follow me," Rock said. "Between the two of you, you've made my day. Let's go see what Liz thinks." Instead of going back through the garage, he led the way and rang the front doorbell. Liz looked confused when she came to the door and saw the three of them standing there, but when she saw the flowers, she hugged all three of them.

"Wait, they're not from me," Doug said. "But on second thought, I'm glad you thought so - I'll take hugs like that any day."

"Don't worry," Rock said, "she's going to hug you

again when you tell her what you told me outside." And she did.

Theo looked annoyed when Eileen brought him out in the pet carrier. "He's going to be fine," she said. "His lungs look clear - I was worried about him getting pneumonia, but I think he's too grouchy for that," she said, laughing.

"That's a fact," Rock said. He wrote a check for the full balance and gave it to the receptionist.

"I'm pretty sure there's no permanent damage," Eileen said.

The receptionist handed him a receipt. "But that's one more life he's used up," she said. He knew she was joking but thinking of it in those terms made Rock feel sad. He had heard that inside cats could live a good long life, but poor Theo, all his mishaps had been inside. He was going to have to start taking better care of him.

CHAPTER 31

"*Self help is no help at all. Self sacrifice is the way, my way, to finding your true self.*"
Luke 9: 24 The Message

Maura had set a simple but elegant table. When Liz commented on the pretty blue and white china, Maura chuckled.

"Green Stamps," she said. "My mother got this china piece by piece with S&H Green Stamps. She always let me lick the stamps and put them in the books. Each month she would get a catalog showing what you could get by redeeming the stamps. When she found something she wanted, she would send the books off to the trading stamp center and a week or two later, we would get a package in the mail. I loved licking those stamps until I heard the glue was made out of horse hooves!"

"Ick," Liz said. "Thank heavens the post office has peel off stamps now."

Holly came from the kitchen carrying a large casserole dish between two oven mitts and placed it on an iron trivet on the sideboard. Abby was right behind her with a big bowl of salad.

"What can I do to help?" Liz asked.

"You can get the salad dressings from the refrigerator," Maura said. "They're on the bottom shelf of the door. Ranch, bleu cheese and thousand island - we're going casual tonight and just serving them in their own bottles. I hope you two like lasagna. We have enough for a small army."

The food was great and the conversation didn't hit any lulls. Sonny and Holly talked about their plans of trying to find a house in town.

"They know they're welcome to live with us as long as they want," Maura said. "But I can understand them wanting a place of their own."

"We don't want to move far," Holly said. "We want Abby to grow up close to her grandparents. I missed out on that. My parents were older when I was born and my only living grandparents were in Nebraska. I barely remember them."

"And don't forget about the cousins," Abby said. "I've never had cousins before."

Liz could see the love shared round the table and thought how blessed Holly was to have been accepted into this family so wholeheartedly. She looked at Rock and was pleased to see him looking back at her with raised eyebrows conveying by eye contact just what she had been thinking. If they decided to rent out the cottage after the restoration, what better renters? They smiled at each other and Rock winked and gave her a thumbs up signal.

After dinner, they brought their coffee into the kitchen. Liz and Maura emptied the plates and put them in the dishwasher as the others gathered around the table and talked. When they finished, they sat down at the table with their coffee. Liz couldn't remember when she'd enjoyed the companionship of friends more, but she was tired. Each time she tried to get Rock's attention to make their excuses to leave, Maura started another conversation. She tried her best not to yawn, but one finally slipped by.

Rock noticed and turned to the others.

"We've had a wonderful evening and I hate to bring it to a close, but I can see Liz is tired. We worked all morning moving things to the parsonage. I'm afraid we're going to have to call it a night. Maura, you've been such a good hostess!"

Liz had noticed that Danny had been standing by the kitchen window for a while, glancing outside occasionally. Now he looked at Maura and nodded his head. How odd, she thought, but then yawned again and forgot about it.

"It's a beautiful night," Maura said. "I want to see the stars. We'll walk down the driveway with you. Do you feel like walking, Danny?"

"I think I'll stay here," he said. "I'll start the dishwasher."

"I do!" said Abby. "Hold up for me."

"We'll go too," Holly said. "I'll get the coats." She came back in with all their coats and they headed out the door.

The air was crisp and clear and the sky was full of stars. "It's a beautiful night," Liz said. "The stars just seem brighter this time of year."

"I can just imagine the star over Bethlehem," Maura said, "how bright it must have been on a cool crisp December night."

"And I can just imagine Rudolph's nose shining so bright!" Abby said. Everyone laughed and listened as she told Liz all the things she had put on her list for Santa. "Mommy says not to expect him to bring them all," she said. "It's just to give him some ideas."

Rock looked at the little group walking beside him

and thought how wonderful it was to live in a little town like Park Place. Good friends, good neighbors and now he had Liz to share it all with. God truly was in this place.

He felt a tugging on his arm and looked around. Liz had stopped beside him.

"Rock, look at that!" She was pointing to the parsonage where the living room curtains were wide open and Christmas tree lights were shining softly through the window. "What....?"

Abby was in Sonny's arms facing backwards towards Maura's house and said. "Daddy, why is grandpa flicking the porch lights off and on at our house?"

Suddenly the shrubs on the front side of the parsonage came to life with lights, and candles simultaneously appeared glowing in all the windows. Liz caught her breath. "How beautiful," she whispered.

A spotlight cast its glow on the front porch illuminating the large wreath on the door.

"Well, let's go see what's going on," Maura said, as she led the way across the street and into their yard. As they ascended the steps of the porch, beautiful music began to fill the air. Suddenly people were coming from all directions singing Christmas carols with Jenny Wilson as their leader.

"I feel like I'm in a Charles Dicken's novel," Liz whispered to Rock. He was speechless. There were at least thirty people surrounding the porch serenading them with carols. The women were all dressed in red and the men had on black coats and ties. Larry Braswell would tell Rock later, "I had to borrow a black coat, dadburnit. There's no arguing with Jenny Wilson. When she tells you to wear black, you wear black!"

Betty Ann Williams opened the front door from within. The carolers were still singing softly. She walked out on the porch and took Liz by the hand. "Liz, I hope we didn't overstep our bounds. The fire had ruined all your decorations and we knew you couldn't possibly have time to re-decorate before Christmas. Tomorrow is Christmas Eve and we wanted things to be cozy and inviting for your first Christmas together. I hope you're not upset with us."

Rock watched as Liz tried to check her emotions, but her voice wavered as she spoke. "Upset? No, but I'm overwhelmed." Everyone got quiet as she turned and faced the crowd. "I knew when I married Rock that he had a wonderfully supportive congregation, but I never realized how important that would be until tonight."

"Well, come on in and see what we've done," Betty Ann said from behind her. Rock took Liz by the arm and led her inside.

"Did you know about this?" she asked him.

"No, I would have never been able to keep it a secret," he whispered. "I've had enough trouble keeping our other secret."

The first thing Liz noticed was her grandmother's quilt on the back of the sofa. Jenny walked over and gently smoothed it. "Clara Hinson took it home and hand washed it in her bathtub," she said. "Then she laid it out in front of her fireplace to dry. We thought it was too delicate to put in the washer and dryer."

Rock looked around the room. For the first time since he'd moved into the parsonage, it didn't seem cold and empty. He had blamed it on the sheer size of the place, the furniture and the neutral color scheme, but now he realized what it was missing. It had been missing the warmth that goes along with good friends, companionship and genuine love. He should have entertained more, he thought. This house was perfect for intimate gatherings and social occasions. When Ron was alive, he and Liz would visit Rock to play cards or checkers, but he'd become somewhat of an introvert after Ron's death when he should have been making new friends. Having people in the house seemed to breathe new life into it.

He had never used the gas logs, but now realized how warm and cozy the room looked and felt with them burning. The only room he had ever really loved was his study. He had personalized it and made it his own, something he had failed to do with the rest of the house.

He watched as Liz made her way around the room taking it all in. Fresh holly and evergreen branches covered the mantle over the fireplace and the stockings from the cottage were hanging. "I thought those were ruined," Liz said.

"I just stuffed them full of scented dryer sheets and dried them on a low setting." Betty Ann held them up to her nose and breathed in. "Good as new," she said and smiled. They do have a slight lavender smell, but the greenery gives it a fresh, crisp Christmassy scent in here, so no one is going to notice the lavender."

Rock was pleased to see the musical pyramid on the table in the foyer. He wound it up and watched as the wise men went in one direction and the shepherds in another. It brought back so many memories. He looked around the room. All the little touches were creative and thoughtful. Rock couldn't believe the congregation had pulled it all off in the two hour time frame he and Liz had spent at Maura and Danny's house. Maura - where was she? He looked around and saw her smiling and watching him from the center of the room.

"You were in on this!"

"I'm afraid so. Danny was keeping watch for the signal saying all was clear for the two of you to walk home. I was worried you would catch on that something was brewing. Danny isn't the most subtle man in the world."

"I thought he was acting rather odd," Liz said. "But I hadn't been around him long enough to know if odd was normal."

Maura laughed at the thought. "He'll get a kick out of that one."

Jenny Wilson was flitting around taking it all in. "Everything is just gorgeous," she said. "This is the first I've seen it. I was busy getting the carolers organized. Our women did a beautiful job. Just look at that tree!"

Liz and Rock walked over to the large frasier fir they had seen through the window. It was strung with soft white lights and gold beaded garland. Floral picks of pinecone and holly were interspersed throughout.

"The ornaments!" Liz said. "They're beautiful!" No two were alike and they were an eclectic mix of old and new.

"We started to just go buy all new ornaments," Betty Ann said, "but Linda here came up with a wonderful idea." She picked one of the ornaments off the tree and held it up for Rock and Liz to see. It was a miniature metal watering can adorned with a red plaid ribbon. "We called everyone we could think of and asked them to choose a favorite ornament from their own tree to bring to the church tonight. There's a total of seventy-two ornaments here and each one means something special to the person who gave it. This watering can, for instance is the one Linda brought. She collects watering cans. Her nephew, who passed away last year, always gave her a watering can ornament each year at Christmas. This is one of them."

"Oh, I couldn't keep that," Liz said, turning to Linda. "It must mean so much to you. You shouldn't give it away." Tears were beginning to well up in her eyes again.

"No, she wants you to have it." Maura said. "You see, it's all about sacrificing something you love to make someone else happy. It wouldn't have made us feel as good inside if we had simply gone out and bought new ornaments." She was fingering the ornament she had taken off her own tree. "If we choose to live by God's words, we make sacrifices every day - little things, really. Like giving of our time to sit with a friend who needs us, or giving up something we want or need for someone who needs it more. But those things are nothing compared to the ultimate sacrifice God made by the giving of his Son so that we could be free of the sins that burden us."

"I'm going to let you preach my sermon next Sunday," Rock teased. He looked at the small crowd still milling about the room. These were ordinary people who had done an extraordinary thing. How could he ever repay their kindness? He knew he couldn't - acts of kindness could only be repaid by passing it on.

"I don't know what to say. There are not many times that I'm left speechless."

Larry Braswell spoke up. "That's for sure. We'll

remember this and when you're still preachin' at 12:15 on Sunday mornings, we'll think back on the day that Rev Rock was speechless." Everyone laughed.

"You all have such sweet spirits," Liz said. I just wish we knew the story behind each ornament. Someday you'll all have to share them with us."

Jenny picked up a basket beside the tree. "We're one step ahead of you. Each ornament does have a story behind it and we all wrote our stories on a Christmas card. You'll have plenty of time to read through them later." She handed Rock the basket. "It was the least we could do, Rev Rock. You give and give and give to us. You're always there when we need you and we take you for granted. And Liz, if you think we have sweet spirits, it's because of your husband. He's been feeding us with his spirit filled sermons for years. Some of it has even sunk in to these hard old heads."

"Plus, we had too many dad-blamed ornaments anyways, what with me and Madge combinin'...."

It was Cap Price speaking. Madge elbowed him in the side as the others laughed.

"Never mind him," Madge said to Liz. "He's a little rough around the edges and I haven't had time to polish him up yet."

"Well, it got rid of everybody's tears anyway - you all were about to make me cry," Cap said, sniffling and then grinning with a full mouth of teeth.

Madge reached over and kissed him leaving her signature smudge of bright red lipstick on his cheek, just to the left of his nose.

The crowd had dispersed quickly when Betty Ann

mentioned the time and the need for everyone to rest up for the next couple of days.

"Tomorrow's Christmas Eve," she said. "I don't know about y'all, but I've still got a lot of gifts to wrap and cakes to bake."

The lights were out. The soft glow from the tree and the gas logs warmed the room in separate ways, but combined to give it a cozy mid-winter's night safe haven as Liz and Rock cuddled on the sofa. Liz had tucked her feet up beneath her housecoat and she leaned against Rock with her head on his shoulder.

"Have you ever been happier than this?" she asked.

"Never," he said.

"Me either."

They sat there contentedly until Rock felt himself nodding off to sleep. "I'm ready for bed, how about you?" he said. When she didn't respond, he lifted her head slightly from his shoulder - enough to see that she was sound asleep. He thought of Liz's question. Had he ever been this happy? No, he thought. Having Liz in his life had taken happiness to a whole new level. He kissed her gently on her forehead and roused her out of her sleep just enough to half walk, half drag her up the stairs.

"Did I brush my teeth?" she asked.

"Yes Ma'am, you did that before you got comfortable on the sofa, remember?"

"I just don't want my teeth to fall out," she mumbled. He laughed. She had once mentioned that her mother told her if she didn't brush before bedtime her teeth would all fall out.

"You never told me you talk in your sleep, Mrs.

Clark." He covered her up, his hands smoothing the blanket over her rounding belly. He slipped into bed beside her and said a prayer of thanksgiving for his wife and the baby, his child, growing inside her. Sometimes it was still too much to comprehend.

His normal routine was to drink his morning cup of coffee in his worn, but comfortable armchair, while reading from his worn, but comforting Bible. He stood in his study uncomfortably, missing both of them. The armchair was salvageable, but needed a good airing out and cleaning, something the restoration company promised to do. Liz had done some research and now had his Bible sitting on a layer of Arm & Hammer Baking Soda in an airtight container in the garage.

"Are you sure about that?" he had asked. He held on to it tightly as she tried to take it from his hands.

"It's what libraries do," she answered, and he handed it over reluctantly.

Settling into the only chair in the room, the recliner, his eyes scanned the Bibles he kept on a shelf. He pulled one out. *The Message* - he hadn't read from that one in a while, but he was choosing a reading for the Christmas Eve service tonight and maybe he should go back to the more traditional versions. He opened it up to the second chapter of Luke and started reading.

Chapter 2: 1-5: *About that time Caesar Augustus ordered a census to be taken throughout the Empire. This was the first census when Quirinius was governor of Syria. Everyone had to travel to his own ancestral hometown to be accounted for. So*

*Joseph went from the Galilean town of Nazareth up to
Bethlehem in Judah, David's town, for the census. As a
descendant of David, he had to go there. He went with Mary,
his fiancée, who was pregnant.*

*6-7: While they were there, the time came for her to give
birth. She gave birth to a son, her firstborn. She wrapped him in
a blanket and laid him in a manger, because there was no room
in the hostel.*

Why not? he thought. *The Message* version was simple
and easy to understand. Why not break from tradition?

Liz stuck her head in the door. "Am I interrupting?"
she asked.

"Of course not, come in."

"Reva's here and she's bringing good tidings of great
food. You won't have to eat Pop-Tarts after all."

"Rats," he said. "I was looking forward to my old
standby."

"Ick," she said, "let's not mention rats when we're
talking about food." She led the way into the kitchen.

"Our angel of mercy," he said when he spotted the
spread Reva had laid out on the table.

"I fixed enough so you could nibble all day. There's
even a batch of sausage balls - I know they're your
favorite." She turned to Liz, "Miss Liz, if you want any of
the sausage balls for yourself, you gonna' hafta hide some
away. He's right greedy with 'em, yes he is."

He loved Reva, he realized, and not just because she
fed him, which she did abundantly, but because of who
she was - a kind and generous soul. And she always made
him smile. He picked up a sausage ball and started
nibbling.

Liz reached over and hugged her. "Reva, you're still spoiling him, but he loves it. This was sweet of you." She looked at all the food - ham biscuits, scones, a breakfast casserole and the sausage balls that were already beginning to disappear. "This is enough to feed us for days," she said.

"Well, that's what I was intending to do, and if you don't have any plans, come over and eat Christmas dinner with our family tomorrow. There'll be a whole house full, mind you, but two more won't make much difference."

Rock knew she meant it and her whole family would make them feel welcome, but what he really wanted to do was have a quiet Christmas Day - just the two of them. Liz sensed his need to be rescued.

"We appreciate your offer, Reva, but I found the most wonderful surprise in the freezer this morning. I had forgotten that we had frozen all the leftover ham, turkey and cornbread dressing from our Thanksgiving meal with Rock's family. It was so good, I wouldn't want to waste it. I took it out to thaw in the refrigerator this morning. Fine china, candlelight dinner - Our first Christmas together - just the two of us."

"And our last Christmas as a twosome," Rock said, grinning slyly.

"Rock!"

"I'm sorry Liz. I can't keep it a secret any longer. Especially from Reva - she's family."

Reva looked from one to the other of them with a puzzled expression, then broke out in a great big smile. For a moment, Rock thought she was going to start doing back flips and he could just envision spending Christmas

Eve in the emergency room with Reva out with her back, but she finally calmed down.

She hugged Rock, then Liz. "Honey, your secret's safe with me. I won't tell a soul - except maybe my Walter."

"This whole town will know by this afternoon," Rock said when she left. "Maybe that wasn't such a good idea after all."

CHAPTER 32

Heather Bartlett pulled a folding metal chair from the supply closet into the small waiting area between her desk and Jess Hamilton's office. "We're a little cramped for space," she apologized. She looked up at BJ, then back at Kit. "Kit, maybe you or Maria should sit in this chair. It's a little rickety for someone BJ's size."

"You calling me fat?" BJ teased.

Heather laughed. "I don't think anyone would call you fat," she said. "You're just a big man, and you know what they say, the bigger they are, the harder they fall. We wouldn't want a lawsuit on our hands." She looked at the closed door to Jess' office. "I'm not sure who's in there," she said. "I just got here about ten minutes before you did. I knocked but he said he was busy and would be out shortly."

"We don't mind waiting," Kit said. "We should have called ahead."

"Nah - he doesn't mind." She turned to Maria. "Can I see your baby?"

"Of course," Maria said. Angelina was in the infant carrier covered in blankets. "We should take some of these blankets off her anyway. It's cold outside, but it's comfortable in here." She peeled back two blankets so that Angelina's face was visible.

"Ohh, look at all the beautiful black hair," Heather said. "Both my babies were born bald as a pumpkin. She's beautiful!"

Maria felt her heart swell with pride. She smoothed Angelina's hair down. The static electricity caused by coming into the warm room from the cold had made her hair stand straight up. Looking at her sweet baby soothed her spirit momentarily, but then she remembered she was in a police station and her fear returned. She looked from Kit to BJ. They both gave her the reassurance she needed when they winked and smiled.

The phone on Heather's desk gave two short rings. "That's Jess now," she said. "He's ringing from his office. I'll tell him you're here."

She picked up the phone. "Yes?" she answered. "Oh, that's a coincidence," she said. "They're all here in my office waiting to see you." She nodded to Kit and put her hand over the mouthpiece. "He wants all of you to come into his office," she said, "and take the metal chair in there with you. Leave the baby out here and I'll watch her."

"She's just been changed and fed," Maria said. "She'll sleep for a while."

Jess opened the door from the other side. Standing in the doorway, he shielded the view from inside his office, but then he moved aside to let Maria go in first. As she slipped inside his office with Kit and BJ on her heels, she gasped when she saw a familiar figure sitting in the chair just ahead. Kit grabbed her from behind. "What is it Maria?" she asked.

At that moment, the figure slowly arose from the chair. "Thank God! I've finally found you."

"Please don't take me back!" Maria cried.

Kit pulled Maria back with her right arm. "You're not going anywhere you don't want to go, Maria," she said, and stepped out in front of her. She looked over at Jess. "What's going on?" she asked.

Jess looked on with confusion. "Perhaps I shouldn't have sprung this on Maria so quickly," he said.

Maria was now crying profusely. "I just don't want to go back to him!" she said. "I'm frightened!"

The older woman in the room had stopped in mid stride as she saw the effect that her presence had on Maria. Her eyes filled with tears. "Maria, my dear," she said. "Ernesto will never hurt you again. I am so sorry for what you've been through." Her tears started flowing freely.

"I was under the impression that all was well between you two," Jess said to Maria apologetically. He pointed to the other person in the room. "Kit, BJ, this is Ann Schrader Ramirez, Ernesto's mother."

Mrs. Ramirez nodded to the two of them. "Chief Hamilton tells me you've been taking good care of Maria," she said. "I can't tell you how thankful I am for that."

Kit looked at her suspiciously. "She needed us," she said. "Your son certainly didn't take care of her." She paused, "except with his fists!"

The older woman acknowledged her. "I had no idea." she said. "He was always such a good boy, but from talking to his neighbors and co-workers in Raleigh, he started drinking and hanging around with the wrong crowd. The drink apparently brought out a meanness in him that we didn't know existed."

"Well, he certainly wasn't a good boy to Maria!" Kit was puffed up like a mother hen, Maria thought. "And I hope he ends up in jail. BJ and I will help Maria fight it all the way through the court system. She is not going back to him!"

"That won't be necessary," Jess said gently. "Ernesto is dead."

Silence enveloped the room. Maria felt as if she had been swallowed up in it and was suffocating. Ann's eyes were filled with tears and Maria felt a new emotion - the emotion that a mother feels for someone who has lost a child. Ann had lost her only son. She ran to her side and the older woman embraced her. The two women were suddenly connected and no words were necessary.

After a moment, Kit broke the silence. She too had experienced the raw emotions the other woman was now feeling. "Mrs. Ramirez, I'm so sorry. I'll admit that I had a lot of ill will towards your son for the way he treated Maria, but I certainly didn't wish death upon him. I know how heartbroken you must be. I lost a child a few years back and the empty spot in my heart can never be completely filled."

Ann Ramirez nodded. "It was such a shock. I just wish I had known about his drinking," she said. "I would have tried to get help for him. And Maria, believe me when I say that I would have taken you out of that situation if I had known. I'm so sorry for what you've been through."

Maria finally spoke. "How did he die?"

Jess spoke up. "I have the police report here. He got into a fight outside of a bar. According to witnesses, he had been drinking heavily and provoked the fight, but the man who killed him is in jail on murder charges. It happened on December 7th, a little over a week after you left home, Maria. This came in on a wire from Raleigh this morning, just minutes before Mrs. Ramirez came in to talk to me."

"His father and I were notified in Honduras and came up to identify and claim the body. We were surprised to find you gone, Maria, but when we talked to your neighbor, she told us that she had heard through the thin walls the abuse that you suffered and that you had finally gotten the courage to leave. She said after you left, Ernesto came home late every night. We found out from his construction supervisor that he almost lost his job because he was not getting to work on time. It breaks my heart."

"I'm so sorry, Ann. I did care for him in the beginning. At first he was a good husband, but he changed. Drinking turned him into a monster. He would say he was sorry when he was sober, but I could no longer trust him. I'm afraid I lost all the love I ever felt for him in the end." She reached for a tissue from the desk. "How did you find me?"

"We found you by accident. No, it wasn't by accident - it was by the grace of God. After Ernesto's burial and settling his debts, Luis and I were on our way to Georgia to visit my sister before we started back to Honduras. We had flown into Raleigh, so we took Ernesto's car after our search for you had failed. We were almost on empty when we pulled off the highway and found the gas station here in town. When we pulled out from the pumps, I saw you walking down the road. You looked so familiar but you had gained weight so I couldn't be sure. We slowed down and when I saw your face, I knew it was you. We stopped, but before we could get out of the car, a truck stopped and picked you up."

"I was sure it was Ernesto's car," Maria said, "and I thought he had found me. It was like a miracle when Rev Rock picked me up."

"Finding you is our miracle, Maria. We would have never rested easy if we hadn't found you. So many things can happen to a young girl traveling alone and we were sick with worry about you. Now we can take you back home with us to Honduras. Ernesto had a life insurance policy and you're the beneficiary. The money is just waiting to be claimed by you. It's a considerable sum and will go a long way back home. You can stay with us or live with your parents - maybe even buy your own home someday."

The news of the insurance money took Maria by surprise. So did the thought of leaving the two people she had learned to love as if they were her own family. With the money, she could attain her dream of getting an education and wouldn't be such a burden on Kit and BJ. But her family - her mother and father and brothers - could she turn her back on them? They were all she'd ever known and she was homesick to see them.

Kit had absorbed the conversation as it unfolded. She wondered what the young girl was thinking. Maria and Angelina going back to Honduras? Just when joy had returned to the Jones household. It would be so hard to lose them. Her heart grew heavy at the thought of it. It was apparent that Mrs. Ramirez didn't know about the baby.

"Maria may not want to return to Honduras," she

said as she looked hopefully at Maria. "She has a home with us as long as she wants to stay."

"That's very generous of you, but she has family back in Honduras. She belongs with us."

Maria's conflictive emotions could easily be read as she looked from one woman to the other. She turned to the police chief. "Mr. Hamilton," she said shyly.

"Yes, Maria?"

"What is my legal status now that I no longer have Ernesto sponsoring me? I need some time to think."

"That's a good question, Maria. We have a lawyer here in town who specializes in immigration." He turned to Kit. "Kit, I'm talking about Bob Clayton." He turned back to Maria. "Bob's a member of our church. I think you should talk to him."

"I think we all need to see him," Kit said. "BJ and I need to ask him about the loopholes of adopting an immigrant." She turned her attention on BJ. "Don't we, Honey?"

BJ grinned. "I wondered when you were going to get around to that subject," he said. "I was beginning to think I was going to have to bring it up."

Maria looked confused. "But who would you want to adopt?" she asked innocently.

"Uh," Kit said to her. "And just how many immigrants do you think we know?"

Maria caught on and grinned broadly. "Me? Really?"

Jess looked worried. "Kit, don't get your hopes up until you speak with Bob," he pleaded. "And please make sure this is something you all want. Maria may change her mind somewhere down the road."

"Yes, and she needs to be with her family!" Ann

Ramirez looked indignant. "I'm sure her parents want her back with them. They would have to approve. They have their rights, you know."

Maria lifted her shoulders and held her head high. "Senora Ann, my father lost those rights when he gave me away in marriage against my wishes. I love him, but I don't want to be put through something like that again. I want to be able to make my own choice if I ever decide to marry again."

Kit could see that Ernesto's mother was trying to do the right thing for Maria, but she couldn't possibly know all that Maria had been through trying to stay alive.

"Mrs. Ramirez, if this is what Maria wants, and if there's anyway possible to make it happen, as a legal resident, she'll be able to visit back and forth with her parents anytime she cares to go. We will encourage it and make sure she has the funds for it. You and I have a lot to talk about." She turned to Maria. "And Maria has something she needs to share with you, don't you Maria?"

Maria smiled. "Yes I do." She motioned to the older woman. "Come outside with me a minute." Mrs. Ramirez got up from her chair and followed her. She left the door open as they walked out to the reception area.

Kit watched as Maria knelt down by the infant carrier and pulled back the blankets. "Senora Ann," she said as she lifted the baby out of the carrier, "I want you to meet Angelina, your granddaughter."

Kit heard Ann's muffled cries and watched as she put her arm around Maria's waist. "Oh Maria! I now see what you've had to face, little one." Maria handed the baby to her and the older woman held her gently. "A little bit of Ernesto still lives."

Ernesto's mother had been kind to Maria. She felt no malice towards her - she wasn't responsible for her son's behavior. She put her arm around her mother-in-law as if holding out an olive branch to appease her.

"Senora Ann, I promise that no matter what I do or where I live, you can always be a part of her life."

Ann spoke shakily. "Thank you, my dear Maria. My only wish is for you to be happy."

Kit was proud of Maria. She marvelled at how mature she was at just the age of sixteen. Oh my, she thought, today would be her last day of being sixteen. Tomorrow she would be seventeen! Her birthday - one that she shared with a King.

CHAPTER 33

Looking at the crowd, Rock wondered if everyone in town had come to Park Place Presbyterian's Christmas Eve service, but then again, it was the only church in town to hold one, except for the Christmas Eve mass at the Catholic Church.

True to her word, it seemed that Reva had kept their secret safe since there were no sly glances or knowing looks from anyone.

Everyone received a candle at the entrance to the church. Rock's reading of the Christmas story was followed by the singing of hymns led by the choir. Then came the candles - each candle was lit from a larger candle to represent the light of Christ spreading from person to person, illuminating the world. All other lights in the church had been dimmed and the procession of the candle carriers as they left the church was a deeply moving experience.

The weather had turned colder, but most everyone gathered on the front lawn of the church to wish each other a blessed and happy Christmas. Kit and BJ were waiting outside. Maria was with them, along with an older woman holding Maria's baby.

"So the white car mystery is solved," Rock said after they told him the story. "I'm so sorry for your loss, Mrs. Ramirez," he said.

"And I'm sorry we alarmed you," she said. We didn't think about our actions looking suspicious. We were just on a quest to find Maria." She put the baby on her shoulder. "And we got a bonus baby in the bargain," she said as she smiled down at Maria.

Kit spoke up. "Rev Rock, what will happen about Maria trespassing on church property?"

"Kit, she was just seeking shelter from a storm and our church just happened to provide it. Case closed."

As the crowd grew smaller, Rock noticed that tiny particles of moisture seemed to cling to the air.

"We'll get us a good dusting of snow out of this one," Cap said, as he and Madge stood with some of the others.

"Nah," Larry Braswell said. "Park Place has never seen snow at Christmas."

"Well, it will this year. I can feel it in m' bones."

"That's just old Arthur you're feeling in your bones, Cap. I've lived here all my life and I've never seen a white Christmas."

"You're gonna' see one come tomorrow morning." Cap said. "I hope ol' Santy Claus has his snow boots on."

Rock saw Sam Owens walking towards him. He met him halfway where Liz couldn't hear their conversation. "I've got your train set in the van," he said. "Where do you want me to put it?"

"I left the side door of the garage open. If you don't mind, wait until we get inside so Liz won't see you drive up."

The fire was glowing softly again, and all the presents had been wrapped and put under the tree and the angel, a little worse for the wear, again graced the very top branch. Rock watched as Liz checked out the newest package. Valerie had wrapped it in a larger box than necessary to keep Liz from guessing it was jewelry. He had wrapped his mother's pearls in a small box. After she had given both packages a good shake, she settled back on the sofa with her hot chocolate.

"Do you really think we'll have a white Christmas?" she asked.

"If Cap's bones have anything to do with it, we will," he said.

Rock heard a sound in the garage as if something had been knocked over.

"What's that?" Liz said with alarm.

"I'll go see. Maybe Theo got out when I opened the door earlier." He hurried to the laundry room and through the door that led to the garage. He closed it behind him. Theo was there, but it wasn't he who made the noise. It was dark in the garage but he heard Sam's voice.

"It's just me," he said. Sam was standing in the middle of the garage cringing - hoping they hadn't heard him.

"I'm sorry," he whispered. "I was holding the train box and I couldn't see my feet. I'm afraid I tripped over your golf club bag."

"Well, that's the most activity it's seen in a while," Rock said. "Can I help you? Liz may be coming out here to check on me. She heard the noise. Here, just set it on this shelf."

"Rock, is everything okay out there?" He could see Liz's silhouette through the open door, but she couldn't see the two of them in the dark garage. Sam stooped down behind the car.

"Everything's fine," he said. "I was moving some things around out here today and my golf clubs must have been left unbalanced when I finished. They just fell over. I'll pick them up and be right in."

He saw the door close. "Whew! That was close. I should just give it to her now, but I want to wait until she's asleep to put it together. I want to see her expression when she sees it under the tree."

"You would make a good Santa Claus," Sam said. "I'll go now. I hope she likes it. Y'all have a Merry Christmas."

"Merry Christmas to you too, Sam. Thanks for being willing to part with it. It's found a good home."

He walked back inside. "We'd better get to bed or Santa will pass over our house without stopping."

"Heaven forbid," she said. "I'll race you upstairs."

Rock was dreaming of a ringing phone, but his body seemed to be made of lead and he couldn't move to answer it. The answering machine was turned off so the persistent ringing finally penetrated his brain and brought him halfway awake. For a moment, he was confused. This was not his bed. Where am I? he wondered, but then feeling the other side of the bed, he found his beautiful wife was snoring happily beside him, and he remembered that he was upstairs in the parsonage. The phone finally stopped ringing. It was still dark outside and he wondered who could be calling him at this hour. He looked at the clock on the bedside table. 7:00 am - that wouldn't have seemed so early if he'd gone to bed at a decent hour. After Liz went to sleep last evening, he had gone back downstairs and worked for two hours getting the train set up. And Sam had told him the tracks were easy, which they may well have been if he had assembled it as many times over the years as Sam had.

He felt around in the dark for his bedroom slippers, and started toward the bathroom when the phone rang again.

"Blast it," he said aloud. "I need my cup of coffee before I can talk," he said to the phone right before he picked it up.

"Merry Christmas!" It was Cap Price on the other end. Christmas? Oh, yeah - today is Christmas, he thought, but still wondered what Cap would be calling him for at this hour.

"Uh, Merry Christmas back to you, Cap. It's sort of early, isn't it?"

"Go look outside," Cap ordered.

"It's dark outside - nothing to look at until the sun comes up," Rock said, growing impatient with his friend.

"Just humor an old man, would you," Cap said. "It might just be gone if you wait too long."

"Okay, I'll look," he said, trudging along to the window. Unless there was another surprise Christmas tree or a bonfire, he knew he wouldn't see anything - and frankly, he was not in the mood for another tree and certainly not a fire of any kind.

He poked a finger through the slats on the blind, and then excitedly pulled the entire blind up. The whole town of Park Place was covered in snow. Forgetting that Cap was on the other end of the line, he put the phone face up on the dresser and rushed across the hall to another bedroom. The church parking lot was one beautiful canvas of snow. There seemed to be no imperfections anywhere in his line of vision - just pure white snow!

He pulled the blinds back down, ran back to the bed

and shook Liz gently on the shoulder. "Wake up, Sleeping Beauty. I have a surprise for you." He laughed as she seemed to be as confused as he had been when the phone awakened him from his deep sleep.

"It's Christmas!" she said with excitement as it suddenly dawned on her.

"Yes, it is," he said from the window. "And come look what Santa left for you."

"A pony!" she said and then laughed at the absurdity of her statement. "Well, I always did want a pony."

"You should have told me," he teased. "A pony in our front yard - just what we need. No, seriously, come over to the window."

"It's chilly in here," she said. "Let me just get my housecoat on." She shrugged her shoulders into the robe that she pulled from the hook on the closet door and walked to the window where Rock stood. He raised the blind again in a quick flash.

"Oh my stars!" she said. "Snow in the South on Christmas Day. Now that's a miracle!" She ran across the hall to the other bedroom just as he had done, not quite believing what she saw out of the front window. "Let's go outside and play and then have some hot chocolate."

"Wait up," he said. "It's a little too early to be cavorting in the snow. It's not even daylight yet. I wouldn't have even looked if Cap Price hadn't called me. Uh, oh..." he said. "I forgot that Cap is still on the phone." He picked the phone back up. "Hello, Cap?"

Cap laughed from the other end. "I'm still here - couldn't help eavesdropping on your conversation with Liz. Sleeping Beauty, is it?" Cap cackled laughing and Rock could hear him talking to Madge.

"Cap, thanks for calling. I've got to go now. Liz and I have a snow date with a pony on the front grass."

"Say what?" Cap said in bewilderment.

"I said Merry Christmas," Rock said and hung up the phone.

Liz bent over double laughing at him. "You shouldn't have told him that," she said. "He'll be riding over here looking for a pony."

"Let him come! We'll give him some hot chocolate."

"Speaking of hot chocolate," she said, "I'm starved! Let's go heat up some of Reva's sausage balls."

"Save some for me," he said. "And if you don't mind, I'll have a cup of coffee instead of hot chocolate. I'm in bad need of a cup! I'll turn on the Christmas tree lights and we'll eat in the living room."

"Splendid!" she said. He smiled. To Liz, who saw beauty all about her, everything was splendid.

He turned on the lights outside and on the tree, then held the plug-in for the train up to the socket until he saw Liz rounding the corner with their coffee cups. He plugged it in and the train immediately started chugging around the tracks and made a loud whistle - all the while emitting a steady spew of steam.

Liz put the cups on the coffee table and ran to the tree. He wished he could bottle up her excitement and the look of pure joy on her face as she watched the train make its way around the tree. If only he could save that moment for a rainy day to be opened and released all over again.

CHAPTER 34

"We remember before our God and Father your work produced by faith, your labor prompted by love, and your endurance inspired by hope in our Lord Jesus Christ."

- 1 Thessalonians 1:3 NIV

"Three inches of snow on Christmas Day!" Cap Price shook his head as he and Madge drove his new four wheel drive pickup truck down Main Street. "I ain't never seen anything like it in all my born days."

Madge corrected him. "You *haven't* ever seen anything like it," she said.

"Yeah, that's what I said. Channel 3's gonna' start beating on my door to be their new weatherman."

Madge laughed and reached over to kiss him. She missed her mark on his cheek and kissed him square on the nose. "You old coot," she said. "If you weren't so cute, I would smack you right on the head. I'm going to teach you proper grammar if it kills me."

He stopped at the one stoplight even though they were the only souls who had ventured out on the roads. He turned around to face her. "Well, you better be plannin' on living a good long time. It's hard to teach an old dog new tricks." The light turned green and he drove on. "Look, Junie's store is open." He stopped in the middle of the street and rolled down the window as Junie was locking the door. "Open on Christmas?" he asked.

"Had to," Junie muttered. "People were calling me at

home interrupting my breakfast wantin' to buy a snow sled. Might be the only snow we get all year so I thought I'd better sell 'em while I they're hot. Just sold m' last one so I'm going home. Why are you two driving about in this stuff?" He waved at Madge through the window.

"Just cruisin' Main Street," Cap said. "Thought we would ride by the church and see what Rev Rock's up to. He said something about a pony when I talked to 'im this morning. He's too old to be gittin' a pony for Christmas."

Madge nudged him. "You're never too old to get something you want," she said and smiled coyly. "You of all people should know that, Cap Price."

Junie tapped on the windshield. "You two lovebirds better get back home," he said. "We can't be havin' all this lovey, dovey stuff on Main Street. Besides Cap, if you get out of the truck, somebody's gonna' be mistaking you for Rudolph."

Cap pulled down the visor and looked in the mirror. He grinned when he saw the neon red lipstick covering his nose. "It's Madge's new Christmas lipstick," he said, "and I'm wearin' it proudly." He closed the visor. "Hope you and Kathleen have a Merry Christmas," he said. He rolled up the window, took his foot off the brake pedal and turned right on Church Street. They drove slowly by the parsonage. "I don't see a pony," Cap complained.

"You must have misunderstood," Madge said.

"Maybe we should stop and pay 'em a visit."

"No, it's their first Christmas together. They don't need company."

"Aw, shucks," he said. "I was hoping to see a pony."

"Why don't we get a pony?" she asked.

"Really?" he said. Madge laughed. She knew what she

would get him for his birthday.

The joy of Christmas had descended upon Park Place. Streets had been closed off and were being used for sledding. The temperature was hovering right below freezing so the snow was sure to stay at least for another day. Families within the town limits were walking instead of driving to Christmas brunch or lunch at the home of other family members.

Across town, a young girl and a baby were the center of attention. Luis and Ann Ramirez had brought gifts for Maria and Angelina on their way out of town. They had also given her a box with the remainder of her belongings she had left in the apartment. There was very little in the box - a few clothes and some trinkets she had brought from Honduras. In the bottom of the box, wrapped in newspapers, she found the figural music box. She wound up the base and the mother Mary and her baby Jesus turned slowly as the music played. She was overjoyed that Ernesto had not broken it. She had been so sure he would.

In the McCarthy household there was a whirlwind of activity. An old snow sled had been brought out of storage and under the watchful eyes of the adults, the children took turns sliding down the steep hill from the house to the street below. The Christmas presents under the tree had been opened and tossed aside in the excitement of the first Christmas snowstorm. "So much for Santa," Holly said as she watched them from the window.

Maura was the happiest she had been in years. All of

her family was together again. This time last year, she would never have dreamed that she would have a new daughter-in-law and an instant grandchild. It had been a miracle - of that she was sure.

Across the street, Rock and Liz had just opened their presents. Valerie, from the Banty Hen had wrapped the antique necklace in four different boxes - the boxes got smaller with each opening. "I think you've only given me boxes," Liz teased, but when the lid came off the final box, she went from being flippant to astonishment in a matter of seconds. "But Valerie said she was holding it for someone!" she said.

He helped her with the latch in the back. "She *was* holding it for someone - me." He stepped back and looked at it as it graced her slender neck. "It looks wonderful with your Christmas pajamas," he said, as he pulled her around to face him. She gave him a long, lingering kiss. Yes! he said to himself. Our first Christmas and I got it right!

When she handed him the biggest box under the tree, he seemed surprised. He had been so absorbed with her presents, he hadn't even thought about receiving one. "Be careful opening it," she said. "It's fragile."

He opened it up and sat there for a moment with his mouth open. He looked at her. "Earl?" he asked.

She nodded. He pulled each exquisite carving out one by one. Earl had hand-carved a nativity set - eight pieces in all. Mary, Joseph and the infant Jesus, two shepherds, two sheep and a stable to hold them. "He ran short on time and said he would finish the wise men in time for your Christmas present next year. I told him not to hurry

– the wise men came later anyway."

"I've never seen anything like this." He held each figure up to the light and admired the workmanship. "Liz, he could have sold these for hundreds of dollars."

"Neither have I," she said, "and I had to practically force money on him. He didn't want to charge me for it at all. It was a labor of love."

They both heard it at the same time. Squeals of laughter came wafting through the window from outside. Rock got up and held his hand out for Liz who was still sitting on the floor beside the tree. They walked to the window and he stood behind her, with his hands on her shoulders. A slushy snowball hit the window and they both jumped back. Cap Price stood amidst all of Maura and Danny's grandchildren and was looking up at the window grinning. For all the world, he looked like Rudolph with his bright red nose. Liz and Rock both laughed at the sight.

"Come on out and play," he yelled. Madge was standing beside him wearing a mink coat, a mink hat, fur trimmed boots and bright red lipstick.

He looked at Liz. "Why not?" she said. "Let's go get dressed."

Park Place was beautiful in the snow. The bell tower glistened as ice crystals formed on the bell. The bright red in the wreaths on the doors popped brilliantly with the backdrop of snow on every roof. Kids with toboggans laughing and playing, little dogs with bright red sweaters running headstrong through the white fluffy powder, and old men acting like kids again. "A labor of love," Rock said to Liz as their boots crunched in the snow. "The church, the children, the first Christmas snow - all are God's handiwork - His labor of love for us."

Liz dropped behind and reached down to pick up a handful of snow. She had worked it into a ball when he turned around. "You wouldn't?" he said.

"I would," she said, laughing. She let go of the ball with a pitch that Rock would have sworn came from a major league baseball pitcher.

"Ouch," he said. It was Christmas in Park Place.

The End

PARK PLACE RECIPES

Although every woman in Park Place has a favorite pecan pie recipe, they all acknowledge that Estelle Walker, the chef at Beverly Hills Children's Home, makes the best pecan pies east of the Mississippi River. Estelle had once confided that the secret to her pies is the smidgen of corn meal she uses to bind it. The townsfolk never got it quite right, so here's the recipe, straight from Estelle's recipe card. I'm sure she won't mind me sharing her secret!

Estelle's Pecan Pie

- 2/3 cup dark brown sugar
- 1/3 cup corn syrup, light or dark
- 2 tablespoons milk
- 1 heaping tablespoon corn meal
- 2 eggs
- dash of salt
- 1 teaspoon vanilla extract
- 3 tablespoons melted butter
- 1 cup pecans, chopped

Mix sugar, corn syrup, milk, cornmeal, eggs and butter together. Mix well. Add remaining ingredients and pour into prepared pie shell and bake at 350 degrees for 35 – 45 minutes or until done.

Wanda Burns, the author character in Sweet Tea and Southern Grace and its sequel, Lighting The Way, makes her mother's recipe for Orange Slice Candy Cake during the Christmas season. Although at first glance, it's often mistaken for a fruitcake, it is like no other cake the good folks of Park Place have ever tasted. Nutty and moist, with coconut and orange overtones, this recipe uses a pound of chopped orange sliced candies and is soaked overnight in an orange juice/confectioner sugar glaze. At church and community functions, everyone has to have a slice of Wanda's cake and it gets gone in a flash. Wanda loves sharing, so here it is:

Wanda's Orange Slice Candy Cake (Adapted from an old recipe card)

Cream until light and fluffy:
- 1 c. butter
- 2 c. granulated sugar
- Add:
- 4 eggs, one at a time, beating well after each addition
- Mix and add to butter/sugar/egg mixture:
- 1 t. soda
- 1/2 c. buttermilk

Toss together and coat all pieces well with flour:
- 3 1/2 c. all-purpose flour
- 1 pound orange slice candy, diced
- 2 c. chopped pecans or walnuts
Note: the smaller you chop all these pieces, the easier

it will be to slice the baked cake.

Add flour and flour coated ingredients to creamed mixture. Stir in a can of Angel Flake coconut.

Bake at 250 degrees F. for 2 1/2 to 3 hours in a well-greased tube pan.

While cake is baking, prepare glaze.

- 1 c. fresh orange juice
- 1 c. powdered sugar
- mix well

Allow to cool slightly and remove from pan. Turn cake so that the rounded side is up. Poke lots of holes in cake and carefully pour the liquid glaze over top, making sure it gets down into the holes. Store in refrigerator until ready to eat.

Enjoy!

AUTHOR'S BIO

Glenda Manus lives in Van Wyck, South Carolina with her husband and their cantankerous cat, Theo. One of her greatest joys is having her children and grandchildren living closeby. When she's not writing, she enjoys reading, traveling and spending time with friends and family. She is the author of *Sweet Tea and Southern Grace* which has enjoyed much success in the genre of Christian / Southern Fiction. *Lighting the Way* is the second novel in the Southern Grace Series. She is currently working on book number three.